Distributed - Heavy Metal ® is trademark and copyright of Heavy Metal Entertainment, LLC © 2022 • Heavy Metal Entertainment, LLC, 2140 Hollywood Way, PO Box 10755, Burbank, CA 91505-9998. All rights reserved. Above the Ground © 2022 Gungnir Entertainment - Licensed print to Heavy Metal Entertainment, licensed digital to Aethon Publishing. E-Book distributed and co owned by Aethon Books Publishing Company.

The Greatest Illustrated Magazine. That legacy comes with expectations, it comes with a promise. That's the honor and the burden of Heavy Metal, to push the boundaries of art both visually and narratively to places even the most gifted creatives haven't dared, THAT is Heavy Metal. When I decided to turn the Greatest Illustrated Magazine into the greatest genre brand it had to be done with the utmost precision. So I took nearly half a decade and crafted mine and Heavy Metal's first novel, Beyond Kuiper: The Galactic Star Alliance.

An Amazon Best Seller which gained notoriety within the science community culminating in the Chief Technology & Innovation officer of NASA Jet Propulsion Laboratory saying this: "Medney and Connelly's Beyond Kuiper is believable, and an important fictional take on the evolution of technology. Much the same way Michael Crichton showed us how taking existing advances and slightly moving them in a few ways previously circumspect could lead to, well dinosaurs, Medney and Connelly show how a few "what if's" surrounding energy experiments, and secrecy could lead to a galactic and multiversal awakening." We did what we set out to do as a brand, and personally as an Author: we upped the ante.

Now, in my sophomore series I wanted to dive deep into something that I hold near and dear to my heart: the preservation of our planet. Above The Ground is a cautionary tale about what can happen if we continue to take for granted our current geopolitical discourse, climate situation and resource management of fossil fuels as lackadaisical as we are. It is paramount to our civilization that we start taking more public care of these tenets, and Above The Ground is a lens into an unfortunate future if we stay the current course.

Above The Ground is also a story of "What If's." What If the Mayans didn't disappear 2000 years ago, but migrated. What If Temporal Manipulation was possible. What If a single scientist held the keys to the future without the support system to realize it. And finally, What If everything we ever thought about the Caldera at Yellowstone National Park was wrong.

I hope you enjoy the adventure and learn a little Mayan history while doing so. Between Bob, Heavy Metal, and myself we couldn't be more honored to share our vision of this dystopian future that lies Above The Ground.

ABOVE THE GROUND

Matthew Medney
Robert Greenberger

To my wife, Alexis-
When I started on the journey of this book we were just dating, and now as I get set to publish it, you are my bride. You are a constant force of inspiration.
— Matthew

This one's for Kate, who continues to keep me inspired, entertained, and enlightened.
— Robert

Forward

Chris Mattmann — Chief Technology & Innovation Officer,
NASA, Jet Propulsion Laboratory

I've been a science fiction fan since as early as I can remember – and bear with me, I've thought about this – and I think it dates back to approximately when I was five years old watching E.T. for the first time. It really became apparent during my early teenage years growing up north of Los Angeles in a small(ish) town when I picked up a novel titled, "Jurassic Park". There was a blockbuster movie coming out directed by the icon Steven Spielberg and as a fan of Indiana Jones and his other works, I had to see it. But even more so, I had to read the novel behind it. This led me to a curious author: Michael Crichton. A former medical doctor, Crichton had penned a number of amazing sci-fi novels – Congo, Andromeda Strain, and other great stories that would eventually make their way to the silver screen like Jurassic Park.

I couldn't put the book down. It was witty, intelligent, well-researched, and hell, it was believable. As a teenager, Michael Crichton was my favorite author of the 90s, and seeing his stories get turned into pictures and blockbuster cinema only further cemented that, especially as I myself was beginning my journey into Science, Technology, Engineering, Arts and Math (commonly referred to as STEAM areas today). So, when Crichton died of cancer at age 66 in November 2008, I was saddened that we wouldn't be able to read and see any more of the well-researched, science fiction-could-be-eventual-reality, pop culture referencing, overall cool style and tone that I had come to love.

Then I met Matthew Medney. The post 2008 Michael Crichton. Matt is a Sci-Fi writer, executive, movie mogul, comic book fan, former iconic event promoter in the music industry (what hasn't he done?), and a dear friend of mine. When he and his co-author Robert "Bob" Greenberger - the author of iconic Star Trek stories, and also a story about a certain hunter alien you may have heard of called Predator - first asked me to review and provide a quote for Above the Ground, I was the one that was blushing. Why would these icons look to me? Sure, I'm the Chief Technology and Innovation Officer at the National Aeronautics and Space Administration (NASA)'s Jet Propulsion Laboratory (JPL) managed by the California Institute of Technology (NASA JPL). But I've never been called upon for these types of consultation by iconic sci-fi writers for their cool stories. They usually like to talk to the folks digging holes in the ground on other planets – which is super cool by the way! Hey, maybe my luck in this area is changing, but watching Matt in total surprise tell me I'm the perfect one to read the early copy of the manuscript and provide a quote, gave me the confidence that led to this foreword today.

Let's dive into the book. You've got a nuclear disaster that imperils the population and is due to rising populism and dictators and scarce resources. You've got a scientific discovery that could be the most valuable intellectual property (IP) ever developed touching on all parts energy, climate food, supply, and agriculture, and as with anything so valuable, an immediate target for populist dictators to expend their blood and soil to acquire it. The technology to create the valuable botanical discovery is enabled by the principles of quantum entanglement. And moreover, you have a setting that isn't the coastal city centers or metropolitan New York, Los Angeles, Chicago, or the United States capitol - Washington, D.C. Instead the primary setting begins in rural Nebraska, and then explores what could (and likely would happen) if nuclear war set in and states, countries, provinces all had to fend for themselves – beginning with the less populous portions of the United States. Living in California, this was very meaningful to me as every two to four years, we get a statewide ballot proposal to redistrict and split up the state, but I digress. Oh, did I mention that all of this is occurring in the wake of the mystical disappearance of the Native American population that may have its origins rooted in the same policies and technology and crises occurring as the book unfolds?

What's amazing about the book is that Medney - like Crichton - is so believable. I've studied Quantum Information Theory and recently completed an activity in this area related to quantum annealing and quantum scheduling. This book feels real in its description of these technologies and flawlessly sets up the supporting story and foundations that make you, as a scientific and technologically capable reader, believe in what you are reading – just like dinosaurs whose blood was recovered in tiny amber stones resting peacefully for millions of years in deep mines. And just like corporations and folks that didn't really consider whether "they should" and instead just focused on whether "they could", to quote Dr. Ian Malcom, the technology, science, policy decisions and foundations of Above the Ground paint a familiar setting, especially given the current state of the world, the rising populism, rising tribalism, and decisions being made without the sound basis and consultation of scientists. It seems like this could happen which makes it all the more riveting and amazing as you read it.

Our story follows David, who creates the botanical technology that could fundamentally change the world's food supply using quantum theory to create Advanced Plant Life Systems. David and his wife Betty journey out of the bunker shelter after an apocalypse in hopes of survival and dissemination of the APLS technology to the right people.. They must navigate state lines, territories, criminals and heads of state who are all trying to get to David and barter with his skills and his technology to gain the upper hand in the new world landscape. It's tantalizing. And, truly, truly believable. With a sound basis on technology and science while drawing from pop culture, music, art and cinema, Above the Ground gives you some things to think about given what's going on in the world today. I loved Above the Ground. And you will too.

Just like all the fans of Michael Crichton did.

Great job, Matt and Bob!

Written on a cool September day in Southern California's Northeast Los Angeles corridor.

CHAPTER 1
A Cold Winter

The temperature was rising, clearly topping 90 degrees, it wasn't even eight in the morning yet. The house's cooling system was struggling to create a comfortable environment. Maybe she imagined it, but the air in the glass enclosure felt cloyingly humid. If anything, her telepresence chamber would be the coolest part of the house while she was conducting the class. Still, the large digital readout on the thermostat, visible from across the room, seemed to warn her to stay inside. Before her, a dozen holographic images floated in the air, a mix of boredom, eagerness, and tentativeness. The cherubic natures she greeted in the fall had already shown the passage of time as baby fat dissolved, features settled into permanence, and weariness replaced anticipation. Puberty had descended in full force, turning her seventh graders into proto-adults as voices cracked, curves took prominence, and acne replaced freckles. Summers were always like this as the school year lurched to a halt. A summer's month off sounded heavenly just then (like the children she taught).

Still, it felt like a perpetual summer in Omaha. The respite offered by the other three seasons felt like passing breaks from the unrelenting heat, which had decades before sucked the moisture from the land. A New Dust Bowl had grown, double the size of the original, with violent storms requiring new methods of emergency preparation. She was required to drill with the students monthly so they knew what to do if the alarms screamed to life on their wrist phones and they were not with their parents. Filtered face masks became the latest in fashion statements along with the ones adorned with political slogans every other year. Appliances adjusted to filter the air, the water, and clothing, so rather than clothes coming out of the washer bright white, they now boasted of being dust-free.

More than usual, the expressions of her students seemed preoccupied, pondering the day, even some serious. Had she missed some major event? As the students were completing a warm-up exercise with circuit board manipulation, she thumbed a side screen to life to check the headlines.

'Celebrations and Memorials Mark Vanishing Centennial' scrolled by, replaced with video of President Fitzpatrick laying a wreath at the memorial in Washington, D.C., and people cosplaying in Native American garb.

The Vanishing. Of course.

Before turning her attention back to the children, she spotted a few more news hits including how the Diamond Coalition walked out of the Senate chamber in protest of the latest water management bill. Border skirmishes with the Canadians over hunting and water rights were also on the rise. To top it all, she saw the warning of a prolonged electrical storm spreading from Idaho to Minnesota.

"Mrs. Anders, what's up with everyone's mood today?" one of the still-freckled-faced, red-haired boys asked Betty Anders, the petite blonde school teacher, who was sporting a light blue dress with her hair in a bun, a look befitting the lover of all things mid-20th century.

"Frankie, one hundred years ago, our great nation saw a mysterious and haunting event occur..."

"Ooo! Mrs. Anders, is this the Vanishing?" Catalina broke in, asking wide-eyed and stark with excitement for knowing the answer.

"Yes, Catalina, but don't interrupt. You are right, though. A century ago, some force larger than anything..." Betty paused and looked up to the cloudless blue sky in wonder before continuing. "We really still don't understand what took all of the Native Americans from the planet. It occurred simultaneously, simply vanishing from wherever they were, thus the name the Vanishing."

"I bet it was aliens," Frankie blurted.

"That makes no sense, you idiot," Joachim sniped. "We haven't found any yet!"

"No name-calling!" Betty said reflexively.

"So, what happened?" Izzy asked.

"Scientists have been trying to answer that for years, It is a dark stain we must live with. It is something that all of you must reflect on and understand so you do not make the same mistakes my generation made. For your generation and for generations to come, you'll need to evolve and learn, not regress. Since we're talking about those who were taken, and before you go to the events in town, let's discuss who originally lived in Nebraska."

"The Arap...The Arak..." Catalina struggled to recall.

"The Sioux," Nyah filled in.

"Very good, Nyah," Betty said as she flicked a finger, activating a preloaded chart. Her own screen as well as the dozen screens at home flashed a map of Nebraska with images of the tribes that once called the land their home.

"The Great Sioux Nation, they were called," Betty continued. "And, Catalina, the name you're searching for is Arapaho. There were also the Lakota, and before the Vanishing, the six tribes, Omaha, Winnebago, Ponca, Iowa, Santee Sioux, Sac and Fox, had inhabited the area."

She continued to review the native tribes that had tilled the land for millennia before the arrival of the Europeans. As she wound down, she shifted the discussion to the afternoon's scheduled events. Betty showed a live camera feed of Omaha's streets - flags of patriotism lined the old town up and down with great long carriages of dancers and musicians, speakers, and poets filled the electric vehicles. Any sense of pride and joy was thrown into the fray in hopes of making this somber day one degree brighter, but it was somber and for good reason.

June 21 had entered the public memory, along with July 4, December 7, September 11, and January 6. No year needed. Of them all, the one that remained shrouded in mystery was what happened a century before. It was most keenly felt in the Americas, but as reports filtered in, it was clear anyone with Native American blood above one-eighth purity simply was no longer there. President Biden inaugurated the memorials and tributes that had evolved over time into the celebrations, attempting to keep the spirit and memory of America's first people alive.

She kept up a bright, positive façade, but she struggled as the pain and sorrow of such massive, unexplained loss washed over her. Maybe it was the oppressive heat outside or the imagined warmth in her teacher's chamber, but something wasn't sitting right with her. It was not like she knew anyone who vanished so far back, but something dark gnawed at her. For a brief moment, she considered calling her husband David during her lunch break. Maybe he felt the same thing or could help her identify what was wrong.

Of course, there was no guarantee he'd be available. His work over the last five years was on the verge of receiving the scientific community's seal of approval and it would finally become public knowledge. Rarely was something so positively radical going to change a struggling world.

David was known as a brilliant student when they met at Harvard. The moment was at a concert, the sparks were undeniable, the attraction was palpable to all who were in the vicinity. They became friends before their relationship blossomed into a full-fledged romance. Before that stunning botanical discovery and before starting their graduate studies, they married. Betty and David shared everything they did, so perhaps David was sharing Betty's sense of dread.

During grad school was when it happened. In 2117, he created his quantum-entangled botany, dubbed APLS– Advanced Plant Life Systems —which she teasingly called "apples." It involved instantly rehydrating plant life, possibly resolving the worldwide drought that had led to fights over clean water and arable land, and threatened the food supply for the nine billion people still on earth. As soon as politicians and military caught wind of the research, David Anders had been pressured to hand it over, but he was protective. He didn't want to offer false hope as he perfected his process, which then was subjected to peer review. Still, he was being pressured to release it so America had a bargaining chip at the UN or the military had a way to feed their forces while opponents suffered. Some cravenly saw it as the ultimate weapon, a way to restore America atop the world power pyramid rather than sharing the pinnacle with four other countries. Its fall from lone super-power still rankled Congress, even though it had occurred long before any of the current members were born. Still, many dreamt of those heady days when the country dictated the world's agenda and protected the weaker nations from aggressive, predatory powers.

"Bring America Back."

It was a slogan that the presidential hopeful had used to capture the nation's voice. Unlike similar slogans in past campaigns, the entire country stood behind this phrase, seeing it as a chance for survival, and then maybe supremacy. Its messenger was Garfield Fitzpatrick, now the 61st President of the United States of America. His direct call to David and Betty was the tipping point of David's decision to surrender himself and his achievements for the betterment of the country as a whole.

It was an imbalance that all knew couldn't last long. Some believed today was a prime opportunity for an outwardly open fight. All of this was reason enough for the American government to insist on keeping David's work confined to their control, for the moment at least.

Even NASA had come knocking, hoping he'd help them figure out if the process could work to terraform Mars. Many felt humanity's future had to be among the stars, as Earth was clearly exhausted. Sustaining so many lives was untenable. The threshold for holding back devastating climate change came and went, and the world was altered. The current global drought had finally led to worldwide famine, malnutrition, and a steep decline in life expectancy. The current population of 9 billion souls was a fraction of the projected numbers from the previous century. All the fears the 20th century had warned about had come to fruition, thanks to ignorance and inaction.

The last five years had been exciting but tense, as David drew within himself from time to time; not even Betty could reach him when he faced a dark mood. He hated the pressure, the appeals to his bank account, or vanity. He grudgingly accepted military protection of his lab until he discovered one of the guards trying to copy the files with a remote ripper. He went through a period of intense paranoia, withdrawing from all public contact, including family and friends, for six months before he finally relented.

The American Association for the Advancement of Science, (AAAS), was finally ready to certify his work, as were similar agencies in Europe, Africa, and Asia. The time had come for the next stage of human ingenuity, the time had come. As the field testing in Egypt, Guatemala, and Texas was at first vexing, David tweaked the formulas ever so slightly and began seeing the needed results.

Long into the night, the two shared wine-fueled debates over where to apply the approved work first and if it was right to give it away rather than profit from it. Betty knew that despite the riches they could have rendered with David's accomplishments, they needed to give back to their great country—and the rest of the world.

Betty realized she'd let her mind wander, so she blinked hard once to refocus. She resumed discussing the 19th-century relocation of the Native Americans and how it now looked like a precursor to the Vanishing. She'd meet up with David later after his return from unassuming Sargent's Spur where the military helped him set up his lab space in a gesture intended to elicit his goodwill. She continued to teach, letting the students distract her, but the creeping feeling of something being horribly wrong would never be far from the edges of her mind.

When he did turn up, unfashionably early, his mood matched hers, which both pleased and distressed her. After a long embrace, she brushed a lock of his brown hair from his eyes and took in his haunted expression. He remained ruggedly handsome in his mid-thirties; just a few lines suggested he had aged at all since college. The thick, dark hair didn't betray the coming of middle age, and his stubble was equally dark. She liked looking at his face, easily imagining them growing old and wrinkled together.

"What's wrong?" he asked.

She shook her head. "Something. Nothing."

"That nonsense with the Senate?"

"The walkout? No, that's them being childish. No..."

"Then what?"

She shuddered for a moment and then looked up into his eyes. "Something. I've felt it all day. There's something wrong."

"Yeah, I've felt off too." She assumed he wrote it off as he did anything inconvenient as pressure over the APLS project, but was quietly reassured they both felt it.

They were separated by a mere two inches, but it was enough for her to look into his eyes and she imagined losing herself there; but today, they were bloodshot, the eyes themselves marred with dark smudges underneath. That was the first signal of the stress he was feeling, so she decided to keep things to herself. Despite all the hours in the lab, he maintained a good regimen that kept him in reasonable shape, especially for a scientist hidden away in a bluff who only saw sunlight twice a day.

"Should we still head into town for the celebration?"

She pondered the question and began to speak, when both were disturbed by the Emergency Alert vibration on their wrist phones. The normal iconography had been replaced with the icon for radiation. A second later, the house computers also flashed the emergency alert with a recorded narration ordering everyone to shelter. Betty grasped the severity of the situation and knew their small house lacked a fully-equipped emergency shelter. Instead, there was one at the lab, courtesy of the US Government.

David had already reached into a wall safe for the rectangular steel box that contained their vital documentation and backup hard drive. He snapped it from the connection to the house wiring and stuffed the drive into his pocket, reaching for Betty with his other hand. Neither spoke, reading the terror in one another's eyes.

The drive to the lab in the Iowa bluffs would normally take about thirty minutes. He knew an alert like this meant the bombs were already flying and—depending on how many and from where they were launched—they had ten minutes, maybe longer, but not thirty. Still, they ran for their car and gunned the electric engine. The solar/electric hybrid leaped from its charging spot and they were off like a shot, kicking up dust and dirt.

"Should I call Mom?" she said aloud.

"First the news," David said. His vocal command brought the emergency band alive. Some man was reading from a prepared statement, a live broadcast, so information was in real-time.

"At least fifty nuclear missiles have been simultaneously launched from the Allegiance, most of which are directed at the coasts. Evacuation is mandatory."

"Those bastards did it," David grumbled.

She fought back the terror and, seeking reassurance, managed to ask, "Are we in danger?"

"It depends how close any of those come to us," he said. "Hey, Jeeves, where are the bombs?"

The always on-call computer AI promptly reported that the nuclear warheads appeared to be targeting the usual suspects: Washington,

D.C., New York, Los Angeles, and Philadelphia. Retaliatory missiles were anticipated to arrive in Moscow, Seoul, and Tehran. After that, additional information was unknown.

"We're screwed," he continued, pressing his foot down despite the vehicle already at its top speed. Their momentum did not change as the highway out of Omaha already began to clog with similarly fleeing vehicles.

"How many can the shelter hold?" Betty asked. She knew it was there but had been barred from visiting the facility for reasons of national security. It was one of the few barriers between the two.

"Really, just us two, so don't make an offer to your mom. But...you'd better call her."

Betty's mother lived in Lawrence, Kansas, once known as ground zero given the missile silos in the area. The call went to digimail, which was fine by her. She didn't feel like seeing her grow hysterical. She was fighting her own dread.

Instead, she flipped the side screen to the newsfeed and saw the night sky of the east coast. As the day gave way to night, an unwelcome light illuminated the night sky across the globe. A bright array of beautifully coordinated destruction penetrated the defenses of the United World.

It started that night. A war that would define humanity ignited like the fireworks on the Fourth of July. Betty watched, unable to tear her eyes away from the explosions. As cameras winked out, satellite feeds replaced them, including one horrifying image of the Western Hemisphere lighting up, looking less like her reality and more like the cinema she enjoyed. She switched channels, but it appeared that regardless of what station their car was tuned to, the communication led to the same voice. A somber-sounding man could be heard, his voice in malicious harmony, a voice that had hijacked democracy and violated the free world, a voice that meant winter was coming, and it was not a winter caused by global warming, or by shifts in the tides caused by a displaced moon. No, this winter was one brought on by the people who needed the planet to survive.

A determined faceless foe whose only goal was to reset civilization and bring life on a journey in time where less involved politics and technology gave passage to humanity and a chance to restart on a new path. A foe with this ideology feared nothing, an emotion that would bring the end of times with their every step. Whoever was truly responsible for dropping the bombs knew this was their calling; this was what they wanted. This foe was the sum of all their fears.

Both drove on in silence, neither noticing the tears streaming from the other's eyes.

The world they knew had just ended. What lay ahead was now a dark tunnel into the unknown.

The car raced toward the safety of the bunker, and after that...they'd just have to wait and see.

CHAPTER 2

Six Months Underground

Betty was growing to hate the lab. She and David had been living there since the nuclear rain fell across America. His access codes admitted them to the bunker, a sealed-off facility from the rest of the research lab. It had two cots, a worktable, shelves stocked with MREs that might have dated to the second moon landing, communications gear, water filtration and recycling, and a too-small bathroom. It lacked entertainment and she regretted not being able to finish reading her novel before the world shattered, a truth Betty didn't want to admit especially as a teacher. While she endlessly grieved for her mother, who died from radiation poisoning two months earlier, she also thought often about her students—who lived, who survived, who wished they were dead? Communication was as difficult as a warm meal these days. Not knowing was half the pain, and when messages were received it typically only compounded that feeling. Betty was reduced to pondering the world's troubles as her greatest ally in life; information and knowledge had been forsaken for some time now.

David had the lab to occupy him, once it was certain there was no serious radiation in the area. They'd huddled in one another's arms those first two terrifying days, believing the worst, and hoping somehow to be wrong. Cut off from the world as radio, cell towers, and all forms of communication were garbled at best. When they let go, they filled the time with taking inventory, making certain the equipment worked, and figuring out how long they could survive in the bunker. Never truly preppers, the Anderses' happenstance preparations that seemingly were promising six months ago had been replaced with a newfound fear as the supplies started to dwindle. First to weeks and now days. They skipped meals to stretch out the supplies, delaying the inevitability of their future, scavenging for rations.

Betty riffled the torn playing cards. She had long ago grown tired of card games but there was nothing else to amuse her. She'd tried to invent new versions of two-player games or solitaire, anything to avoid the tedium. On day three, David cracked their titanium alloy door open and the built-in Geiger counter indicated the air was safe enough. He refused to let her out, caring too deeply for her safety and protection from the radiation, though he needed to move quickly in the sun to the adjacent lab. He was gone for hours, leaving her to worry and imagine the worst that might have happened to him. When he had eventually returned, her grief had turned to anger at being left behind.

"We're in this together. Don't you dare do that to me again!" she screamed through tears. She threw herself at him, but he enveloped her in his arms and hugged her tight, letting her cry it out in silence. After sobbing her last tear and using the back of her hand to wipe away the snot, she looked up into his brown eyes and pleaded, "Not again." He nodded and held on to her.

That night, she resolved never to be that weak again. The world had changed, and to survive, she'd need to deal with reality. As he returned to the lab the following day, she made it her mission to find out what was left of their family, their friends, and America itself. It had become clear that the Midwest was spared the worst of the destruction. The haze in the air was rolling in from both coasts, coating the already parched land with radiated dust and debris. The sun shone weakly through the cloud cover, which, over the last few months, had barely cleared, causing the frigid temperatures. The borrowed jumpsuit that was found in the lab was a nice extra layer of clothing because she certainly hadn't shopped for a nuclear winter.

She insisted they stay healthy, so she forced them to do exercises and calisthenics each morning. It was clear that David did it more to humor her, anxious to get to the lab. She instilled this routine, making it clear they needed to function in this new normal, so as not to lose what little sanity and normality there were. Rising with the sun, exercising, eating together.

Then he was free to work in the lab or keep her company. They'd do some other form of exercise after lunch and then each did their own thing in the afternoon until dinner. After that, they'd play games, enjoy a sultry night, or invent stories. For what it was worth, Betty wasn't all that depressed with the situation. If truth had been told, she had started feeling guilty for enjoying the new paradigm a bit too much, spending more time with David than she had in years. Even if it was just sitting in the same room as him, it was a blessing she kept telling herself, a blessing that they had each other.

Betty spent days using the computer, which thankfully had a satellite uplink given its military design and construction, to try to locate information. The worldwide web had been broken, its filaments tattered, so connectivity was iffy, and what worked one day didn't the next. First, she found websites with books and music, downloading what she could to bring some culture to her day. She even managed to find a copy of the novel she left unfinished at home, which brought her a pang about what was left behind. Once she secured things to help keep her sane, she focused on the rest of the world. What she managed to piece together was presented each night over their foil pouches of dinner. Using plastic chopsticks, she fished out some steamed vegetables and chewed on them as she began the report.

"The Alliance didn't just fire the nukes," she began as she chewed, "they had been secretly mobilizing forces, both land and sea." The moment the missiles flew and everyone was in a panic, they launched massive invasions of their neighbors. It was like the blitzkrieg tactics the Germans developed in World War II. Japan, Myanmar, Vietnam, Turkey, and other countries fell quickly. There were some skirmishes, but essentially, the Alliance appeared to have conquered most of Asia and parts of Western Europe. Once they settled, the Alliance cut access to the internet, expanding China's fierce firewall. As a result, distant cousins and many of David's scientific colleagues were now ghosts.

She managed to piece together that the Alliance now controlled the Pacific along with the South China, Baltic, and Mediterranean Seas. The strategic ports that they had seized control of spoke to a longer, more thorough plan than just pressing the reset button. The need to memorialize these thoughts, as the constant teacher she was, found her scribing some notes daily to hopefully use as markings of the time.

A few nights later, David frowned as Betty recounted what she had determined about the United States. President Fitzpatrick, Vice-President Radwitz, and most of the cabinet and Joint Chiefs managed to get to their secure locations for continuity of government. Given the devastation along the coasts, there were so many pieces to pick up that a sense of paralysis settled over the government. FEMA and the Red Cross did what they could, but there weren't enough radiation suits, not enough medication... just not enough.

"I think some of the governors had prepared for this day, whenever it would come," Betty observed. "Within a week of the attack, seven states declared themselves a new nation, seceding from the union."

That stopped David mid-forkful. He frowned, his brows knitting together, darkening his already smudged eyes. He looked haggard, spending so many hours in the lab, so many hours adjusting and pushing the formula forward, she knew he felt like he was humanity's last chance. Betty knew the only way to get a conversation out of him, was to drag him out of the lab for meals. Killing two birds with one stone, only as a teacher could do.

"Yeah, we're now living in the new country of the Seven Flags," she said.

"That's a dumb name," he muttered.

"It is if they intend to ever add to their size. They even introduced a snappy motto: 'To survive, we must unite. To thrive, we must divide.'"

"They sound like an amoeba."

Betty grinned at that. "Well, the country is certainly embryonic. Even though there are seven states now running the damn thing, the man at the top isn't a governor, isn't a celebrity, or a statesman, but a military man."

"A military man?" David said, peering over the crescent top of his coffee. He contemplated the dark liquid before continuing. "So, he broke his oath to America?"

"He sounds like an opportunist, honestly. Guy's named Holtzer and—"

David's head snapped up and he glared. "Holtzer? Rodney Holtzer?"

"Do you know him?"

David laughed bitterly, but something warned Betty that there was history here, a history he had kept from her. There were gaps he never told her about, and clearly, this Holtzer was a part of it.

"What is it?"

"What did you call him...an opportunist? That may be the least of the adjectives I can use for the bastard. Who else is part of this new country?"

"Nebraska, Colorado, Wyoming, Kansas, Iowa, South Dakota, and Missouri," she said.

"I guess North Dakota wasn't invited," he murmured, his mind clearly not entirely on the conversation but in the past.

"They're a country of dust. Nothing was growing and now there's even less of a chance of reversing that," Betty noted. "Millions died, but millions more will die because there's no food being grown. Canned goods are now more valuable than gold."

They grew ever more grateful for the food, ignoring its questionable quality, but as the weeks dragged on, the shelves were growing bare and both kept putting off the difficult discussion, the hard decisions they would need to make. Instead, Betty played cards, tried to get news, even celebrity gossip, anything to break the tedium. The problem was, the celebrities were no longer worth anyone's interest. Instead, scientists from across the ideological spectrum were featured, predicting mutant plants and animals that were a threat or a solar flare that would cleanse the skies. Most wrung their hands, fearing the worst as radiation sickness turned communities into mass graves and survivors became roving packs that crumbled the foundations of modern society. Criminal organizations that survived stopped selling drugs and took over the supermarkets, hardware stores, pharmacies, and liquor stores. Jewelry and gold were still good for currency—people still liked shiny objects—but bartering became commonplace. Digital currencies were useless given the intermittent digital network and people couldn't access what cash was left. Libraries had become lumber yards as people raided the shelves to have something to burn for heat wherever gas or coal could not be found. Though for the darkness that had consumed man, there was still some glimmer of hope. Organizations could be found throughout the network, aimed at saving critical books and history. Both David and Betty knew the only thing that differentiated them from the animals was the invention of history. And this apocalypse wasn't going to change that.

Betty tried with little success to reach out to her fellow faculty and her students. Memorial websites listed names she knew, each recognition a slice at her heart. She openly sobbed when she saw her principal had been burned alive when he refused to let squatters into his home. When she finally made video contact with her student Catalina, she almost wished she hadn't.

The girl looked wan, a scar across one eyebrow. Her cheeks were smudged with badly applied makeup, but she smiled broadly when she came on screen. "Mrs. Anders! How are you?"

"Fine, Catalina. But what about you? Your parents?"

Catalina's eyes immediately brimmed with tears and Betty regretted the questions. Clearly, she'd had it far tougher than she and David. This was what privilege felt like and it didn't fit her.

"Dad's gone...missing, and Mom, Mom is hurt," her student said hesitantly.

"Where are you?"

"A shelter in Omaha. It stinks here."

"I can imagine. Are you healthy?"

"Enough."

The answers signaled hunger and something more. Something she wasn't saying. Betty feared the worst after studying the haunted eyes.

"Has something happened?"

There was a long silence and she almost missed the brief dip of her chin. Betty wanted to ask a million questions, wanted to offer comfort, but she sat in silence.

Finally, the teen said, "When we got here, the organizers were over-whelmed...a gang took over. They wanted tribute even for water. Mom wouldn't let me...Mom did what she could...but then she got hurt, and well, medics aren't as available as before..."

Betty was filling in the blanks with growing horror.

"Are you being fed?"

"Enough, when I'm up to it, which honestly, isn't that often. Look, I gotta go...but it was nice to see a familiar face."

Catalina cut the connection, not before Betty saw the tears stream down both cheeks. Her own tears blurred her vision, frightened that her student would be considered lucky, a survivor. But at what price?

She'd been reading up on the roving bands of gangs that looted, raped, and pillaged, much as barbarians did centuries before. Fitzpatrick and Holtzer both seemed powerless to stop the harm being done. Neither seemed capable of re-building a framework for society to cling to and rebuild. But she knew the time was rapidly approaching when she and her husband were going to have to leave the bunker and lab, and take their chances in the chaos.

The Seven Flags had declared victory by seceding and then immediately imposing martial law to protect their borders, or so they claimed. It was the first step away from democracy, but maybe that was what was needed right now, a strong hand to guide things until society got back on its feet. The true test would be once the soil settled, once the ground was ready to rebuild, would the leaders restore democratic rule. Too often countries were liberated by a strongman who decided he liked the taste of power so much, he became the very thing he overthrew. From David's reaction, she suspected Holtzer was not one to cede power so easily.

One night, David grabbed one of the few remaining MREs from the dusty shelf and sat staring at it. He'd been putting in even longer hours in the lab, preferring his solitude, which had led to more than a few arguments followed by uneasy silence as both went to bed, apart. He played with it, tossing it from hand to hand, distracted.

Betty sat with her own unopened bag, a vegetable medley she detested that used too many radishes and lima beans. But, she couldn't avoid it any longer, as the other options were nearly gone.

"It's time," he said finally. She knew what he meant and wasn't looking forward to the conversation.

"Where to?"

"Not a clue. I can't stay here. Once we leave the lab, we're in Seven Flags territory and I can't be here."

"What did Holtzer do to you?"

David let out a sound that was laugh and sigh. "To me? Nothing. I'll tell you later. Right now, we need to pick a direction and get back to what's left of America."

"David, it's ugly out there. Gangs. The criminals in control. It's a mess. Neither one of us is trained for this. I can't teach my way out of this. You're no marksman. How do we do this and live?"

"We're not staying here and starving to death. It'd be a sad irony."

"Will the apples work with irradiated soil?"

David paused before answering then gave her a small smile. "I think so. That's what the last week has been about. Testing the air, soil samples, mixing them with water to see what happens. It's promising."

"Then that's your bargaining chip."

Betty tore open the pouch, willing to down the distasteful mix now that she knew there was some hope ahead.

"I have to get it out of here and to America, to Fitzpatrick. But he needs to know about it and that's the catch. How do I get to him and how do I make him listen?"

"I suppose a demonstration is out," she said between mouthfuls. Both had taken to eating more slowly, stretching out the food, letting them fill on food and dreams.

"There have to be some DOD scientists I can reach out to, ones who know me and my work. We just have to find them." He took a mouthful. "How much time do we have?"

"Did you intend on bringing some of this with us, to get us started?"

He looked at the near-empty shelves.

"Maybe a day or two, so we'd need to leave in two days, three if we stretch it."

"And then what?" she probed. "It'll be a day or two to get through this country and across a border, presuming we don't need a passport, blood test, or something worse." Catalina and her mother flashed before her mind. She shuddered then pressed on. "From here to Washington would take at least a week. If we bring two days' food, then what? It's not like there's a roadside barbecue joint to stop at for lunch."

"God, I miss Bryant's," David said to himself.

"Not the time for that," Betty said, refocusing him. He'd taken to revisiting all the places he liked to eat, all the foods he missed. Sometimes it was a pleasant daydream between meals, other times it was sheer torture to think about all that was gone.

"Here's what we do," she said in her teacher's voice, giving instructions to her prize pupil. "Give me names and departments, I'll do what I can while you finish your work. If, after twenty-four hours, we can't make contact, we need a Plan B. East or west?"

"East, I suppose," he said. "If there's anything left of the government, maybe I can find them in person. I can bring lab equipment and supplies for barter, I suppose."

After they ate, he left her a list of names, titles, and agencies and retreated to his cot to rest. Fueled with urgency, Betty didn't join him, but instead began searching the web. Site after site was down, the high speed slowed to a crawl, so frustration grew with the late hour. If she reached someone's email or agency site, she left a message in David's name, hoping that would be enough. She didn't dare mention the APLS until she was certain she was in touch with someone he knew and trusted.

Her computer whirring and beeping repeatedly awoke her. It was 3:30 in the morning and she had fallen asleep at the keyboard, something she hadn't done since college. Her eyes were crusty and her neck ached, but she stretched herself back into shape. Several messages were awaiting her, all from one Dr. Choi from the FDA. Each one bore the same message: "Thank god you're alive, David. Is your work available? We desperately need it."

She padded over to the cot and shook David's shoulder, first gently then with increasing impatience. He finally cracked an eye open and stared at her quizzically.

"Dr. Choi?" she said.

"Ryan, yeah. He alive?" His voice was thick but his eyes were brightening.

"Come see."

David read over the message and considered his response. Finally, he dictated to Betty, who was always the better keyboardist. "Work available and prime for conditions. Will give it only to Fitzpatrick after we make a deal. Can you help get me through to him?"

To their surprise, the answer came back almost immediately: "I'm on it."

Both were now too awake to even consider sleep, so they jubilantly played strip poker. Betty happily lost within five hands and took him to their cot.

It was late the following afternoon when Choi got back in touch, confirming a satellite link with the president was being arranged. They were given a frequency and time, then he ended the conversation, avoiding any further discussion. Not even a status of how Choi himself was faring, which David took to be odd and Betty saw as ominous.

At the appointed time, their screen flashed with the presidential seal, which quickly dissolved to the craggy, lined face of President Fitzpatrick.

"Mr. President, David Anders."

"And Betty Anders," she added when it was clear he wasn't going to introduce her.

"I am so glad you've both survived," the president began, his voice that pleasant baritone that gave gravitas to his speeches, easily winning over people. "How are you?"

"We've been in a bunker at my lab for the last six months. I've actually been working on my project, testing its efficacy given the new environment."

"I understand it works," the president said.

"The small samples here in Iowa look promising. But, that's the problem. I...we're in Iowa."

Fitzpatrick frowned and leaned away from the camera to listen to an aide or adviser.

"I want to help. But, we need safe passage. If I can get us across the new border, how do I get it to you?"

"What about transmitting your data in advance so my people can verify it while you're en route? There's no air traffic and won't be for a long while. So you and your wife would need seven to ten days to get here. Do you even have a car?"

"Yes, the one we used to get here. I checked and the batteries are fine."

"What are you looking for exactly, Dr. Anders?"

"Safe passage to you and you alone. I won't be handing this off to anyone else. Then, I want guaranteed access to a lab plus housing for me and Betty. I keep the patent if that ever matters again."

"Not unreasonable. What about my request to begin studying your current formulae?"

David narrowed his eyes. "What about my not unreasonable request? I'll take the risk of getting out of Seven Flags territory if you get me the rest of the way."

There was a pause. "I don't know if I can make that guarantee. Our resources are stretched thin."

"Think of the people this will feed, sir. Doesn't that require an alteration of priorities?"

"You think highly of yourself," Fitzpatrick said, looking very unhappy.

"Of course, I want to feed millions, which is why the sooner we can begin confirming your work, the sooner we can begin growing crops to feed them all. Famine may do a better job than radiation in killing us all."

"Sorry, sir, I won't be just giving away the one thing I possess that someone else may want."

He paused and looked at Betty, mouthing, "Of course, love you too."

She winked back at him, but then resumed studying the president, who was looking increasingly unhappy.

"I'm not asking a lot, sir. I need peace of mind."

"And I need a nap, but we both may be disappointed. I don't want to promise you something I can't deliver on. I don't work that way."

"I don't give my research away for free," David replied.

"My understanding is some of that research was federally funded, giving us some claim to the work. Be reasonable and let's make a deal."

David and Betty exchanged glances, aware they were not going to get the escort they felt would keep them alive.

"No escort, no data," he said.

"Damn it, man, we're on the precipice here. Every hour counts, so why waste the time?"

"Because, sir, I become expendable the minute I share the formula, and I would rather have some protections."

There was an uneasy silence that stretched, time slowing down, both sides hoping the other would blink first. Neither did and the intransigence became increasingly apparent.

"If you make it to the east, re-establish contact with Dr. Choi. We'll bring you in and deal then. I wish you Godspeed."

The screen went dark before an astonished David could reply.

The new silence settled over the couple for a minute. Then two. Finally, David said, "Plot us a course. Somewhere east, somewhere you think will harbor us. We'll leave when you're ready."

CHAPTER 3

Meanwhile,
in California

"CQ CQ CQ DE THX1701. THX1701. THX1701. K."
"CQ CQ CQ DE UKB9081. UKB9081. UKB9081. AR."

"THX1701 DE G3YWX GM OM ES TNX FER CALL UR RST 599 599 = Name is Reid—Romeo, Echo, India, Delta—ES QTH Costa Costa = So HW CPI? AR UKB9081 DE UKB9081 KN."

"THX1701 DE THX1701 FB OM ES TNX FER RPRT UR RST 599 599 = Name is Mike—Mike, India, Kilo, Echo—ES QTH NR Solvang. Solvang. = SO HW? AR."

Reid leaned back, a smile crossing his dark features. He made a minute adjustment to the digital readout and the static cleared. Mike was a mere 35 miles away, but these days, that could mean a whole other world, a different society, or even a country. As they exchanged information on frequencies and equipment, the real conversation could begin.

"How are you?" Reid asked in a low hum.

"Alive, so there's that. Alive and uninjured, a little hungry."

"How bad is it?"

"Solvang is a mess, nothing is working, no one seems to be in charge. There's been some cleanup, some fighting, some cooperation. You?"

"Not sure, to be honest. I'm in a shelter, well, more of a homemade bunker, but yeah, I've been here for the last six months. This is all that's keeping me sane."

"That is not all!" a third voice cried."

"You got company?"

"My wife Linda. So yeah, she keeps me sane too."

"I am sooo appreciated."

"Yeah, I have my wife Suzy and...two of my three kids. Even managed to keep the dog with us."

"Sorry," he said.

"I miss pets," Linda called from behind Reid, who ignored her.

"What do you hear from the ARRL?"

Over the last six months, Reid Costa had kept in touch with the outside world only via his ham radio network, which, thankfully, survived largely intact and had proven more reliable than the internet. The American Radio Relay League found one another from coast to coast, from the Canadian border to the Texas gulf. As the FM repeaters and other bands crackled from radiation, Reid was relieved to see how many people maintained their equipment in such a way that they survived the multiple EMPs from the nuclear blasts. He had constructed an elegant Faraday Cage for his equipment years before, and despite Linda's mocking it as something that belonged on the Earth Space Station, successor to the original ISS, it meant they could talk to the world despite the pair living in a fallout shelter he built with his own hands on weekends and vacations during the first five years of their marriage.

As he made contact with one operator after another, he began to understand what had befallen the world. The rise of the Alliance, of a foreign superpower growing in the shadows, didn't necessarily surprise him, but one growing domestically, that caught him off guard. The Seven Flags was a reflection on the broken hope he had for Americans to band together, but instead, they had splintered. He wanted to see patriotism rival or outmatch the fervor that followed Pearl Harbor, something he always drew inspiration from. The country had been devoted isolationists, keeping their heads in the sand as Europe fell into shadow. Then the surprise attack by the Japanese was as if a light switch had been thrown and the country was jolted out of its torpor and went back to work with a vengeance. It would have made the last six months motivating, and yet, nothing seemed to be working. It was as if the house of cards had not only fallen but it was made of glass. He spent long hours thinking about how it had come to this as each new report arrived. Of course, Canada and Mexico closed their borders. Non-contiguous states Hawaii, Alaska, and Puerto Rico were cut off and virtually independent, left to their own meager devices.

California's coastline was devastated as the naval yards in San Diego and Silicon Valley up north took the brunt of the Korean attack. Los Angeles, now merely an entertainment generator, suffered just one nuke, but that was more than enough. The yield from these warheads ruined the coastline, turning beaches to glass, sickening the people, killing the fish. Santa Barbara was just far enough north of LA to have time to flee or go underground before the Santa Ana winds brought the radiation with them.

What could be gleaned about the rest of the world was less certain, more speculation than hard fact. The bastions of democracy—London, Paris, The Hague—had crumbled with starvation and chaos. The Alliance continued their lightning march across Asia and now Europe, consolidating power and marshaling their resources. The loyal would be healed and fed; the disloyal were left to wither.

The operators living within the newly formed Seven Flags chafed at the martial law, the curfews, the rationing. What amazed them, though, was the new nation had a constitution, government structure, and iconography ready to roll out. They clearly seized an opportunity when it was handed to them, but it was frighteningly clear that this had been in the planning stages for some time. Reid and some of the others wanted someone to blame, but after 350 years of lies, misinformation, and false history records, maybe America's bill had finally come due. But, others argued, England, Switzerland, Germany, and other countries managed to survive more centuries and even a millennium. His stock reply was always, "I'm a theoretical physicist, not a poli sci major."

It was clear, though, that as America jerked back to life in fits and starts, life within the Seven Flags was being regimented, dictatorial no matter how they gilded their speeches and laws in flowery language. It was always for the good of the people, the survival of the nation, and even the human race. Submit and do as you're told, and you will eat today. Pockets of resistance, including more than a few of their ham brethren, died as a result. Law enforcement had been given extraordinary freedom to judge and mete out justice, often resulting in resisters being shot, their bodies heaped atop a growing mountain of corpses, each mountain located at the border of the new country, a flesh and bone wall to warn any thinking of immigrating in or out.

Reid and Mike kept the contact short as Mike was strategically positioned to act as a relay hub of information up and down the California coast. They agreed to resume the conversation in three days.

After signing off, Reid scanned the frequencies, picking up faint or garbled chatter, background noise that reminded him of how far removed from civilization he had become. He sat, brooding in silence until slender hands began massaging his temples. The rhythmic motion always relaxed him and he sat still, letting Linda's fingers ease his concerns.

When she finished, he swiveled in his chair to look at his wife. When they married, she knew he was not easy to live with but loved him regardless. He first started talking about building the "shelter," which she quickly dubbed the Panic Fortress, a name that stuck, mainly because Reid always wore PF Flyers. While she scoffed at the need, she knew he firmly believed disaster was always lurking behind the next sunrise.

And unfortunately... he was right.

He even took a second job, teaching introductory physics, which he hated in its simplicity, to afford the equipment and day labor he needed to build the space. It was eventually connected to the main house with a staircase that could be sealed magnetically with a lead shield. He consulted with others at the lab to determine the right meteorological gear to install to monitor air conditions and water safety. In time, he was dubbed the doomsday prepper, but ignored the barbs, refusing to show off his plans let alone let anyone see the finished compound. It was a high priority to him, something Linda had recognized early during their courtship.

That was why she never stopped him from digging up their backyard and even began helping him, especially as his initial plans were particularly Spartan ones. The 1000-square-foot space was eventually doubled, giving them living and working spaces, a far more spacious shower (for two, of course). There was one spare bedroom because neither had given up on the hope of children. He even built her a private space where she could do as she pleased.

That was when she began making suggestions to add touches that would make the place more palatable than just merely surviving. By the second year, she had begun buying the supplies they'd need to stock it, insisting on colorful sheets, blankets, décor.

"If you're going to make me live with just you, it can't be a black and white world," she told him the first time she came home with bright, primary-color towels.

Her support only made him love her all the more. He knew he lived in an orderly world, one of science with chaos not far behind. She gave him a reason to live and their five years together were happy ones, marred only by three miscarriages. The doctors were uncertain what the issue was and only encouraged them to keep trying and try they did with gusto.

"So, now what?" she asked, hands on hips, ready for something, anything.

"I was going to get back to the book," he began before she cut him off.

"Oh, no, not again. How many times have you read that? I know you've read it to me twice and I still only understand a third of it." He suspected she was exaggerating because she was not a trained physicist but was, indeed, a social worker. She understood how people worked in ways that he didn't, while he could ponder the mysteries of the universe for hours, leaving her wondering. Despite the advances in over a century of research, Brian Greene's The Elegant Universe: Superstrings, Hidden Dimensions, and the Quest for the Ultimate Theory was, for him, a concise treatise on the theory of everything. When he was troubled by the current theories being argued, he returned to the book, as much for comfort as for confirmation of the foundation of the theory of everything, building on Albert Einstein's pioneering research.

Green's work was later supplemented by the work of Michio Kaku, who once described it as, "Let's say chess is the rules of the universe. After two thousand years, we finally figured out how the pawns move, how the bishop sliced across the board, and how the cosmos said, check; and then I suppose one day we'll have the God equation and that'll tell us how the whole chessboard moves and then we'll become grandmasters and we'll tell God, checkmate. We'll be able to apply this to answer some of the deepest unsolved questions in relativity. For example, is time travel possible? Einstein's theory says yes, but is it really true? We don't know what happened before the Big Bang, before creation itself. What lies on the other side of a black hole? All these questions cannot be solved with the present under-standing of physics, but that's where string theory comes in. String theory is a theory of everything."

It was the notion of universes beyond our own, beyond time and space, that truly intrigued him. He desperately wanted to understand the order of things. Order was his guiding principle, his interest in physics and outgrowth of his personal compulsions, the OCD that dictated his life. Getting used to his routines and the need to maintain that order nearly kept Linda from marrying him, but she loved him for his soul, she said; the rest, she could handle. He, in turn, adapted his routines to accommodate another human being in his world.

After six months together in the fortress, he realized how much he needed her. He likely would have lived on his own, studying physics as the world deteriorated around him, uncaring about others because his mind was on larger matters. She grounded him and was his conduit to his fellow man.

And there she stood, waiting for him.

"What did you have in mind?"

"Puzzle?"

He shook his head. That, to him, was a last resort, despite the orderli-ness of putting the jumbled pieces back together.

"Stratego?" They'd only selected two-person games and she'd never mastered chess, but would always beat him at this antique.

"No, what about backgammon?" There, at least, he had a fighting chance against her.

"Fine, loser cooks dinner," she said and turned on a heel, heading for the rec room.

He examined his equipment before powering it down, conserving battery life. With a fresh cloth, he wiped it all down then his chair, ensuring any germs that might have aberrated during his time in the lab were eradi-cated, finally washing his hands for a solid two minutes before joining her.

Later, after beating her two games out of three, Linda was in the kitchen making pasta. He went back to his workspace and turned on his computer, carefully cleaning the screen and keyboard before settling himself before it. The internet had been particularly iffy lately and he suspected one of the switching nodes had been damaged or taken offline. Still, when it worked, he sought fellow scientists, hoping to continue refining his theories with their help.

On one message board that was active as of five hours ago, Reid was scanning a variety of topics, all of them seeming to be related to issues of the nuclear fallout. There was a vigorous debate raging regarding when the skies would let the sunlight through and how long mankind could survive with reduced agriculture. Animal life was increasingly endangered as they had nothing to graze on and were quickly slaughtered for meat rather than letting them grow and procreate. Milk was in short supply, with goat milk becoming the go-to choice for infants. Others noted the rise of insects as rotting human and animal corpses fattened them up. Of course, there were the usual jokes about how the cockroaches would outlast all other life while others guessed how large the rats would get.

He rarely read more than the subject lines, hoping to find someone to talk about the future of humanity after the disaster and where our place in the universe is. Reid was particularly pleased that the colonies on the moon, Phobos, and Deimos, were still intact and intermittently transmitting. While there was some concern about their viability with Earth in chaos, the planning for the next supply ship to Jupiter's moons for colony construction was still a go. If we destroyed this world, he was optimistic mankind would survive elsewhere in the solar system. And maybe get it right this time, he thought.

"Dinner!" Linda called, her voice making it clear in that one word she wasn't going to wait if he got lost in work.

"Coming," he called as he reached to power down the device. As he reached, though, one final subject caught his eye. It wasn't scientific in nature, not at all. Instead, this was a plea for help. Someone trapped in the Seven Flags, based on the geotag, so he looked at the detail. The sender's name jarred a memory, a familiar name. He'd heard something about him and his research, but it was in another field, so he hadn't committed it to memory.

Testing his wife's patience, Reid called up a second window to refresh himself on who David Anders was.

CHAPTER 4
First Contact

"How do you feel about strays," Reid asked over the pasta and vegetable dish. Linda seasoned the food sharply this time, hot peppers burning as he chewed. She liked things far hotter than he did, but he indulged her taste buds every now and then. Being consigned to making the meal for losing the game, this was her revenge.

"You don't like pets; they are all dirty to you," she said. Her hair, six months longer than she liked it, hung below her shoulders, auburn curls catching the light above the table. He had grown to like it, running his fingers through it after it had been washed and dried. He would bury his face in the mass of curls and sniff deeply when he was feeling amorous.

He chewed and then drank some water uselessly to try and cut the burn. "No, I meant stray people."

She paused at that. Initially, when they heard the alerts and grabbed their go-bags, which were refreshed every three months, she asked if their next-door neighbors could take shelter with them. He refused, worried about their germs and interrupting his studies. Jarring changes to his routine required processing time and with the bombs coming, there was no time for him to even think about other humans sharing the shelter. He argued that neither knew if they were home and besides, they wouldn't be prepared. With finality, he ran into the garage for fully charged solar batteries, emergency packs of traditional batteries, and the carton of water purification tablets.

"What changed your mind? Tired of me after just six months?"

"Never." He stared at her until he realized she was teasing him again. "No, it's just that, there's a scientist and his wife in Iowa "

"That's awfully far to go swinging."

"What? No, nothing like that. Really, Linda."

"Sorry. Okay, not swingers, scientists. Got it," she retorted with the slightest of grins.

"Well, he is. I don't know about her. Anyway, he's been in a bunker that is now running out of supplies. He's looking for safe shelter away from the Seven Flags."

"Yeah, I don't blame them for getting out of that shithole country. But Iowa is far," Linda thought out loud.

"And I don't even know if it's really him or why he wants to come west." Ever since he read up on Anders and the APLS research, he was intrigued. While he studied the cosmos, Anders was doing practical research that might actually help America heal. That alone meant he was someone worthy of help. But they'd never met, came from different circles, and for all he knew, the man was an impostor, using the man's recognition to get help.

"We can't go get them, but I suppose if they got all the way here, we couldn't turn them away," Linda said, finishing her dinner.

"No, that would be cruel." After the bombs stopped falling but before the winds brought the radiation to Santa Barbara, Linda had climbed to the surface and went next door to see if the neighbors were safe. No one answered the door. They never found out what became of them and a part of Reid later came to regret not offering aid. He promised himself he would do better next time, and "next time" had arrived. Still, he couldn't just invite a strange couple to their shelter, not without some sort of verification.

"You're serious," she said.

"I think I am. He has this amazing project, something that could help humanity. After everything science has produced, and the current state of things, the nukes, Linda, the nukes have left a stain on science," Reid said, sighing with pain at the prospect of science being mankind's doom. "Apparently, he has a method to encourage rapid growth of plant life regardless of terrain using quantum entanglement. At least that's the gist of it."

"Well, that's pretty damn amazing. So, he could grow tomatoes in the backyard, radiation and all?"

"Something like that."

"Wow, imagine large, freaking mutant tomatoes the size of beach balls in our backyard," Linda said.

Reid laughed at that then shook his head. "I have no clue what he could actually grow, but I doubt it will be anything like that."

"This man I gotta meet," Linda said. "Go vet him. I'll even clean up."

"No, I've got it." Reid, as Linda fully knew well, was fussy about cleaning after a meal. He gathered their plates and glasses and brought them into the kitchen. He set the recycled water to blistering hot and filled the shallow sink. He meticulously washed one plate, rinsed it in hot water, and carefully hand dried it before moving on to the next one. Not only did he gain a sense of assurance in the act, but it also let his mind work. After all, this man's work was significant and could truly help humankind. All of it. A man like that needs to survive, he needs protection. Reid knew that since APLS hadn't been circulated, it suggested that the work was not completed. The short reading he had done suggested Anders had been working on this for some time, but it wasn't ready for mass use.

If he checked out, he would find the inner strength to invite strangers into the world. And while he would never grow tired of Linda, he was sure she would appreciate someone else to speak with or lose at backgammon to.

Once everything was dry, the counters wiped down with disinfectant, and his hands washed again, he returned to his computer. The message board was in place complete with a contact link for Anders. "Computer, establish contact." While others named their computer AI or bought celebrity-endorsed AIs, he left his at the factory settings, not caring about it. Every now and then, Linda tried to suggest something for a change of pace, but Reid wasn't a fan of change.

There was a lag, then the connection was interrupted and he needed to reestablish an uplink to the net, and minutes ticked by as he felt himself beginning to second-guess his decision. At the screen to his left, a window resolved itself and a scratchy, imperfect human face appeared. He looked like Anders, an older version than the one he saw in The Journal interview. The handsome face still looked youthful even with beard stubble and dark smudges under the eyes. His unruly brown hair was annoying, but it was the intensity of the man's gaze that caught Reid's attention.

"David Anders?"

"Yes."

"I'm Reid Costa out in Santa Barbara."

"Wow, some portion of the west coast is intact."

"More than you think. What's your real situation?"

Anders frowned at that. "It's as I described. My wife Betty and I have been in a bunker adjacent to my lab for the last six months. We're down to three days' worth of food and water, and I need shelter, sanctuary, something to keep her safe and to finish my work."

"Why not work with the new government of the Seven Flags?"

"You're shitting me, right? Do you have any idea of what's going on here? I've been in a box and could tell you that it's martial law and ugly. I have zero interest in working for Holtzer."

"Holtzer?"

"The bastard running things. I need to get out. We need to get out. Do you have crash space, even for a week? We need to get out and regroup."

Reid was discomfited by the clear desperation felt through the screen and his heart went out to the man's plight. Still, trust but verify.

"How do I know it's you?"

Anders blinked.

"What do you need? My DNA?"

"Just tell him about the apples," a voice—Betty's, he presumed—was heard in the background.

It was Reid's turn to be stunned into silence unless it meant he was successful. "You've grown apples already?"

Anders let out a bark of a laugh and shook his head. "Nah, not yet. I'm still tinkering with the stuff at a quantum level."

That caught Reid's attention since quantum physics was a language he understood. "But you're a botanist."

"Well, yes. But I am using biotechnology at the quantum level to rehydrate any plant life with self-replicating quantum cells. It's at a very delicate stage, but I am close to being able to use this in real-life conditions."

"This is based on Vertigan's work?"

"Yeah, I've been finding the sweet spot between..."

"...near-Planck-times to as slow as Cosmological-Constant-time. Then it self-replicates..."

"Allowing me to synthesize artificial self-reproducing quantum-entangled prebiotic kernel systems to promote new growth."

"I think our two men are in love," Linda brightly said from over Reid's shoulder. "Hi, I'm Linda."

David Anders nodded in her direction and then turned his attention back to Reid, an expectant look on his face. Reid was intrigued at Anders' process and the idea of having someone to talk quantum theory with. He definitely seemed legitimate and certainly desperate.

"We have one room..." he began.

"And he's got lab space," Linda chirped.

David cut back to the point. "The further away from the Seven Flags the better, so California here we come. Seriously, under normal circumstances, if we shared the driving and didn't stop except for battery swaps, we'd be there in about 24 hours."

"These are not ordinary times," Linda said, now beside Reid, her hand approvingly on his shoulder.

A blonde woman peered over Anders' shoulder, tablet in hand. "Hi, I'm Betty the navigator. It's roughly 1500 miles from here to Santa Barbara. If you give me your GPS coordinates, I can refine that and plot us a course."

"How long do you think it will take you?" Linda asked Betty. Reid leaned back and Anders made room. It seemed the women were now in charge of the conversation.

"A week is my best estimate I have until I know what's really out there."

"Do you have any defenses?"

Betty blinked. "Guns? Ha! No, nothing. If he lets me, I can pack the kitchen knives and we have crap to barter."

"My equipment is not crap," Anders complained.

"Drive safely." Linda chuckled, appreciating that Betty dealt with similar tendencies with her man as she did, something else she noted would be a welcome conversation to share in.

"Anders, you'd better get a move on it," Reid said as he transmitted their coordinates, the one detail he prized at present. His safety and anonymity were on the line, but Anders' process was important enough to take the risk.

"We'll be in touch as much as we can from the road," Anders said. He was about to cut the tenuous connection when he paused and leaned into the camera. "Thank you, Reid." Then he turned to Betty, who leaned in with him, and in unison, they said, "Thank you, Linda" before severing the connection and beginning their journey.

CHAPTER 5

Field Journal:
Entry 9

Writing in her journal, Betty noted: "Clearly, the one-week estimate was a wild dream. More of a hope, I suppose. We had no idea what we were getting ourselves into. It's now day nine and, as my loving husband constantly reminds me, the radiation shielding we managed to apply to the car was rated for, at best, seventeen days. So while we need to get to Santa Barbara before then, it'll be a bit of a moot point, because we only have enough food currently for the next five days. But hey, if we manage to fast for the remainder, at least we'll become thin glowing corpses," she added, half for her own self-indulgent humor.

"We've found another building with a fully fueled generator, so we can recharge the TAV's batteries. For that, I am grateful, because I need to stretch. I'm doing a lot of walking now, charging my internal batteries, before getting into that cramped car again. I don't think this model was designed for long drives. God, we certainly didn't need a long drive in Omaha. As it is, finding ways to charge the TAV has proven even more challenging than dealing with my pessimistic husband or finding water." She continued to ponder in her journal. It was the only thing that kept her sane, the ability to spew her thoughts onto the endless page, the only constant in this new world.

"David's grown gloomier, either from the cramped conditions or the conversations he's had with Reid, who strikes me as a tad paranoid and certainly a Doomsday prophet. I mean, who builds their own hideaway by themselves? At least it looks nice enough from the videos." She did have some comfort in the destination, Linda seemed lovely, and someone that she'd be friends with, even if these weren't the circumstances. And the videos that had taken three days to download looked like they were going somewhere that was prepared for the unknown. That gave Betty some much-needed relief.

Betty paused the journal but continued walking. They were in the remains of a factory. She couldn't begin to guess what kinds of electronic components were made here, but David had been gathering more items to barter, which was good because their supplies had dwindled. How this place hadn't been ransacked was a mystery to her. It was nestled among a dozen other buildings in this industrial park and they all seemed largely overlooked.

As it was, once the TAV, their trusty four-year-old Tridar Automation Vehicle, was packed and they hit the road, the AI mapping program couldn't find a clear route—it couldn't access the network of traffic sensors and drones that would have normally provided one. Instead, Betty had anticipated this and had programmed in multiple options using older maps, and these proved useful. They drove south from Iowa and found backroads through Nebraska that allowed them to slip out of the Seven Flags territory into Kansas, south but at least back into the United States. Apparently, despite the lightning-fast establishment of the new government, securing all its borders had yet to occur, so they slipped off the main highway and took circuitous smaller roads that let them slip through.

David seemed particularly easier once he knew he was beyond Holtzer's reach. Their history continued to nag at her and he kept saying he wasn't ready to talk about it. Any time it came up, he deflected, so they talked about everything but his military past despite the specter clearly hanging over their heads. So they talked about what they saw, and as he drove, Betty wrote. She was chronicling their journey with meticulous detail, partly to stay busy, and partly to preserve this perilous period in their lives. She signed on to their married life knowing there were secrets and figured they'd eventually be shared. Up until the bombs flew, it wasn't an issue; however, with every passing day, it now seemed more important. She knew there were government secrets and missions that haunted David's past, things he did or was asked to do, that he wouldn't relive. But at this point, Betty was growing tired of that, and with each passing hour out in the unknown of this apocalypse, she yearned for a human moment, for feeling close to the one person that mattered to her. And for that, she needed him to open up about his past.

The Midwest may have been spared nuclear annihilation, but the shattering of the supply lines along with the persistent drought had left the American middle barren. Smaller towns were now ghost towns and the roads, streets, boulevards, avenues, throughways, and highways were littered with broken-down vehicles of every make and model imaginable. Most had been stripped for spare parts and their inhabitants among the army of walkers, destination unknown. Those with the means fashioned signs begging for rides, food, and even water. With the skies clouded, temperatures had rapidly dropped so the normal temperature in this region, from 65° to 75° Fahrenheit, had plummeted a good twenty degrees. David explained it was a good ten degrees worse in the Alliance countries. Europe, Canada, and South America all had it worse and the worst had yet to come now that true winter has arrived.

Reid, who had made a study of the projections and computer scenarios, had warned them that there would be no food grown in North America, and most of the world, for over a year. Between radiation sickness and famine, the nine billion people of 2121 Earth would rapidly decrease to a small fraction of its former glory, as the survivors fought over scraps. Hearing that chilled Betty's blood and made her all the more grateful Reid and Linda were welcoming them. It also reminded her that the man driving and arguing with her over what music to play held the one possible solution to mankind's survival. No pressure.

As it was, their rations ran out on day three, as expected, and every time they pulled over to begin foraging for energy of some sort, they also scavenged for any other essentials they could find. They lost a day to being unable to drive very far when Betty caught food poisoning from something that went wrong with a tin of tuna they found under an overturned grocery store shelf. Water was also a rare commodity, so the notion of bathing became a dream and the TAV began to stink beyond the air conditioner's ability to refresh the cabin air.

They were tired, and with every passing mile, seemed to grow incrementally more irritable with one another. It began with little things such as fighting between classic rock of the 20th century to the Mozart sonatas she preferred for soothing her nerves. When he wanted to torture her, he played the sharp electronic melodica he used when working out. It jarred her nerves and forced her to place her hands over her ears as he cranked up the volume and tried to sing along. David was wonderful in so many ways, she could forgive him for his inability to sing. When she sang along to her favorites, Shaka or the Gibson Twins, he indulged her, limiting himself to merely humming.

Normally, they'd mix in music with local news or audio narratives, but these days, they couldn't seem to find common ground. He wanted nothing light and fluffy that belied the horrible circumstances the world found itself in while she needed something distracting. They tried the works of Austen, Burroughs, King, and Mack, but after a few chapters, one or the other shut it off.

The first in a series of arguments began over a disagreement over directions. Overturned trucks blocked the road they were on and her tablet map suggested picking up a different road, but it meant turning around. He wanted to skirt the trucks, risking damage over the rocky terrain past the road's shoulder. Anything that he deemed a "waste" of their precious energy was anathema to him. She acquiesced since it wasn't a big deal that time, but subsequent battles over directions grew more heated.

"I'm a fucking scientist, I can figure this out," he shouted at her one time.

"This isn't some plant you're breeding," she countered. "Just turn left here."

And so it went, day after day after day. They fought over music, stories, directions, and even how long they should sleep. He feared they made easy prey whenever they were not in motion and wanted to push themselves for every mile possible before catnaps. The teacher, though, knew the value of longer rest and cognitive restoration, so that became a new battlefront after four days. Here they were on day nine and neither were happy, with their individual behavior or their spouse. The uneasy periods of quiet stretched like a yawning chasm between them despite the close quarters. What kept them from truly getting nasty was that life outside the TAV was worse. The roads were starting to be littered with the dead, as exhaustion or dehydration began to take its toll. Where there were corpses, came the very hungry predators and scavengers alike. Humans took clothing and personal effects, the animals, birds, and insects took what remained, piece by piece, layer by layer. Grisly images dotted the roads and even the places they stopped to relieve themselves or recharge.

"I hate this," David said on only the second night, setting the tone for the entire journey. He held the service weapon he kept after his time with the US military. He'd kept it locked away, away from Betty, away from her even knowing of its existence. David never bothered to clean it since separating from the service, but an hour before they left the bunker, he carefully took it apart, not missing a beat as if he was gearing up for an upcoming mission, cleaned and oiled it, chambering a round and tucking it into the holster, which now hung at his hip. The sight of it kept them from being attacked twice now, and he hadn't even had to withdraw it. On the third day, they were bartering electronic components for the right to top off their water bottles at a running river. David insisted on testing the water before even considering a trade, and once the results showed it was safe—enough—he agreed. The people hoarding access to the stream now wanted double. He casually pulled back his jacket to show the holstered pistol and cocked an eyebrow. The original deal was honored. Might was making right and they were left alone. But he still hated carrying it and feared using it. Not only couldn't he sing, but he also wasn't a very good shot. He didn't want to play the odds, though, thinking to himself, "How many more times will that work in my favor before it doesn't?"

The one thing they agreed on was that humanity had quickly devolved into savagery and he grew to understand how Fitzpatrick could not guarantee him safe passage. The helping hand that was normally on display after disasters was absent this time. Those who remained in their homes had barricaded doors and windows, and those on the move traveled in pods that were either predator or prey. One productive conversation they had was over whether or not the reduced human population would fare better once the crop growing could commence in a year or two. The devastation from the attack left a gloomy outlook to the preservation of life, but it was in some of these moments that David pondered the will of man, and how the species could endure, and would.

So it went until here they were, on day nine and just entering Wyoming. Betty suggested detouring on Route 76 to stop at Fort Collins, hoping for a safe place for a good night's sleep if not also some fresh electric fuel. Once again, David argued, preferring to take Route 80, further north of the Fort, even if it deflected them from their western direction. However, as they neared Cheyenne, once again, they had to course correct, heading even further north on Route 80 to 25, heading further north to Casper and Yellowstone Park, and further away from Santa Barbara. David feared the lack of directness to Reid but understood he needed to ensure absolute safety. So even with the fear of adding more time to the journey, he knew this was the only option.

Finally, Betty bubbled over. "Why do you have such hatred for the military? What on earth happened? You cost us days at least by not taking my advice."

David brooded for a few slow miles, not responding, and she waited him out. His shaving cream had run out and he had a five-day growth of beard that surprised her with how much red was coming through. The long hair remained a lovely chestnut brown, but the red seemed out of place. He looked exhausted, tense, and anything but the man she fell in love with.

"The APLS needed sophisticated equipment the university lacked," he finally began, his voice low, tone even, almost monotone. "I needed funding and equipment to even see if this was remotely possible. So, I made a deal with the devil. I approached the government, the Office of Science, and I was directed to the Pentagon."

"Why the military for a botany project?"

"I asked that very question the day I got the call," he admitted. His eyes remained fixed on the road, which was as littered with debris as every other road. He swerved around hunks of metal and rotting meat melting off the bone. "I was told they had the very equipment or means to develop any needs I had, along with staffing who could help me determine if this was a pipe dream or a real breakthrough."

He drove on, a haunted look filling his eyes. Betty would wait him out, finally learning of what happened during those years. Being a teacher taught her patience, waiting out recalcitrant students and forcing them to fill the void with an answer to her question.

"I worked with an R&D team and my theories were looking promising. I was given carte blanche access to equipment, even some assistants. In turn, I was required to make monthly reports to the military. And that's when Holtzer heard about the APLS."

"What's he like?"

"Look up utter bastard in the Dictionary and it's him," David grumbled. "He is your stereotypical war hawk. Everything is a threat. Everyone is a threat. Everything can be weaponized. He lives, eats, and breathes combat."

Betty blinked at that. "But we haven't had an actual war in decades."

"He's old, saw combat in the last conflict with Sudan. He served two tours there then another when it looked like Bolivia was about to erupt. There's always something smoldering and he's the first to volunteer to piss all over it."

"He sounds lovely."

"Anything but. The first few briefings, he seemed like he'd rather be anywhere but at my briefing. But, the third or fourth time, he was paying attention, and by the fifth, he was asking questions."

"How do you turn hydration into a weapon? Drown the enemy?"

"No, the slick bastard wanted to know if it could be reverse engineered and use the APLS to withdraw water from living matter, dehydrating the enemy into submission without risk of life."

Betty shuddered at the thought then looked over to see his face. He was clearly reliving those conversations and they pained him. The frustration they'd been feeling for one another was melting away, no quantum processing required.

"I told him no, it couldn't be done, or if it could, I wouldn't be a party to it. That was when I realized I needed to get out of there and find proper funding in the private sector. But I needed time. Holtzer wasn't going to give me any and began dropping by the lab, 'inspecting' my work as if he could understand anything other than plants are green. He even began asking my assistants for copies of my research. When I realized some preliminary notes had been passed over without my authorization, I went over his head and complained to the Secretary of Defense. She almost laughed at me for complaining about Holtzer, one of her most revered advisors. I did, though, get her to agree to ask him to back off.

"I returned to the base and had the assistants reassigned and increased the data encryption on my research, pulling the backups from the cloud and resorted to downloading the backup to a hard drive each night, then carrying it in my pocket."

He fell into silence and they drove on for a few more miles, dodging gaping potholes and with tight lips, avoiding making eye contact with any of the hitchhikers. Not that there was room even if he wanted to help out.

Betty waited.

Finally, the narrative resumed. "About six, seven months go by, and Holtzer had backed off the lab visits, but continued to attend the briefings. He just watched me, the falcon to the mouse. There was a smile he had that irked me, one that suggested he knew something I didn't, and that pleased him. Finally, it was maybe a year total, he shows up in the lab unannounced, that idiot smirk now a grin.

"He announces that my data was good enough for his own tech people to figure out that the dehydration could work and they had been field testing it. It wasn't quite right, so he gained authorization from the Secretary herself to re-task me to help him refine it.

"I complained as high as I could, appealing to my Senators, my Congressmen, anyone who might listen. But I was some kid with a promising plan going up against a decorated soldier. He practically crowed when I reported to his office to see what I could do. I couldn't sabotage the project, but I figured if I could refine his project, maybe it'd help me with mine. The work was actually good and I had to admire his people, who were never introduced to me. He compartmentalized everything so only he knew the big picture.

"We managed to make it work on mice, then birds. It was grisly, horrible stuff. I think I had nightmares. I know I didn't sleep. Anyway, one morning, he announced we were ready for human trials. I had to laugh because we weren't at war and capital punishment didn't exist anymore so I asked where the volunteers were coming from. Then he laughed and said he didn't need volunteers. The world was filled with enemies and we'd try it out on selected targets. I knew we had adversaries, rivals, whatever you want to call them. I also knew the Alliance was taking shape and Fitzpatrick was shitting his pants over the aspect of a war. So was the UN and, well, any sane person.

"Holtzer said he had one subject in mind, one he wanted us to test the technique on. Korean premier Bin Yun-Seo. He was coming that September to address the UN General Assembly, so it was an ideal time to reach him. I refused to do any further work on it. I was not going to be a party to cold-blooded murder. My work was to preserve life, not be an assassin. We argued for days over it, each of us refusing to budge. What he didn't realize at the time was that I had begun unwinding my work so when things blew up, I could walk away."

Betty stared at him, a flood of emotions washing over her. She knew something happened when he returned, how it set him back a good year as he scrambled for funding and a place to resume his work. He'd been withdrawn with their friends and family and only seemed receptive to her. She comforted him, knowing better than to pry, and on more than a few occasions, she awoke to his nightmare thrashing and needed to coo in his ear to calm him down. She'd been waiting for him to reveal what had happened, and now that it was here, she was properly horrified.

He seemed to deflate, having bottled this up for so long, and now it made perfect sense why his very name bothered him and why he wanted as little to do with the military as possible. She reached over and placed a comforting hand on his shoulder. His left hand crossed over and caressed it as he continued to drive forward, his right hand white-knuckling, the tension for today remained steadfast. Betty, stricken by the revelations, felt for her husband and his sanity, but thought to herself, as she added the notes in her journal, "I finally feel that emotion again, I feel comfort, I feel the need to be strong for someone who is being vulnerable, I feel love again."

David knew what the problem was, given the state of the world. The military were the only ones who were disciplined and trained well enough to restore order. For America, that was going to be life under Fitzpatrick's orders. For those stuck in the Seven Flags, it meant everyone would dance to Holtzer's tune.

CHAPTER 6

The Seven Flags

Cigars were becoming an endangered species, much like the rest of the world's commodities, but today, Rodney Holtzer allowed himself one. Today was a good day, one worth celebrating. After six months of hard work, things had come together and were now running smoothly. He had been laying the groundwork for the Seven Flags for a decade in Kansas City, Missouri. His office was strategically placed at the Marine Corps Mobilization Command, a base that had been deactivated in 2011 and remained unused by anyone, barely maintained. The place was a ghost town. When no one was looking, Holtzer had begun rerouting materiel and supplies to the base, ensuring it received upgraded utilities, from plumbing to broadband. He had hidden the costs under other expenses, outright lied to the men who did the actual work, promising them news that the reactivation would be forthcoming, but for the moment, it was "need to know."

He adjusted his brown and green jacket, the newly commissioned emblem of the Seven Flags on the right shoulder, his name stitched in gold across the left breast. The starched sage green shirt was open at the throat, revealing the beginnings of an eagle tattoo and a thatch of gray hair. He had piercing black eyes that betrayed his age, the gray in his hair conveying his experience. There were crow's feet at the eyes, a scar on the right cheek marring the weathered skin. The crew cut was old-fashioned, but keeping it short was simple, and he liked things simple. The datapad at his wrist flashed incoming messages and requests for conversations, all of which he had ignored.

Looking out the window, he saw a fleet of helicopters lined up, ready for action. Off to the right were armored all-terrain vehicles capable of ferrying twenty men apiece, most anywhere within the land now controlled by the Seven Flags. Beyond them were the tanks and other troop carriers. To the left were barracks filled with men and women who swore allegiance to the new nation, most believing in his ideology, others willing to act as ordered in exchange for food and shelter, ideology be damned. The units had mustered out as needed, quelling rioting, enforcing curfews, and making criminals pay in Old Testament fashion. Punishments were handed out in public, with whippings being the first level, all the way up to hanging (with bullets now a precious commodity, the rope could be reused).

A decade ago, although it felt so much further in the past, Holtzer was watching with alarm as Russia awoke from a decade's slumber, and once more the bear roared, demanding attention. A restive China had just finished assimilating India, expelling Buddha from their land, while Korea forged alliances rather than take on the larger foe. Iran had overrun Iraq and Kuwait fifteen years earlier and was looking to expand, enveloping and eventually extinguishing Israel, which finally admitted what everyone knew for a century, that they had nukes. What surprised the world was how many had been stored in tunnels once used by smugglers. They'd found innovative ways of miniaturization that made them envied and feared.

In conversation with Garrison White, a soldier turned politician, the then-governor of South Dakota seemed to be a like-minded man. They fretted over what was an increasingly likely collaboration. Neither expected the forces to become the Alliance, but they had spent many late nights talking global politics over tumblers of scotch. It was White who complained about the sleepy Executive Branch and he feared America would be caught with their pants down and take it up the ass from some foreign foe. Finally, White visited Holtzer in Washington, when he was in town for a governors' meeting with newly elected President Fitzpatrick. There, over steaks and scotch, White said he'd found others who shared their worldview, including Scarlet Wolf, a financier from Colorado, and Kane Roza, another military man, based in Iowa. He suggested they all get together at his retreat in the Badlands, shoot some buffalo, and talk.

From these meetings, the beginnings of the Seven Flags formed, bringing in Army demolitions expert Bowie Cormac from Nebraska; Gunther Fitzgerald, a Missourian who worked with Holtzer for thirty years; Luna Knox, a Kansas corporate powerhouse; and Elsa Ember, a Wyoming humanitarian, who saw a radical approach to saving lives. For nearly ten years, the group of rebels turned their talking into action, each carrying a digital alarm that was synced only to these eight people, and whenever it was activated, they'd swing into action using plans that were revised every six months, reacting to world politics. To their surprise, President Fitzpatrick got himself re-elected and remained passive as the Alliance coalesced. In Washington, Holtzer did his best to remain loyal, using his contacts throughout the Pentagon to be prepared for the Alliance. Some acted, others demurred, following their Commander-in-Chief's lead.

It was ingenious, carefully crafted, and meticulously engineered. All eight hand-selected candidates from their states would serve at the state and federal levels, getting entrenched in the politics, ensuring power over the localized governments. So, when the time came, each of them had voices, but more importantly, votes for secession. It was these men and women who increasingly began to object to legislation as a block, conditioning the American public to see these seven states as one with a voice. Some called them nuisances, others revolutionaries, but the truth of the matter was greyer. The country had stagnated, Holtzer wasn't wrong there, and to bring disruption into the mix would, in the long run, be cleansing for a governing body that had outgrown its effectiveness.

Knox had the new military uniforms mass-produced, saying it was for a dramatized action series she was financing, while Wolf hired designers to come up with everything a new nation might need, from logo to highway signage. Whenever they'd gather, their constitution was drafted, American laws rewritten to fit their paradigm, and a strike force assembled and trained, so when the day came, they would seal their new borders at bridges, tunnels, and waterways, close the airports, and train lines, plus seize the media apparatus. It had been reviewed and revised, even rehearsed as a War Game.

Then, the bombs flew.

It was White who activated the alarm, summoning the others

to action. By the time New York and San Francisco began to burn, the Seven Flags had been born with military precision. Men took the time to switch their uniforms to the ones from the new government while pre-recorded broadcasts began, announcing the new country's existence. They'd even selected and groomed a woman to arrive at the United Nations with notarized documentation, presenting her credentials for admission, requesting observer status for the moment.

The media had seen nothing like it, a new nation arising from a national conflagration, refusing a coast-to-coast call for aid and support. Instead, Holtzer, speaking for the new government without claiming a title, announced martial law and began shutting things down in the name of public safety. He eventually took to calling himself Chief of Staff while his allies took control as governors of the seven regions that once called themselves states. Holtzer harbored no illusions that the seven would be loyal to one another as long as it served their agendas in these early days of the nation. There would be, in the coming months, more splinter groups, secret alliances, and possibly betrayal. The only one he knew to be completely loyal was Gunther; everyone else was a possible liability. They just needed to hang together and give the new nation some roots, so when the inevitable fallout occurred, the Seven Flags would still stand.

The previous six months saw the well-organized operation preserve life as the skies clouded, the temperatures plummeted, and resources grew scarce. Their stockpiled goods, from blankets to canned vegetables, endeared them to their new citizenry. As a result, few protested, and the organized attempts to resist were quickly and publicly quashed.

He was pleased and didn't mind when Knox wandered through the door without knocking. She looked stunning in a turquoise dress that accentuated her ample figure, her blonde hair piled in a sensible bun. Jewelry dangled from ears and wrists; an ankle bracelet jangled as she walked. Her confident stride was a hallmark and people had trouble keeping up with her, despite her being in her forties.

"Good morning," she said.

"It is, isn't it?"

"They finished the census analysis last night. Here are the highlights," she said, handing him a tablet.

As things settled, Knox's people coordinated a name-by-name census, ascertaining who survived, what their skills were, and how valuable they would be to the Seven Flags. They saw the same projections Anders had, that food would not grow for years, and death would rule. A triage of their countrymen would be required in the coming months and this represented the first analysis.

Holtzer nodded as he accepted the tablet and saw the report had been organized and cross-referenced. He needed geniuses who could make food grow in labs and greenhouses, computer techs who could rebuild fried computers, even janitors to clean up after the dead. Knox helped herself to tea, coffee having become too precious for daily use even by the leadership, and sat in a surprisingly comfortable chair. The general thumbed his way past glass blowers, actors, and beauticians, and paused at scientists. His eyes scanned the screens until they paused at one name he recognized. Someone he knew had the genius to save the people of the Seven Flags, if not the continent. This person would do what was best for mankind and do it under Holtzer's command.

He tapped his wrist datapad, and within seconds, Iowa governor Roza responded.

"Send a team to Sargent's Spur and bring me a scientist named David Anders."

CHAPTER 7
The Passage Beyond

For David, it felt like a dam had cracked. Once he revealed to Betty what truly happened during his brief tenure with the military, he felt more relaxed. The weight of what had occurred, the time it cost him, and the threat that remained out there with his research had sickened him. The idea that his research could be perverted sickened him. He was a builder, not a destroyer, and if anyone died as a result of his work, he couldn't imagine bearing that guilt.

It now felt like it was all he was talking about as he finally shared the details with his soon-to-be-host Reid. Each day, they would check in with one another, via radio, video transmissions, whatever was working that day. They used the time as a tool for getting to know one another. Mixing in with the discussions over quantum theory and Reid's own search for meaning in the universe, there were the more traditional trading of backgrounds. Whereas he went to the Ivy Leagues, Reid was a product of the California colleges, getting his undergraduate degree at the California Institute of Technology followed by a quick Masters at Stanford. He'd put off his doctorate program after he met Linda and got involved in his work for the University of Santa Barbara. There, he was left to do research, a bevy of grad students doing the scut work year after year.

In turn, Reid also disclosed his OCD, which made living with him a challenge, but one Linda seemed more than up for. "We all have our burdens," David assured him.

With every passing day, David described the desolation and despair that marked every mile. With Reid's help, they figured out adjustments to their course. Whenever Betty's mapping failed, Reid offered tips he picked up from nearby ham radio operators and David even tried resorting to celestial navigation whenever there was a break in the cloud cover. That proved elusive and frustrating, so he put it aside, thinking about those who made their living on the water. What must it be like for them, he wondered.

"You know what I miss," David said one night as the TAV was charging at an auto supply shop in Wyoming. "I miss baseball."

"Too slow," Reid replied. "I prefer hockey. I watch it and imagine the puck is a proton or electron, bouncing against other molecules and forming new elements for the briefest of moments. The speed is thrilling."

David chuckled at that.

"For me, it's the outdoor summertime, the grass, and dirt, that the game has endured for three centuries, and someone from the 1800s would still recognize it for the most part. Although the gear they wear these days makes them look positively cybernetic."

"Do you ever do anything with cybernetics?"

"Well, I toyed with cyber enhancements to root systems before I put everything aside for APLS. You know, the 1800s was such an exciting time."

"If you call the Civil War exciting. Weren't there a lot of diseases too? Yellow fever epidemics and the like?"

"Okay, the Civil War was certainly a dark time, but think about it. The century started with the steam engine and ended with the motion picture projector. In between, there were incredible advancements in magnetism, physics, and inventions. It changed society in dramatic ways."

"David, you sound like a historian," Reid joked. To physicists, historians ranked low on the sciences scale. But that wasn't for a lack of appreciating history. Reid, like many scientists, didn't believe history was a science, more an invention of man, to prop up the victor, and tell the story they wanted to tell, not the unabridged truth that would garner using such a word as science.

"I firmly believe in knowing the history of my field, those who came before me. It's interesting to note that while I find American ingenuity impressive, the real botanical work was done by the Europeans during that period. Very few Americans made noteworthy contributions during that time."

Reid imitated a snoring sound, which made both David and Betty, who had been trying to wipe the windows clean, laugh.

"Okay, you've put Reid to sleep. Put Linda on," she insisted, coming closer to the tablet.

Much as Reid and David spent time getting comfortable with one another, Linda and Betty insisted on equal time since, after all, they argued, they were going to be stuck with one another while the men hid in the lab.

"Hey, girl," Linda said that night.

"Want to talk 1800s fashion?" They giggled.

"Not at all. Before they get lost in their reveries over bouncing electronics..."

"Electrons," Reid shouted from the background.

"Whatevs," Linda said in a bored tone. "Seriously, if your husband is going to pull his weight here, he can use that botanical genius to help us with a hothouse. You wouldn't believe the seed types Reid squirreled away. The best thing about marrying a Doomsday prepper is that when Doomsday arrived, he was ready."

Betty had already shared how spartan and drab their bunker was. She endured it, of course, but she craved something with color and some additional space. Before leaving, she noted there was enough wear on the concrete floor to show the patterns of her exercise walking. "I swear, it gave me flat feet," she complained early in their chatting.

By now, they talked about their past lives, the loved ones most likely gone. Anyone who lived near either coast was automatically assumed to be dead until proof was offered. Each had grieved in their own ways and now commiserated with one another.

It turned out they were close in age, so their pop culture frame of reference overlapped. From that foundation, they discovered a shared interest in fiction and instrumental jazz, although Linda mixed in pop and even country, while Betty leaned toward classical. Despite being the younger of the two, Linda declared she had the older soul.

David took comfort in knowing Betty would have an actual friend when they arrived in Santa Barbara. He knew that once he resumed his work, he'd be putting in his obsessively late hours, something that he seemed to share with Reid.

As they closed the connection, David looked at Betty, who seemed genuinely happy rather than tense. He wanted to sustain that mood, tired of arguing, tired of stress. He checked the gauge app and saw he was about done charging the TAV.

"I'm feeling pretty good; want to push on for a few hours?" He smiled encouragingly at her. They had eclipsed the thirteenth day now; David was determined to get to Reid as soon as they could, knowing that this streak of good humor would pass in time, and didn't want to go through another cycle of what they had just emerged from.

She seemed to pick up on his meaning; she was always good at reading him. With a nod, she stretched herself before climbing back into the car, which had its doors open, airing out the human smell. They desperately needed proper bathing, but there had been nowhere safe to stop. Her hair was a greasy mess, her clothing soiled from the times they had to climb over or around debris to find food or energy. There was no time to pack more than a few outfits and two had already been bartered when things got desperate. To him, though, she looked like a stoic pioneer, rough for wear, for the game.

Under all the stress and anger and frustration, he still desperately loved her, feeling very lucky to have her in his life. And with the final secrets now shared, he could truly relax around her. It was a balm to his soul, one he didn't realize he needed.

They resumed their trip on Route 25 with David having reconciled himself to the delay. With the hazy sun having set, the night sky was shades of gray, the roadway dark except for various TAV headlights here and there. He'd drive a good twenty or thirty minutes before seeing another vehicle. The hikers had found shelter for the night, so the animals and insects were the only ones on the move. As a result, when pairs of headlights appeared in the distance behind them, David didn't pay them much attention. Instead, he let Betty pick the music and he relaxed, listening to her sing along.

However, the two vehicles neared then remained fixed in distance behind him. It was unusual for there to be cars in parallel like that, neither gaining nor falling behind. There was something precise about it, almost... military. That sent the hairs on the back of his neck upright and his hands gripped the steering column tightly. He tried to slow down to see what happened and the vehicles fell back, maintaining their distance. That convinced him this was nothing good.

"I think we're being followed," he said.

Betty paused singing and looked over her shoulder, unable to really see out the back window given their belongings piled high. She swiveled back and asked, "What makes you think that?"

"Instinct or paranoia," he said.

She quickly consulted the tablet, which approximated their position given the lack of strong satellite connections through the haze above. Her fingers scrolled, stretched images, and finally, she traced a path.

"There's a spur up ahead; it's a right onto 95, a state road," she said.

He nodded in confirmation, having already seen a road sign indicating the exit. He gunned the engine and they went from a steady 45 to 65 in seconds, although they rattled and shook over the rough roadway. It clearly needed repair, and the higher speed punctuated every divot and pothole. As the car jerked ahead, his fears were confirmed anew as the cars paced them.

He hated wasting energy and going out of their way, adding to their journey, but getting there safely was better than being waylaid by road pirates. If that was what they were. His mind briefly flashed back to Holtzer, who was exceptionally proud of the tactical team he had ready to assassinate the Korean premier. He inherited the tactical team when he assumed command and renamed them the Ghost Squad, having them trained to be swift and deadly, leaving few traces of their existence. If this was anything like that, he had every right to be worried. Holtzer had bragged to him how they stole secrets, laid traps, and committed extralegal acts, and no one was the wiser.

His mind refocused from the past to the present as the right-hand turn came up fast, and he jerked the wheel at the last second, kicking up gravel, and took 95 straight north. As he pushed the car to 70 on the pitch-black road, he gained some distance, but sure enough, the twin pair of headlights also made the turn.

"Shit," he said, which sent Betty scrambling over her tablet.

He didn't know what they wanted; they had nothing of much value. They were as average as every other vehicle still moving on the highways. The chill spread from his heart through his limbs as it was clear the only unique thing was him. Someone knew who he was and where he was and someone wanted him. Considering he just left the Seven Flags a week earlier, he was now convinced that this was a Ghost Squad, sent by Holtzer to retrieve him and the APLS. He felt himself breathing harder and faster, worried now about having a panic attack and crashing.

"We're so fucked," he said.

"Focus. Next right West Carter," Betty snapped. "Gun it to 9th then another right."

"Where..." he began but focused on not hitting a flock of carrion birds picking over what might have once been a dog. Candles burned in several windows of the small buildings and homes he raced past, his eyes desperately scanning to find the sign for 9th Street. The headlights remained behind him, but they had definitely lost some ground and needed to travel single file.

As 9th approached, he re-gripped the steering and added power as he turned, skidding, but still in control.

"Back to 25, no, it's now 26. You want to get there and turn right."

"There is a plan, right?"

She didn't reply, studying the tablet as he kept switching from the windshield to the rearview mirror.

One of the cars looked to be gaining, which made David curse, feeling sweat trickle down his right cheek.

"Left on West Aspen," she snapped.

Without hesitation, he jerked the wheel and continued going faster than he felt comfortable.

"Right on 7th."

He obeyed, feeling she had a plan but didn't dare question her, not without losing focus. The car skidded over something he missed in the dark and he righted the vehicle, which clipped a bench. He overcorrected and the car fishtailed a bit before coming back under his control. The pursuing vehicles had definitely lost some ground. But he was visible, and there was no way to dim or kill the exterior lighting.

"Seventh gets us to 26, cross it, and the post office will be on your right."

"What's there?"

"I'm hoping bays for their trucks where we could hide. If they don't see us cross 26, we should be fine."

"Don't you think they have the same maps?"

"Yeah, but there's nothing behind the building. We can always ditch the car and hide in the brush."

It wasn't the best of plans but the only one they had, so he followed her instructions and crossed Route 26, and the headlights shined over the dark, two-story post office. Both scanned it as the vehicle moved, but Betty jabbed an arm across him, showing he needed to make a left into the parking lot, not the loading dock. At the edge of the lot were trees abutting a cluster of homes. He killed the lights as they coasted to the last parking spot and scrambled out of the car the moment they could. She handed him the pistol as she got out and then she dashed into the trees to the left. He shoved the "alien" weapon in his hip pocket and went right. Amidst the rustle of branches and dead leaves, he could hear engines and tires, so he sprinted a bit more until he found three closely positioned trees and leaped up, grabbing a branch. He was in nowhere near as good shape as Betty, but desperation mixed with adrenaline gave him the power to scramble up and then up one more branch, putting him a good ten or twelve feet off the ground. He hugged a trunk and tried to control his breathing as he strained to hear the enemy.

All he heard at first was his own rapid breathing and then a branch snapping to his right. There was something above him, probably birds whose sleep had been interrupted. A dog barked from a house nearby, answered by one further away. There were wheels, then a soft skid, then the doors slammed closed. Footsteps on gravel, then grass, then leaves. No voices. No flashlights, meaning they might be using night-vision gear, which only served to reinforce his conviction it was Holtzer's team. The footsteps were steady, several people, but he couldn't count distinct footsteps or guess how many were searching for him.

He was comfortably above them, hugging the tree and controlling his breathing. He was as safely positioned as circumstances allowed, but he had no clue where Betty was and feared they'd find her and threaten her to force him to surrender himself. He couldn't bear anything happening to her. His mind went to dark places and he shivered against the rough bark, grit affixing itself to his sweat-soaked face. There was most definitely a chill in the air and he wasn't exactly dressed for cold weather but reasoned his survival instinct would keep him alive, chattering teeth and all.

The scientist lost track of time and didn't dare check, so he thought about music, the Boston Red Sox, anything but Holtzer, or what might be happening to his wife. Every time his mind drifted toward dark ideas, he shook his head as if he could physically loosen the bad things, shake them out. He guessed it was thirty minutes or more as the men wandered the grounds, coming near then going further away. Finally, the sounds grew fainter, so they were heading away from him, into the neighborhood in a widening search pattern.

Finally, who knew how much time had passed, but he heard the footsteps returning, passing directly beneath him, and then heading back to the parking lot. Minutes later, he heard a series of car doors angrily slam shut and engines whine to life. Tires crunched and the vehicles were on the move, the sounds fading into the night.

Still, David didn't move, fearing one was left behind, but as the minutes passed, he heard nothing human. He lowered himself one branch and paused, straining to make out anything. He wanted to whisper or shout for Betty but didn't dare. So, after a count to 120, he lowered himself to the ground. He hurt all over, was starting to shiver from the cold night air in addition to the fear that continued to grip him. The adrenaline had faded, leaving him feeling drained. Driving was unthinkable now. Instead, he wanted to sleep; anywhere warm would do fine. He stood in place and listened and then decided that rather than seek Betty in the dark, he'd head back to the car, praying she'd be there.

She wasn't, and waves of panic rolled over him, but then his rational mind reminded him that to get to the car, she'd be making noise, which he would have heard. Instead, he was making the noise that would hopefully attract her.

He leaned against the dented fender and tried to regain control of his body and emotions, arms wrapped around himself to try and stay warm.

He waited, fighting the fear that niggled the back of his mind and bottom of his spine. After what felt like forever and a day, he heard leaves being crushed. With no evidence the enemies were nearby, he dared to loudly whisper her name.

The footsteps quickened their pace, and out from the trees burst Betty, her hair wild, her face wet with tears. She rushed into his arms and they held one another for a long while. He held her tight as she let go of the bottled-up emotions, heaving sobs against his chest. He soothed her, stroking her hair, trying to smooth it out, picking twigs and bits of leaves from it.

"You're a wild child now?" he finally said after a while.

She glanced up at him, but then he showed her a handful of natural debris plucked from her and she laughed.

They walked back to the car and noted it had been searched, probably seeking anything that might contain APLS data, but the hard drive never left his pocket. He was impressed they didn't sabotage the car so they could sleep and start fresh in the morning.

Betty had reached for a canteen and they each drank, then locked up the car and headed for the post office, hoping it was deserted and they could sleep there unmolested. Hand in hand, they walked to the shelter, realizing things had changed and the next few days were going to be even more dangerous.

CHAPTER 8

We're Being Followed

Rodney Holtzer was looking forward to the morning. He had assembled his governors for a status meeting and was feeling good. Things were going pretty much as they had planned, confirming for him the value of time invested in planning and patience. It took just over a decade to be ready but when disaster struck, so did opportunity, and he seized it, wrestling it to the ground and making it his. He always kept the big picture in mind, refusing to get caught up in regional issues. There, he deferred entirely to his governors, who knew the territory better. He had been reaching out, as technology allowed, to other nations around the world, seeking recognition, and with that, validation of country, validation of borders and security.

It was going to take a lot to ruin his morning, so of course, that was exactly what happened.

An adjutant entered the meeting room, a converted amphitheater, retrofitted with a massive round table, plush chairs, and two walls filled with screens and another wall with shifting images from whichever broadcast facilities managed to operate, including screens from America, Canada, and Mexico. Most of the time, there was static, but when they could get a signal, operatives watched, taking notes for a follow-up briefing.

Holtzer was finishing a cup of tea—leaves easier to find and maintain than coffee beans—when he was interrupted. He cocked a graying eyebrow at the woman.

"Message from GT One," she told him.

He waited expectantly.

"Target not acquired. Bird bugged."

He glowered at her, but trained personnel were in short supply, and shooting the messenger was no longer an option. Still, he waved her away and glowered into his cup. Anders' APLS could give his new nation an edge, make them a superpower way ahead of schedule. It was not all bad; they'd been found. Even in America, he could send his team after them because the country was in disarray and no one would complain. Before turning back to the others, he did wonder why they were in Wyoming. He anticipated Anders would make a beeline for Fitzpatrick, wherever he was ensconced. He didn't like mysteries; they gave him a bellyache.

"Trouble?" Gunther Fitzgerald asked.

"A promising asset fled the country and we're retrieving him," was all Holtzer would admit to.

The others gave him quizzical looks, but he ignored them and returned to the agenda.

"Minnesota keeps knocking on your door," Kane Roza complained. "They keep wanting to make nice."

"Why?" Luna Knox inquired.

"Mostly because they want us to reopen the I-80 border and let transports through to get to the other side of the US. Problem is, they don't want to pay my tariff."

"What are you asking for, human sacrifice?" Scarlet Wolf asked.

There were some polite chuckles and then Roza said, "Fifty gallons of water per ton of vehicle weight."

"Doesn't sound too bad. They've got lakes, right?" Knox said.

"And to them, every drop is more precious than helping the other states," Roza said.

"Let's just say we're negotiating."

Holtzer turned to Knox and said, "Tell us about diplomatic outreach."

Knox, wearing her trademark dangling bracelets and today a burgundy and gold coat, said, "I'm about done training the first dozen ambassadors. Good people and we'll start making outreach contacts to the NATO nations first, build new allies." As she went on, Holtzer surveyed the room, noting how quickly Roza got bored and was trimming his nails with a pocketknife. A wiry-haired blue-eyed Bowie Cormac was taking notes, or doodling; he couldn't tell. Fitzgerald was paying attention, evaluating the choices of contacts, tallying allies and foes. White was doing the same, but Scarlet Wolf and Elsa Ember seemed bored, pretending to focus.

While the majority of their attention had to be on securing borders and instilling order, the rest of the world continued. Cities were rebuilding or suing for peace, the Alliance was continuing to annex countries and quash rebellions. Every move outside their borders needed to be tallied, plans adjusted.

When the report was done, Holtzer took up supplies, but Wolf interrupted him. "What's got you all hot and bothered?"

"Nothing," he replied.

"Nah," Wolf said. The woman had a hawk face, lean and angular with a prominent nose, dark eyes, and permanently knit eyebrows below a shock of dark red hair. She was older, more experienced than the others, and recorded more kills while serving as a Green Beret than any soldier in American history. Wolf was not a politician and couldn't care less about most of the Seven Flags' goals. What interested her was the idea of forging a new nation out of the American ashes. As the plans took shape, she insisted on Colorado for her territory, knowing of the hidden missile silos, the underground network of facilities within the mountains. Holtzer knew she was a power to be reckoned with and needed to keep her leashed for now, but leashed animals do not like being captives. She was wild and dangerous, and if he feared anyone in the new government, it was her.

"You're worried about this asset. Tell us why."

Holtzer thought he had schooled his features and mannerisms, but she knew. She had animal instincts that befitted her family name. Better to be truthful than earn Wolf's distrust.

"This man, David Anders, has promising research into rehydrating plant life, rejuvenating withered crops. Imagine if we could produce fresh food for the masses. Imagine having enough food to avoid rationing and growing more to export in exchange for power. He was working in Iowa when the shit went down."

"And..." Wolf pushed.

"He sheltered in Iowa, according to the census, and when I ordered his retrieval, he had gone on the road. I sent a Ghost squad after him."

"He got away? A botanist?" Fitzgerald asked.

"I don't know how or care," Holtzer said evenly, not letting the others get to him. It wasn't easy, but he needed unity, not politics. "We know where he is and I sent more men."

Nods around the table, some with smiles. They heard enough to see why this man was valuable.

"There's something personal in this," Wolf pressed. All eyes swiveled his way and the general met them.

"The DOD funded him for a while and we crossed paths. I wanted to try an experiment with the method and we had a disagreement. I don't like being defied," he said with a slight emphasis, getting his point across to those assembled.

"I imagine not. So, he's old business, from the old country," Wolf said.

"But, if he's perfected it, we win."

"Only if you retrieve him," Wolf finished.

"Once you get him," Ember interrupted, "how do you get him to provide the work?"

"Bribery? Torture? Threaten his wife?" Roza suggested.

"That wins us nothing," Ember shot back. "He's a scientist, he's growing new life. He has a moral obligation to the human race. We use that. We give him what he needs, whatever that is within reason. We give him food, water, sex if it comes to that. We also keep Rodney away from him. I get the impression the enmity may go both ways, so someone else can make him see a way to working with us."

"You?" White asked.

"Let me read up on him and I will answer that. Right now, he's an unfinished puzzle. Getting him is the first step," she said.

• • •

The gray skies had lightened, suggesting day had arrived. David didn't feel particularly well-rested, but he was warm and not being hunted, so the day was already off to a good start. Betty slumbered beside him, under a winter coat rescued from the TAV. He was sore from the tree climbing, hungry, thirsty, and worried. Rubbing the sleep from his eyes, he looked about the abandoned post office. Automated kiosks stood dark, conveyor belts still, walls covered with digital displays that remained black. Pieces of furniture had been taken, some graffiti marred a wall, and a sneaker was near a garbage can.

He sat up and stretched, wincing at a sore muscle. They needed to get moving, with greater haste than the day before. Whoever was after them had failed, but that didn't mean they wouldn't come back or weren't staking out Route 26. He needed Betty to find them an alternate. Letting her sleep, he rose and put his shoes on before heading outside. There was no one outside in the chill morning air, but candles continued to flicker in the odd window, the smell of wood smoke in the air. He loved that smell and wished he could sit beside wherever that fire was, reading or napping. Instead, he trudged through the parking lot to examine the TAV.

He was down to 60 percent power already, thanks to the high-speed shenanigans from the night before. David examined the body damage and deemed the car drivable. He would activate the diagnostics before they left to make certain. It was clearly the most damage the body of the car had sustained so far, along with all the other dings and dents they collected on their drive. It was a miracle the thing still drove, let alone turned on. The hunters didn't slash his tires, which he found surprising. Unlocking the vehicle, he reached for the canteen and finished it, grabbing a full one and a protein bar for Betty's breakfast. They'd need to find more food before dinner, but they also needed to get rolling. He had hoped to get more miles under him last night, but that was not to be, so he wanted to make up for it today.

Upon reentering the building, he saw that Betty was sitting up, a worried expression on her face. Seeing him, she grinned and reached for the canteen. She drank greedily, pausing with the last mouthful to swish it around and gargle before walking over to the deactivated water fountain to spit it out.

"So much for brushing my teeth," she said. "How are you?"

"I'm fine," he said, not really feeling fine, but his job today was not to worry or provoke her. They were being hunted and they needed to put the tensions of the last thirteen days aside and be a team.

"Liar," she said, reaching for the protein bar. It was gone in three bites.

They each went to the restrooms, appreciating indoor plumbing that still worked, and then climbed back into the TAV.

"Home sweet home," she said mockingly.

David was relieved to find the car powered right up and the diagnostics didn't show any internal issues. One tire needed air, but they could drive on it for now. Betty was already reviewing the tablet for directions, scrolling one way then another.

"Okay, we can reorient ourselves, taking 26 to 220, which brings us southward, and then 287 to Jeffrey City, where we can find energy."

"You hope."

"I always hope," she said with a smile. Apparently, she was trying too, which lightened his heart.

"And away we go," he said, putting the TAV into gear and hitting the highway. They drove in silence, no music, and watched as mankind roused itself. Hikers took the shoulders, some pushing carts or strollers with belongings. Many held signs saying they were willing to do anything, and David guessed they really meant anything, for food. He had to ignore them, get to Reid's lab, and finish his work so they could all eat again. It broke his heart to see them, to see the misery and hopelessness in their eyes.

The car rumbled at anything over 50, which wasn't something picked up on the diagnostics, so that slowed him. He inwardly cursed at more time being lost when time was more precious than water.

When they eventually got to the turnoff for Route 220, by Casper, they saw wrecked cars and an eighteen-wheeler blocking the way. He glanced Betty's way and she shrugged.

"Stay on 26 for now," she said.

As he drove, she consulted the maps and reported back after a few minutes.

"We can pick up 287 again at the Wind River Reservation. No one is likely to stop us." Because, after all, just over a century earlier, the Native Americans had vanished.

However, as they got to the intersection, the road was chewed up, like a machine literally took bites out of the asphalt. They slowed to examine the damage and decided to stay going straight on 26, into the national parklands that loomed ahead.

As he drove, David's paranoia returned, and he finally turned to his wife and spoke his mind, hoping he didn't sound crazy. "Isn't it more than a little coincidental that both paths to 287 and our optimal route are blocked? Do you feel like maybe we're being herded?"

She didn't reply immediately, which he took as a good sign. Instead, she consulted the tablet and craned her neck to look at the wreckage once more.

"You feel that way, don't you?"

"Look, Betty, I'm trying to be rational about this and take two plus two plus two and get six. We were followed and two ways south were blocked, forcing us to go straight."

She considered this and then asked, "If they wanted us, why didn't they just wreck the car and wait for daylight?"

"Maybe they bought time waiting for instructions," he suggested, to see how it sounded out loud.

"That sounds very organized," she offered without certainty.

"Doesn't it? Holtzer told me about his trained Ghost Squad, better than the Green Berets, deadlier than Seal Team Six; you get the idea. He was going to send them in with the anti-APLS..."

"The poisoned apple," she said.

He blinked and processed the reference then nodded. "Send them in to do the wetwork. Now he's in charge of a country and you don't do that without help."

"Are you suggesting he sent trained assassins after us?" The alarm was instant in her voice which he winced at, not wishing to scare her, but instead, to share his concern for the apparent situation.

"They do what he says, and if he is after me, he wants me and the APLS formula."

"So, you elude them, they radio for instructions, and now they are herding us. To where?"

"I guess we'll find out," he said, his voice soft, the fear clear in each word. "Raise Reid; he needs to know."

It was unusual for them to talk while they drove, but maybe that would punctuate the urgency. Reid was all smiles as his fuzzy image appeared on the auxiliary screen near the passenger seat. One look at David's face caused the smile to evaporate. In brief terms, David filled him in on the last 24 hours and the expression on the physicist's face continued to darken, storm clouds gathering in his eyes.

"You want to bring that shit to my doorstep?" The tone of his voice was new, anger mixed with fear.

"Of course, I don't want to do anything of the sort," David countered, afraid of losing his safe harbor.

"Well, if they follow you here, that's exactly what will happen. Sorry, man, but I can't do this to me and Linda..."

"Listen, Reid, maybe we can lose them," David countered.

"Now you're an Indy 500 driver? You're a scared botanist who has something very valuable in his head. Those people get here, we're collateral damage."

Betty and David shared a concerned look, both scared that they were out of good options.

"And where should they go? Huh?" Linda's voice was clear despite being behind her husband.

"It's not our problem," Reid countered.

"Sure it is, hun. They're fellow humans in need; you geeks are both scientists who understand each other's babble. If they get him and the apples—"

"APLS," David corrected but was talked over. Betty chuckled from her seat.

"—then it's game over for America. Do you want that? I don't want that. The shelter is secure. All they need to do is lose their tail."

"How the hell is he going to do that?"

"They're smart and avoided them yesterday and can do it again. Right, Betty?"

Betty nodded into the camera, a smile fixed on her face, but David saw the tension in her eyes.

"As long as this tablet keeps me updated with maps, I'm good to go."

"And you're armed, right?"

"A pistol isn't going to mean much if I'm right about who's following us," David admitted.

"Better than nothing. You keep coming west, we'll be here."

Reid shot her a look David couldn't see, but clearly, the stare-down between the couple was an old one. Moments passed and the man's shoulders sagged in defeat.

"You're still welcome," he said with a monotone.

"You won't regret it, Reid," David assured him.

"I do already," Reid said and cut the signal.

The pair drove in silence, every pockmarked mile bringing them closer to the Bridger Teton National Forest, on their way toward Yellowstone National Park. The millennia-old wilderness had remained largely untouched over the last few centuries thanks to various ecological and environmental movements. Neither had visited it previously, and from what Betty could glean, it was one of the first places people fled to when the bombs went off. She'd read about campers and groups settling to fight for space with the wildlife. Once the hell rained over America, Park Rangers were re-tasked for emergency services, and whatever law-enforcement existed had largely been overrun by refugees.

While many could happily live off the grid, the TAV was going to need energy once they crossed the hundreds of miles of parkland. At best, they'd stop for water and to relieve themselves, but the goal was to remain moving, emerging from the other side and then beelining the best they could to the California coast and safety.

"Take 191; it'll parallel Jackson Lake and we can fill the canteens," Betty said.

They drove in silence, both marveling at the old-growth trees that had endured all manner of weather since their birth. Their leafy canopies often provided relief from the hot sun, but now they merely provided a barrier between the ground and the gray skies overhead, which lightened enough to tell day from night. Sure enough, as they approached the oblong lake, the edge was dotted with campers, RVs, tents, and even the beginnings of a log cabin. People washed clothes in the water, and most sat around campfires, warming themselves from the cold. No one could be seen eating, and their gaunt faces suggested the last six months did away with the easiest food.

At one spot, they parked, quickly refilled their water supply, and took care of their personal business before climbing in. They avoided looking at the curious people and just drove steadily up 191, trying to enjoy the scenery despite the dying plant life and lack of wildlife. In David's mind, this would be an ideal place to try out the APLS, but that was for another day. Instead, he drove steadily, but slowly, north on 191, following the curve into Yellowstone proper. There were signs that explained the difference, but the terrain looked all the same to him.

"No time to visit Old Faithful, is there?"

David was also curious to see the natural formation, but shook his head, refusing to stop. Instead, they drove by the West Thumb Geyser Basin and began to loop from 191 onto Route 20. As the TAV began the curve, their way was barred by three large, dark vehicles, the windows tinted, the license plates missing. Green-and-brown-uniformed men spilled out of the passenger vans, weapons out and taking position between the TAV and their vehicles. Each person was identical, almost exactly the same size and shape, pretty close to clones of one another. There was no insignia to identify them, but the colors were enough to say they had come from the new nation and therefore were there by Holtzer's order.

This was Holtzer's famed Ghost Squad, and they had come to collect him.

The goosebumps rose to attention on his arms and he tightened his grip on the wheel even as he slowed to a stop. Their battered, trusty vehicle felt small compared with the three hulking vans. David felt for the pistol, which was as useful as a water gun against the dozen people assembled before them.

"Shit," Betty whispered.

"Any ideas?"

"Surrender, Dorothy," she quipped, a reference he didn't immediately get.

"David Anders, we have orders to return you to your rightful nation," a woman with dark skin said from the extreme right of the dozen.

He lowered the window and replied, "I'm an American!"

"All citizens in Seven Flags territory at the time of its independence are automatically citizens of the new nation. We have a warrant for your arrest and extradition."

"You have got to be shitting me," David called. "I'll challenge it in court, thank you very much."

"Who are you going to file the papers with?" Betty called from her window.

The woman chose not to reply to either query. Instead, the man next to her gestured for them to leave the car.

Betty looked over at David, worry marring her beautiful features. "Am I expendable?"

"What? No! You'll stay alive, a bargaining chip to get me to do Holtzer's bidding," David seethed.

The man gestured one more time, then, in unison, the dozen took a single step forward.

"Shit. Shit. Shit," David chanted, his mind frantically considering options. None of them left him or Betty alive. His heart sank that they had gotten so far, had freedom in their sights, but were being dragged back like common criminals. But, as long as he held on to the APLS data, they'd leave him mostly unharmed, especially if he surrendered. What choice was there? He couldn't let them harm Betty, which he had no doubt they would do in order to get him to comply.

There really was no choice.

"We're coming out!" he called, shrugging at Betty.

He opened the TAV's door and stood beside it, Betty following a moment later. Four agents, magnetic handcuffs visible, approached.

"I'm so sorry," he told her.

When the quartet was within five feet of them, there was a loud whooping and hollering. Bursting through the brush were a man and a woman, colorfully clad in animal skins, carrying round shields with intricate designs. Bands of red and black paint were visible here and there. They wore some sort of quilted armor, and instead of helmets, they wore feathered headdresses. Each carried what appeared to be a wooden club with dark, black blades on both sides. They continued yelling as they threw themselves at the four unprepared soldiers. The male said something in a language David didn't recognize and swung the club, which sliced right through the body armor underneath the uniform, treating it like tissue paper. One soldier crumpled while the other reached for a pistol, only to lose a hand in the process, blood spurting onto the dirt. His cries mixed with the war chants still being uttered.

The woman swerved away from the four, seemingly confident the man could handle such a small number, and stalked the others. Pistols were aimed her away, but she acrobatically twirled in midair, avoiding the first fusillade of bullets. Landing on the balls of her feet, she used her own club to hamstring one soldier, spinning and using the top to break the nose of another. She moved quickly, efficiently, almost balletic despite the savage cries.

David and Betty crouched together behind the open driver's door of the TAV, puzzled by this bizarre turn of events. He couldn't begin to imagine who these people were. Their dress suggested Native Americans of some sort, but he thought they'd all disappeared. Had they merely gone into hiding?

The man used the magnetic cuffs to tie two of the soldiers together before using the deadly club to hamstring them, their bellows and screams of pain now louder than the rhythmic war chant.

One of the soldiers managed to get an arm around the man's throat, but he merely turned his head and bared his teeth, which turned out to be sharpened to points. He bit deeply into the arm, forcing the man to let go, but their rescuer grabbed the arm and flipped the man over his shoulder before stomping on the soldier's throat, killing her, gurgling blood spraying from her mouth. A swift kick to the midsection sent the last of the quartet into a nearby tree, knocking the wind from him.

He joined his partner, who didn't really seem to need his help despite the overwhelming numbers. She was a sight to behold, a whirling dervish with a deadly club that slashed and sliced, whistling through the air. David was trying to analyze them both, to try and find clues as to who they were, but as he was constantly being reminded, he was a botanist. It didn't help that they were in constant movement, a matched set, clearly accustomed to fighting side by side with one another. Each move meant their backs faced each other, presenting no clear line of attack. Their feet moved like those of dancers, sure-footed, pivoting on the balls of the feet, directing the rest of the body.

It struck him that their heads were elongated, not shaped like humans' or any Native American tribe he knew from the recent history books, nor did he know of a tribe with filed teeth. They were a complete mystery to him, and when he shot Betty a questioning look, she merely shrugged, barely taking her eyes off the pair. David had a fleeting thought, a faint memory of an ancient group. But no... they've been extinct for 2000 years, he thought to himself.

There were just two soldiers left standing, the other ten having been taken out in rapid succession. One was firing wildly, missing with each loud crack of the pistol, as the woman crept nearer. The man hounded the other soldier, who tried to turn and run, only to find the club hurled the short distance and cleaving into his back, shattering the spine and causing him to crumple like a puppet with cut strings. Left by herself, the woman tossed her weapon, raised her hands, and went down on her knees.

The colorfully clad woman stood over her and laughed.

"Coward," she spat at the kneeling figure before reaching into her belt and withdrawing a pair of mag cuffs, which secured the hands behind her back.

David slowly rose to openly stare at the pair. They were panting somewhat, their breath forming steam in the cool air, but they didn't appear menacing. Who were they and why did they just rescue them? His head was swirling with a thousand questions, uncertain what to ask first.

"It's safe," the man said in English, switching from whatever it was he was speaking to his companion. He gestured for them to come closer. His English was solid, with just a trace of an unrecognized accent. Maybe Mexican? Two words was not a large enough sample for David.

Betty rose beside him and gripped his hand. Whatever happened next, they were in this together. They both began walking toward the pair, who remained in place, their heads taking in the carnage around them. Frankly, David was sickened to his stomach at the blood and guts that casually littered the ground.

As they neared, the man suddenly tensed and twisted, looking just past them. The soldier who hit the tree had recovered enough to withdraw his pistol and fired four shots wildly. The rescuers dodged their torsos, evading the shots.

Betty gasped, her hand tightening its grip instinctively as her body spasmed. She sagged into David, who gasped and reached, catching her in motion, as he gently laid her down, his eyes frantically searching her body for the entry wound. Blood was leaking through her coat, onto the dirt, from her side. He was only dimly aware of footsteps, then a cry and the snapping of a neck.

A moment later, the man was beside David, his fingers probing Betty's limp body. She was grunting in pain, breathing shallowly, each breath cutting into David's soul. The man reached into a pouch at his hip and pulled out something that resembled a bandage or cloth. He did something underneath her dirty, torn shirt, and then tugged the shirt back into place. He then scooped her up and turned to his partner.

"Follow us. Quickly," the man said.

David numbly followed; all thoughts about their identity cast aside. The thousands of questions he had moments ago coalesced into just one.

"Who are you?"

CHAPTER 9

Pure Imagination

The man carrying his wife didn't respond to the question, focusing instead on walking back the way he and his partner came. David risked a glance over his shoulder to see that the woman was disabling the guns and securing the bodies on the ground—those that were still breathing. Whatever noises they made clearly scared off not only the wildlife but any other humans who might have been in the area. Thankfully, the APLS hard drive was in his pocket now that he was abandoning the TAV. He would actually miss the smelly, dented vehicle.

They trudged around trees, through bushes, and across barren stretches of ground. Within minutes, the woman had silently rejoined them and only an exhalation of breath signaled her arrival. She was ninja-silent, which spooked him a bit, but he preferred that to the crazed warrior war chants. Their eyes met for a moment and he realized she was studying him, weighing how much of a threat he might pose. He knew the answer was none at all, not as long as the man was effortlessly carrying the small figure in his arms.

In turn, he studied them. He was taken with the sloping forehead that elongated their heads. Both had pierced ears from cartilage to elongated lobe; wrought metal designs made their ears reflect the dull ambient light. She had something silver through her septum, a bar of some sort with carvings, symbols he didn't know. When she spoke, he saw her pointed teeth were also decorated with green gems of sorts in each incisor. Each had large, almost beaked noses. The man had something turquoise dangling from the left nostril.

Despite the sweat, their black and red body paint had not streaked. He got the sense she was tattooed under her quilted vest, which struck him as some sort of layered cotton batting. The man was more obviously tattooed with intricate designs on his hands and forearms. Everything about them spoke of some alien, martial culture; one he did not recognize at all. What was oddest, though, was the feathered headdress, kept in place by some band in the back. The bird feathers were attractively designed, his in blues and blacks, hers in yellows, oranges, and black.

"Where are we going?"

"Kasper," she said, her voice quiet. It was a commanding voice, one used to being obeyed.

"The city of wonder," the man said from ahead.

Neither piece of information helped David, but they knew what they were doing and he had to trust them.

"Is there a doctor nearby? We have to hurry!"

"Do you want to carry her?"

"If you need help," David said, unsure of how long he could manage her weight.

"I do not," he said. "But thank you." So he was a polite killer.

"We go for three miles," the woman said. David estimated that to be at least an hour if not more and worried Betty wouldn't live until then.

"The injury is serious, but I applied a patch that will compress the wound, staunch the blood. There's even a mild anesthetic to help her rest. She will live until a doctor can tend to her."

"Look, my name is David Anders, and I appreciate your help. How did you know we were in danger?"

"I am Ponco, that is my husband Karuk. We knew there was danger in the woods and came to stop it."

"You live in a commune or tent city or something?"

"Kasper is nothing like either, David Anders," she said.

"David is fine." If they were going to be friends, he was okay with just first names. They seemed to have one name, so this leveled the field a bit.

"How did you know... about the danger?" The words just fell out of

David's mind into an audible rendition of thought.

"We knew. There were signs, so we sent out eyes to locate you," she said.

"Wait, you knew in advance I was the target and you came looking for me?"

She looked at him with a smile. "You've trusted us this far, David. Trust us a little more and we can have it all explained. Right now, our goal is to save your wife."

What amazed David for the next hour was how they had been seen by no one. Karuk seemed to instinctively know where to turn, which copse of trees would effectively hide them all from sight. The ground beneath his feet didn't seem well worn, no obvious path that others had flattened down through repeated use. Karuk adjusted Betty in his arms every now and then, but she didn't whimper or say a word. She was clearly out from the anesthetic and he kept scanning the ground for blood, but never saw a drop. Still, Karuk would shoot Ponco a glance and David could read the worry in his eyes. Still, his pace neither quickened nor slowed, speaking of his incredible strength and endurance. He was getting winded from the pace but refused to budge, figuring he could collapse once she was safe with a doctor.

To make conversation, he asked, "What was that weapon you used so effectively?"

She lifted the club and he saw the wide wooden shaft was decorated with pictograms, polished to a sheen. The ring of eighteen obsidian blades were still stained dark red with dried blood. "It is the macuahuitl. The weapon has been in use for centuries although this version is modified. Where it was once sharpened stone held with adhesive to the shaft, it is now a metal alloy, encased in wood, and sharpened by lasers to within microns of sharpness, able to rip through most anything or anyone."

Lasers? There was so much more to learn about these people and she seemed so casual about it, but as he asked other questions, she silenced him with a finger to her lips. She was clearly on the lookout for any living impediment to their goal.

Ahead, David could make out some rocky cliffs, which he didn't realize would be there. But then he remembered that Old Faithful was not the only amazing aspect of Yellowstone. There was a volcano there too. The rock was the cooling result of some ancient eruptions. It was clear these rock walls were their destination, but he saw no signs of life, no electric lines, no smoke or steam from vents, nothing to suggest life. If anything, the gray walls seemed devoid of life. Still, they were heading straight for it and a part of his mind was thrilled at the idea of someone living within a volcano, like something out of the movies he loved as a kid.

Sure enough, they reached one section that seemed especially craggy, like it folded in on itself. As they neared, he heard a rockslide, a deep rumbling sound, and then he noted an entire section of the basalt wall had shifted four feet, creating a passage. Two women rushed out, each less gaudily attired, but with the same nose and forehead, with a variety of piercings. They relieved Karuk of his burden and hurried Betty within. Once free of carrying her, Karuk slumped against the wall, breathing hard. His macho act got them this far, but he was clearly straining and exhausted.

David approached him and crouched to meet the slumped man's eyes.

"Thank you. You saved our lives."

"I've saved yours," Karuk said. "I hope we got her here in time to join you."

"Come, let me show you our world," Ponco said, gently touching his shoulder.

"I need to be with Betty," David insisted. She laid a firm, strong hand on his arm, directing him away from the women carrying Betty off to some recess.

"She will be cared for and you cannot visit while they operate," Ponco said. "Instead, let me take your mind off medical matters. Let me show you Kasper, our world."

"I hear it's a city of wonders," David repeated and all Ponco did was grin and lead him further into the cavernous space. Karuk had vanished, leaving the two alone.

"As I said, I am Ponco, nacom, or in your tongue, supreme military commander for the Mayan culture."

David paused, almost stumbled actually, and stared at the dark-haired woman. "Mayan? Weren't the Mayans wiped out like 1000 years ago?"

"Our culture left the surface world approximately 1400 years ago," she admitted.

"Wait... you were native to Central America. What are you doing in Wyoming?"

They walked further, the ground sloping so they were descending, and it was clear each rock wall was well-lit from some sort of recessed lighting along the top of each side wall and those walls bore intricate carvings and designs, none of which looked new. Some were geometric shapes; others were colorful images of people hunting animals or making war. The path they walked was smooth stone, neatly maintained from all appearances. No one else was visible, but there was the sound of activity ahead of them, which reassured the scientist.

"My ancestors withdrew from a world that was threatened by invaders," she said. "We outnumbered them, but they had firepower we had never imagined."

He knew she meant the Spanish, the conquistadors who ran roughshod from Central America downward onto the South American continent. Dim memories told him the Mayans vanished, a great mystery, and in the last 150 years or so, remnants of their cities and temples and pyramids had been found and restored by archeologists. None yielded an answer as to where the once-great people went.

Apparently, the answer was Wyoming.

"I am not a historian, but if you desire a lesson, it can be arranged. Know for now that we are here, occupying the land beneath the caldera. There are four adjacent calderas forming what you would know as the Yellowstone Supervolcano."

David gaped at the concept of an entire hidden society living underneath a volcano. All that was missing was some action-adventure hero to protect them or fight them. He was, though, utterly fascinated because it was clear this was a sophisticated society, not some collection of refugees cosplaying as Maya.

"How far does this go?"

"We are in the northwest corner of Wyoming, but we have tunnels that would allow us to exit in the Uintah and Ouray Reservation."

David whistled at that. "That has to be hundreds of miles."

"We've had plenty of time to expand our home, preparing for guests."

At first, he thought she meant people like him and Betty, but an instant later, he remembered the Vanishing. "You mean all the Native Americans didn't just disappear; they came here."

"Everything can be explained, but really, let me show you the city. I'd like you to absorb our culture a bit before I present you to our Council."

He had questions, lots and lots of questions, but decided to let her direct him, suspecting they'd be there for a while. After all, they seemed determined to find and rescue him, they needed him, but for what reason? Did they, too, want the APLS? He had his doubts but couldn't imagine why else they'd want him.

His thoughts were interrupted as they made a sharp right turn and the tunnel widened into what felt more like a boulevard. He wasn't sure where the illumination was coming from, but it felt like noontime, and before him stretched a neat, orderly small town. There was a uniformity to the structures, rectangular shapes that were neatly arranged in a grid pattern, suggesting careful planning. As he peered closer, he saw each building had elaborately carved doorways, all painted in primary colors, similar to the Egyptian pyramids he visited as a college student. Streams of smoke curled up from a few chimneys, and to his left appeared to be stalls for some sort of shopping center. The thoroughfares were jammed with people in a motley assortment of clothing, from attire similar to Ponco's and Karuk's, to others in loincloths or feathered dresses. Some, but certainly not all, bore the elongated heads and body adornments, others veered for simpler styles, more recognizable to him as Native American attire. All mingled happily, no obvious class distinction. Their skin tones were pretty similar from dark brick red to lighter browns, with almost all sporting black hair, worn long, in a mohawk, or decorated with shells, beads, and feathers.

"Welcome to Kasper," Ponco said.

"Kaa...sper...? What... wow...aaaamazing," was all he could manage to say. After staring some more, he began to note bits of technology carefully embedded in the buildings, the ornate doorways glowing or sparkling with moving lights. He even caught sight of a hologram being projected near the market that seemed entertaining for the young. Clearly, time had not stopped, but modern touches were integrated in traditional styles.

They walked further, joining the throng on one street, and passersby genuflected in respect to Ponco, while others openly stared at the white man in their midst. None stopped to talk, none appeared worried about him being there. A few glanced at his hands and noted he was not bound and was therefore presumed not to be a threat or a prisoner. He watched as potters and weavers worked in spaces by the homes or seen through windows. Other craftsmen were at work, including one using a soldering torch to repair a circuit board. His mind racing, trying to absorb it all, the technology, the people, "the people" he thought, "holy shit, The Vanished." His faculties threatened the moment though, daring to take him, as the overwhelming sensory information overloaded his synapses as he was filled with his worry for Betty.

They walked in companionable silence, David not ready to ask any of his questions yet, just wanted to take it all in, just experience it all. He thought to himself, The world just ended, and my wife was just shot, and I'm in a volcano, with a bunch of extinct Maya who clearly never went extinct and just have been living here.... He slapped himself in the face, which got Ponco to jump, making sure he was okay.

"Just making sure I am not dreaming."

She grinned, turning back around and continuing on her route.

A short time passed and they neared the market where the sizzling smell of something tasty was being cooked. His mouth instantly watered and his stomach reminded him that man did not live on protein bars alone. Just as he was about to ask for something to eat, a young boy, maybe five, clearly a Maya, rushed to Ponco and threw his arms around her legs. He babbled something in a language he did not recognize.

The woman leaned down and returned the hug then spoke in the same tongue as the boy looked directly at David, who gave him his friendliest smile.

"Hello," he said in English.

"Hello, I'm David."

"I am Poxlom," he declared.

"My nephew," she explained.

David looked over to Ponco, who explained, "We retain our home language, but as more and more people came to live with us, it became clear we needed a common language. In time, it evolved to be English and Spanish. The Maya never had a single language, much as your Native Americans had hundreds of tribal tongues. It can sound confusing, but once we know what people can speak, we adjust."

He nodded with approval and leaned over to the young boy. "What are you up to today?"

"We were being shown stories about our ancestors," Poxlom said, jerking a thumb toward the holograms. Now that they were closer, David noted they were sharper in definition than anything he had seen in America. Their technological prowess was quite impressive.

"Why are you here?"

"I wish I could tell you," David admitted, reminded of the primary question on his mind.

"Ooh, secret stuff."

"Go on then," Ponco said, shooing him on.

"It is secret stuff, isn't it?" he asked as they resumed walking.

"Not really, but it is not for me to discuss. I am to get you cleaned up and ready to present to the High Council. I am indulging in this brief tour, so you see we are not a threat."

A trio of men and women approached and saluted their leader. All seemed to be in their twenties, one man with a bright red, apparently fresh tattoo on his left bicep, a leopard head of some sort.

"This is David Anders. Please bring him to the baths. Have him cleaned, fed, and dressed. Cacoch, please find out the status of his wife and inform him. I must report back to the Council, but I will collect you when it's time to meet them." She turned to leave, but David impulsively reached out and grabbed her arm, an act the trio thought a threat, as various knives were rapidly drawn.

"Ponco, I can't begin to thank you. I don't why I'm here, but I am thankful. You saved us both and have acted honorably."

"I'm glad you feel that way," she said, her right hand gesturing for the others to stand down. "There will be much to explain before we even begin to answer your questions. A man of science such as yourself lives to ask." She smiled and resumed walking away. The woman, Cacoch, went off in a different direction, leaving him with the other two. They escorted him through more streets, letting him absorb more of the amazing culture, blending of centuries and societies. After a series of rapid turns, they stopped before a smaller building, one without windows, but with a stone door that was once again decorated with shapes and symbols he couldn't begin to fathom.

The man said, "Come with me to the zumpul-ché."

Inside, he felt the instant change in humidity. "Take off your clothes and enter the room. It is mostly steam, but there are soaps, perfumes, and oils. Indulge yourself while fresh clothing is brought to you. Then you can eat and be ready for Ponco."

It all sounded reasonable until he realized it meant emptying his pockets, which would include his precious hard drive. While copies of his research, in theory, resided in the cloud, accessing it from here seemed problematic. He trusted Ponco, not yet anyone else. But, to his surprise, the man pulled a large wooden box, inlaid with tiles that formed a red dragon in flight, and handed it to him. The man handed him a beige body towel and gestured for him to enter.

"Put your things in here. They'll be safe."

Not having much of a choice, David did as he was bid and when ready, stepped into the steam bath. He had no idea where the water was being heated nor were there obvious grates, but there was plenty of steam that seeped right into his pores, instantly relaxing him. He sagged in a heap on a stone bench, letting the heat and moisture work their way into his body. After a few minutes, he reached for a tightly woven basket that was filled with glass and ceramic bottles, most labeled in languages he didn't recognize, but the iconography was clear enough. He let the towel drop on the bench then rose, lathering himself with a fragrant soap that seemed to fizzle against his body. After a minute or two, the moist air seemed to dissolve the soap, leaving him feeling refreshed.

A sign pointed to an exit in the opposite direction and he entered the equivalent of a locker room. To his surprise, there was a table with a basin, pitcher, and basket filled with more familiar toiletries, including a toothbrush and cream. If he intended to address the High Council, having fresh breath certainly seemed to be in order.

Atop a bench were a pile of clothes, soft leathers, and tanned skins, well-worn but comfortable-looking. A pair of moccasins were on the floor and he slipped his feet into them, finding they fit him perfectly.

He emerged from the building—doubting he'd ever master the Mayan language—to find Cacoch awaiting him.

"Is she..."

"Your wife is resting. She needed surgery because of the gunshot, but it missed her vital organs. I am told they had to operate delicately for she is small in size, but will recover. She will be sore but can function."

Despite the toxins cleansed from his body, his soul remained shrouded, awaiting the news, and now that psychic weight was being lifted from him. He exhaled, a physical manifestation of his emotional state.

"When can I see her?"

"Later," Cacoch told him. "You are to eat now and then be brought before the High Council."

She led him to another building not far away, some sort of communal center with long tables and benches. A kitchen of a sort was in the rear and the woman signaled their arrival with a rap of knuckles on the stone table. Immediately, a boy of maybe twelve emerged with a bowl of steaming vegetables. Another followed with a tray bearing a pitcher and mug. Both were placed before him and the first server produced a wide wooden spoon and handed it to him. Cacoch sat beside him as he settled in to eat.

He knew he was hungry and intended to pace himself so as not to cramp in front of what he presumed to be the government. He sniffed and noted heavy spices but nothing set off any alarms. The spoon slid into the bowl and he took a small amount into his mouth. The explosion of flavors made his eyes bulge and the woman laughed, pouring him a glass of juice.

"We don't usually spice our food so heavily, but today's cook comes from a tribe that believes in putting heat into everything. Well, everything except the juice."

"Guava?"

She shook her head in agreement and he appreciated how it helped cut the burning of the peppery stew. Still, his hunger won out and he silently apologized to his taste buds as he scalded them with every mouthful of the meal. She watched in silence, although he could easily see the amusement in her eyes, which bore traces of makeup, enhancing the whites of her eyes.

"What is the High Council?" he asked as the bowl emptied.

"They rule Kasper and consult with the King and Queen," she replied.

"How does it work?"

"Work? The High Council controls all the day-to-day functions of

Kasper and oversees the other conclaves further south."

"There's more than one Kasper?"

"There is but one city of wonder," she said with pride. "But, from here to deep into South America, we have colonies, built over time, to house all those we brought home."

David stored the knowledge, not wanting to get off track. "So, what function do the King and Queen have?"

"They are our rulers," Cacoch said with some surprise. "They speak for the gods; they have the responsibility of overseeing all the peoples."

"They're the Big Picture type?"

"Big picture?"

"Long-range, long-term planning."

Cacoch processed the unfamiliar terms then decided they fit and nodded. "Come, you will learn for yourself."

"I will meet the King and Queen?"

"In time. First, the High Council. Come, I am to hand you off to Ponco."

Both rose, and as they did, two boys hurried out from hiding to bus the table. David instinctively felt like he needed to leave a tip but felt foolish not knowing what currency they would even use here. Together, they left the building and headed for the rendezvous, and from there, his meeting with the leaders and still to his shock, the royal family. His thoughts were divided between intense curiosity, concern for Betty, and rage over Holtzer.

CHAPTER 10
Elsewhere

"A dozen dead?" Holtzer bellowed.

The messenger nodded once and then backed out of the office. A wise move, as the general was seething with outrage. When the Ghost Squad did not report back, a precious drone was dispatched to survey the area, a risk, considering how the charged atmosphere played havoc with the delicate electronics. He didn't care; he needed answers. Hours passed, and finally, as it came into range, the governors, still present from their meetings, gathered to see for themselves. The main screen in the conference room came to life and showed the parkland then lowered as it neared the signal still being output by the three vehicles.

There were bodies scattered about, none neatly lying on the ground, all showing evidence of grievous wounds, blood, and bits of bodies everywhere.

"Your botanist has teeth," Roza said. He was a large man, heavily muscled, his neck tattooed in red, white, and blue with the symbol of his Army division. He preferred a shaved pate but let a graying mustache stay in place. Despite running a portion of the new nation, he remained dressed in fatigues, ready to wage war, which seemed to be his constant preference.

Holtzer whirled on him, his eyes ablaze. "You think a fucking scientist could do this?"

"Of course not, which means someone else is involved. Someone came to their rescue," Roza said, meticulously studying the image.

"Something sliced and diced these ghosts; no gunfire was involved," he mused. "Someone who knew what they were doing."

"Not preppers or gangs?" asked Elsa Ember.

"Savage, yes, but trained," Garrison White agreed. "What do you think we're dealing with?"

"I don't know. But Anders is gone, probably rabbited while everyone fought. I put the Ghosts under your control, Kane. They failed!"

"We sent them into hostile territory and gave them no time to reconnoiter. This is not on me or them," Roza said. The challenge was in his eyes, but he and Holtzer went back years, so it would never come to blows. But he needed to keep Roza under control, use him as a weapon, an extension of his will.

"This tech is still out there," White said. "If you were a scientist on foot, without resources or allies, where would he go?"

Roza had called up a detailed topographical map of Yellowstone Park and they all studied it. Carefully, the drone's data was added so they knew where the dead soldiers were, where the TAV had traveled, thanks to the bug planted the night before. With his hands directing, Roza examined the terrain, noting the four calderas, Old Faithful, and other landmarks. He added more data, a human's average walking speed, and created a timeline, an ever-widening radius of where they could have walked. He shook his head and Holtzer silently agreed: there was no shelter beyond the human tents clustered here and there.

"How much longer does the drone have?" White asked.

"Twenty minutes before it has to return," a tech in the rear of the room read from a computer station.

"They want to get clear, not hunker down," Holtzer said. "Plot the most direct route out of the park and have the drone follow it."

A second screen flared to life as the drone's camera broadcast real-time images of the park, the wildlife, and the scattered humans. Holtzer looked carefully for a shape that might be Anders, but as the minutes ticked by, nothing presented itself.

"Your little botanist seems to have gotten away," Bowie Cormac said.

"With no sign of his helpers," Roza added.

"Five-minute margin of error," the tech called.

"Damn it." Holtzer slammed his fist on the table. "Recall the drone," he grumbled. The defeat hurt his position in the eyes of the others and the loss of the APLS dashed his hopes of a quick victory. Blood in the water is never a good thing, especially when one's going through the fires of expansion. He thought to himself

"There's a new player on the field," White said quietly as the second screen went dark, followed by the main screen. "A new variable to consider."

"The Ghost Squad lost a dozen men with nothing to show for it," Ember noted. "We don't have enough trained soldiers to try that again, Rodney. Next time, we need a sure thing."

"This was a sure thing," he snarled.

"There's always the X-factor you can never account for," White said quietly. "This proves that to be true."

They turned their attention to other matters, but the bitter taste of defeat would not wash away and Holtzer seethed. He needed David, the technology to stabilize his rule over the people, and his generals. As the hours turned the sun into a distant memory of the day, Holtzer contemplated the situation. Where did Anders go? Who was helping him and why? These thoughts burned in his mind as others, like Roza and Cormac, chalked it up to a failed mission and moved on, looking at the next crisis that needed to be solved, not sparing another moment on the situation that just came to pass.

Roza moved throughout the main village, across two markets, and to the back of an unmarked building. He slipped through the crowds as if he was never there, arriving at White's lockout room.

"I'm concerned," he started.

White indulged him, motioning the man to continue his plight.

"Rod, he's fixated on this Anders guy, on this science. We have other matters to attend to. I'm worried."

White raised an eyebrow, sizing up Kane. He paused for the next words were carefully constructed, carefully placed after a long moment of silence. He looked Kane square in the eyes, took a swig of his cantina, and began. "Empires rose and fell for centuries before America came to be. At the heart of each civilization were a core belief system and some iteration of science for the time. Without both, you fall before you even crawl. Rodney is fixated because he believes David Anders is his scientific breakthrough, his reason for the Flag's having power over the world, to be respected as a nation. We need science, at a level unknown to the world of today, so we can pave the world of tomorrow. That is why he is fixated."

Roza paused, unsure how to process the information delivered; while he agreed with the sentiment, he was less convinced that David was this prophet of science Rodney was hoping he would be.

"And why should we believe that this man is what we need over any other?"

At that, White processed the inquiry, tempted to take the bait. He always was quite indulgent at playing the all-knowing role. "Well, Kane, we should believe it, because Rodney Holtzer had David in his unit, ready to take out Bin Yun-Seo with his 'science,' as Rod called it, something that would change black ops forever while also being a hand of God and using his science to feed the masses. That kind of science is worth killing over; that kind of science is empire-building science."

• • •

In Santa Barbara, Reid was worried that David and Betty had not checked in. He knew they were in danger; he knew he was inviting them against his better judgment, but he worried all the same. When an hour passed without contact, he took to his ham radio network and put out the call to anyone between California and Wyoming, to see if anyone matching their decryption ID had been seen. Over the next few hours, his heart sank as each negative report was called in. Reid knew David and Betty were attacked at this point; looters, scavengers or worse had taken the Anders off course, that was certain. The only question that remained for Reid was, were they still alive?

Faint footsteps crept closer and closer as the sound reverberated across the lab. "Reid honey, dinner. It's been on the table for two hours now. Please, come eat." Linda, unknowing of the situation, came into view, slightly annoyed, but more so endeared to love the mad scientist in her husband. However, as she saw his face and the various communication tools sprawled across the lab, she snapped into a more serious tone. "Are they okay…"

"Don't know. They didn't check in at the last call time, and no one has heard anything about their whereabouts for the last four hours or so. Something happened." He trailed off somberly.

"They'll make it. David might have what you need, but Betty, I know Bettys. Heck, I'm a 'Betty,'" Linda stated, half to keep herself from breaking down, half because she knew they couldn't be dead. "Yes, you are probably right, they got attacked, but look, they've made it six months in this brave new world. They are survivors."

As Linda went on, talking more to herself at this point than to Reid, he started thinking about David's work. Based on what the two scientists had discussed, along with what he managed to find in the archives, Reid had gotten a good idea of what APLS was all about and he believed the hype, excited about the technology's promise and what it could mean for regaining control of society to start the rebuilding process. It really would be a game-changer, a victory not only for mankind, but for America, in its darkest hour, to have this brightest light. It would be significant. But all that excitement had started to fade into memory. Reid knew the prospect of seeing David now was bleak, regardless of how much Linda tried to convince him otherwise.

With each passing hour, his optimism continued to fade, finally abandoning the optimism in place for full-on depression. He took to wiping down his equipment, meticulously cleaning everything with fresh cloths and cleaning solution. It settled his nerves, gave him purpose in the moment, and reassured him that when work resumed, everything was ready. He played music to steady himself, anything to shove the dirtiest thoughts from haunting him.

As he cleaned, Linda watched. Far gone were the days of her convincing words of safe harbor. The time between communications had created a deafening silence, replacing her joyous tone for the every-so-often smiles of distant hope. She hadn't given up hope, not yet, though even with her more subdued demeanor, she would have to remain optimistic for the both of them.

CHAPTER 11

The Palace Beneath

Ponco looked him up and down, evaluating his appearance. "Clean, presentable," she determined with a firm nod.

"The High Council is in session?" David asked as he fell in line beside her, examining everything he saw with fresh, rested eyes. Amazing what a bath and some food could do for your outlook on life.

"They convened just to meet with you," Ponco said. As they walked, he noted how many reacted to her presence—her badge of office evident to the people of Kasper—and soldiers saluted; others seemed to bow from their waist. Few ignored her and everyone stared at the white man who walked with her. He had never felt so self-conscious in his life, even at his fraternity hazing. He did come to admire the rigid precision of the streets, the buildings, and the markings. There had to have been hundreds, if not thousands, of the pictograms that made up their language. With a clear mind, he began to recognize some, and as they passed a few streets, he came to recognize signage in multiple languages: Spanish, Portuguese, and English. They were simple signs with sure-handed calligraphy that clearly identified a doctor or dentist, a lawyer even. The questions flooded back into his mind but he suspected Ponco was still not going to answer any of them.

He noted that they were headed toward the center of Kasper where stood the most massive structure of all. It was tiered, roughly pyramid in shape, recreating the grand temples and palaces he knew marked the Maya culture. There were seven levels, each with thirteen doorways that he could count, and nine evenly spaced windows letting the inhabitants look at the city from all directions. It was a pale stone, well-weathered, and it clearly had been here some time. The notion of an underground civilization, the idea that a mass group of humans could thrive beneath the cities and towns, the villages and pastures, unbeknownst to the people above the ground had been the stuff of bedtime stories and novels, fictional movies and conspiracy theory videos, so he supposed it was inevitable one really existed.

Guards fell in beside the pair as they neared the building as other similarly attired people opened the wide, thick stone walls. It was somewhat cooler on the inside, with low lighting from, again, some unknown source. In his leather footwear, his footsteps were silent, but the boots the soldiers wore echoed on the pristine stone hall. They walked about ten feet and were led into the interior, which surprised him with small courtyards and a series of smaller buildings circling a tall tower. People were tending the gardens, which were a riot of colorful flowers while others sat studying documents on benches. Guards were everywhere, notably around the tower, which was where he presumed the High Council sat. The buildings on the southern side of the tower appeared to be public spaces given the volume of people coming and going. Next to one was clearly a heating unit, so he wondered if these were other steam baths.

Ponco continued, down the path in silence, escorting him to the tower's entrance. The gates were beautiful—Mayan inscriptions laced the finely carved edges. Once through, the vestiges of the outside world faded into ritual garments and proper salutes for the ranking of which Ponco held. The guards that accompanied them took positions beside the others, remaining outside the tower. Now they ascended a wide staircase that took them up a level and into a chamber. To David, all seats of power were clearly evident and there was nothing different. The council of seven men and women sat in a semicircle on a raised platform so they looked down on whoever appeared before them. A series of stone tables and benches were positioned in the well before them. Several earthenware mugs and a steaming pitcher sat on one table, which was where Ponco steered him.

No one spoke, and clearly, they evaluated him as much as he did them. In the center was the oldest of the group, so seniority mattered here. The man was ornately dressed in reds and purples, white feathers in a spray around his head. His lined face suggested age and wisdom, as did the piercing eyes. With a hand gesture, he indicated the pair should sit. As he took his place beside Ponco, David immediately recognized the aroma from the pitcher. Chocolate. The Maya, he now recalled, introduced the cocoa flavor to the world, for which billions through the centuries were forever grateful, himself included. The two mugs were simple, with images of a human scribe and a god of some sort both decorated in simple black, red, and cream. She poured the thick brown liquid into two mugs.

David blew on the steaming mug and took a sip. Hot and bitter, not the sweet milk chocolate he had been raised on. Betty, though, would love it.

"Sip it slowly," Ponco told him, sotto voce. "Being served cocoa at a meeting like this is a rare show of respect."

He nodded, now intending to drain every drop so as not to offend his hosts.

"Welcome to Kasper, David Anders," the man said in a rough voice.

No one coached him on what to say or how to act, so he tried his best to be diplomatic and respectful. "Thank you, sir. I appreciate the rescue in the park and for the care you are providing my wife."

"She will survive," the woman to the man's right said. She was middle-aged, with black hair going gray, her clothing in silver and blue, and the most amazing set of pierced ears he'd ever seen; every millimeter was covered with earrings of various sizes, set with polished stones and gems.

"Again, you have my thanks. I am in your debt," he replied.

"You are a man of science and my experience tells me men of science have many questions," the man continued. There was even a hint of a smile, making him appear grandfatherly, less intimidating.

"Many," David admitted. "Starting with, whom am I addressing?"

"Ah, yes, introductions. It has been some time since we had a visitor," the man said. "I am Hadwin, leader of the council, serving King Hakan Miwok and Queen Dakota Miwok. On the far right, we have Aaapo, Gabor, and Itzel. On my left are Xoc, Zac-kuk, and Akna. No doubt, you will have the opportunity to get to know us all." As he spoke, the other members of the council nodded or raised a hand to confirm their presence.

"Thank you for that…"

"Hadwin or Presider will do," the old man said.

David decided to stick with formality, for now, easing into familiarity later. "Presider, I have the impression you knew we were in danger and dispatched Ponco and…"

"Karuk," Ponco prompted.

"…Karuk to rescue us. How did you know?"

"What could a Caucasian know of our ways," scoffed Gabor, younger than most, with jet black hair slicked back, curling behind his well-adorned ears, claw tattoos on both hands. He had a thinner nose than most of the others, and he seemed to wear a permanent sneer.

"To the outside world, we were the first to vanish," said Aaapo, another middle-aged man, with a clearly broken nose and a scar on the left side of his face. His eyebrows were strewn with hoops and his wrists jingled with a dozen bracelets on each arm. His peacock green cloak hid the rest of him.

"We were hunted, nearly slaughtered by the Spanish, so of course, hiding was our response," Gabor, with white hair, a smooth, ruddy face, and neck tattoos of various birds, said. "And we have remained hidden ever since."

"Old arguments," Hadwin said, silencing the bickering that David's presence ignited. "David Anders, the Maya are a proud people. A clever people who knew when to retreat to survive. And thrive. We were wise enough to take what worked on the surface and apply it below the surface. Did you know that we developed roads that connected our far-flung cities? We encouraged trade among our allies and used the roads to slay our enemies, chukking our enemies for the priests."

With a jolt, David was reminded that the Maya believed in human sacrifice. Whatever chukking was, it involved humans to be used for their prayers. He doubted he was being cleaned and fed just to be sacrificed, not after the rescue. Still, it was good to be reminded that these people were as alien to him as conquerors from Mars might be.

"There are prophecies that guide our culture," Hadwin continued after gesturing to cut off a comment Gabor was ready to make. "Our priests and philosophers, our kings and Queens have all had time to consider what they meant. A prevailing interpretation, along with events on the surface, led us to act."

"Even if you are white," said Xoc, a very dark-skinned man, maybe thirty or forty, jowly and wearing a rainbow of jewels along his large ears, some sort of stone necklace around his ample neck, and wearing something closer to caftan than robe or shirt. His eyes blazed with contempt.

"Paler than the conquistadors, darker than the politicians," Gabor quipped. "Whatever are we to do with you?"

"Enough," Hadwin snapped. Clearly, this was a well-worn byplay.

David processed what was being said as they bickered. The Maya, like so many ancient cultures, had their prophecies, some of which actually proved to be true. But was Hadwin really suggesting the Maya had a prophecy about a botanist from Nebraska?

"So, there's a prophecy about me? How is that possible?"

"I will leave that to the rulers to explain," Hadwin said.

"They should never have been brought here," Xoc said, voice rising and echoing off the stone. To hide his worry, David sipped at the hot drink. "In fact, they should be banished to the surface to suffer with the other white people."

"That is cruel," Itzel said. "I will point out the whites weren't the only people to launch their missiles. The Chinese and Koreans are not white."

That filled in one blank for David, the fact that the people of Kasper were aware of surface events. They had some means, either electronic or human or both.

"Have you been keeping an eye on us since you...relocated?"

Xoc thundered, "Of course we have! We have to protect our way of life and now we have our brothers and sisters to protect."

"Only the ones whose blood we deemed 'pure' enough," Gabor needled the older man. "The rest, you left to burn or starve."

Several of the councilors reacted to that gibe. Clearly, the decision as to who was to be saved and who wasn't was far from a unanimous one. That decision, whatever it was, was 100 years in the past. Could these people be arguing about something three generations earlier? David pondered to himself as the thoughts of what all this was continued to flood his every molecule.

Of course, the various Native American tribes and the American government were also parsing bloodlines to determine who qualified or who did not, a debate that had gone on for nearly two centuries. At least each counted as a whole person and not the absurd three-fifths compromise the Founding Fathers enacted to preserve the Thirteen Colonies. Ever the scientist, he knew race to be merely a social construct, but a universal one that even seeped deep beneath the surface.

Akna, a woman who had stayed silent, cautiously observing, seemed the youngest of the councilors, maybe still in her twenties. He couldn't exactly tell given their foreign appearance. Still, she wore the least jewelry and seemed to have the fewest scars. To compensate, perhaps, she wore the most primary color palette, all reds and golds, with orange feathers fanned out over her right ear. She was also the most attractive of the group and absorbed everything with her wide eyes. She finally spoke up, her voice at a high pitch, making her seem even younger.

"Were you perpetrators or victims?"

"If you know anything about me, you know I am a botanist. I study plant life. I was nowhere near the attack and certainly don't know the attackers." Of course, had he agreed to Holtzer's crazy scheme, he would have been directly involved with the Korean premier, but he kept that to himself. "I, that is, my wife and I were victims in that we lost friends and family. Our way of life is forever altered."

"And for that, I grieve with you," Itzel said. He nodded toward the woman with appreciation.

"Is there some way I can be of help?" David suspected it was the APLS, but for all he knew, there was some other reason. Hell, it could have more to do with Betty than him, which might be why she was saved.

"You can," Hadwin said, although Xoc made a dissenting snort. "I asked Ponco to bring you before us in order to formally offer you and your wife sanctuary among us. Our King and Queen will provide details, but it was proper for you to meet us and, as you await your wife's awakening, you had the time." He smiled at that as if David had something better to do than meet with his rescuers.

"He knows nothing of us, our ways. You intend to let the serpent in the garden?" Gabor asked. David later found out he would not make a Christian allusion unless he was showing off or identified with the serpent.

"I intend to welcome our guests, who are here after the Council voted its recommendation to our sovereigns," Hadwin said, putting Gabor in his place. "David and Betty Anders are our guests, and of course, it's all new to them. I will ask Ponco and Karuk to act as their guides to protect them..."

"...and us," Xoc interrupted.

"From you, certainly," Gabor added.

"We do not anticipate needing our supreme commander, and since you have gotten to know one another, this seems best," Hadwin continued, ignoring his colleagues. To David, though, the back and forth over the last twenty minutes had been illuminating. David, astute as ever, even in the current situation observed who said what, and who was speaking with their body and not their lips. There were definitely alliances and rivalries. Gabor, he decided, needed to be watched most carefully since he seemed to merely stir the pot for his own amusement. Whatever he truly intended, he kept to himself. He was someone he didn't want to play poker with. Ever.

At some point, when he wasn't paying attention, Karuk had slid in and was positioned between them and the chamber entrance. Now he joined them at the table, standing at attention. Ponco nodded at him and then rose, David imitating her.

"All will be explained, David Anders. You will have to trust in us," Hadwin said. As he considered what he'd been told, David realized he hadn't been told much at all. This was a courtesy call with the real information to be doled out by the real rulers. A time to be presented to the royal family was not mentioned, which meant he was likely going to stay underground for some time. At least Holtzer couldn't harass him down here. Had the general known about this place, he'd have invaded. Or tried to. From the glimpses he'd seen so far, there were hidden technologies that suggested something beyond what the surface had managed to accomplish.

Flanking the scientist, Ponco and Karuk escorted him from the chamber, down the stairs, and out to the southern court. They were alone among the statues and greenery. He saw a healthy variety of plants and flowers, a few varieties unlike anything he had seen and would love to study. With no direct sunlight, something was letting them grow and thrive, again suggesting there was more to these people than they had revealed to him. Depending on how long he was a "guest," he hoped they'd let him take cuttings or give him access to a microscope.

"Did it go well?" Karuk asked Ponco.

"Well enough, my love," she said. "The usual bickering. They were actually somewhat rude."

"People like me, I gather, are a rarity," David said.

"You're not the first Caucasian here, but it's been a long time," Karuk admitted.

"Any news on Betty?"

"She is healing and resting. We're having her brought to your house soon."

He began leading them away from the tower, but David paused. "House?"

"House may be too grand a word, David," Ponco said. "It is small, but clean, and a good place for Betty to rest. I think you'll be happy with the speed of her recovery."

Another clue. He was eager to see her for himself because, so far, all he'd heard were words from others. As a scientist, he liked to see things for himself. And as a husband, he was insistent upon seeing his wife.

"I am a soldier first," she told him as they resumed walking. "But I am also a spouse, so I am not entirely immune to your feelings."

David found a new emotion for Ponco, as they crossed eyes, understanding one another more deeply in that moment.

"I'm also not like the council. I have sworn an oath to protect Kasper and all its inhabitants. There has never been an incursion, never an insurrection, never an assassination," she said proudly.

"That she knows of," Karuk added.

"That is true. No doubt with a millennium of records, some secrets have been kept."

"Like, why me?"

"Actually, no. That is not a secret, at least not something intentionally kept from me. The Council and our sovereigns understand the protests of the prophecies far better than I. I am a soldier. I understand the field of combat. I understand the enemy."

"What do you make of me?"

"You are no threat from a physical standpoint," she said without hesitation. "It's why you traveled with just one gun and no defensive measures." She stopped then turned and tapped the center of his forehead. "It's here that may be the threat. And things in there are things I cannot anticipate and prepare for. So you may yet be a threat to our society."

"What's in there?" Karuk asked, teasing his wife.

"Ideas," she said as if it scared her.

"Hope," David countered. "If my project can help grow food to help mankind survive, then we may yet survive our capacity for destroying ourselves. You have an abundance here, don't you? Would the Council consider sending aid?"

Karuk chuckled at that. "Help the surface? Admit we exist? I doubt anyone would be in favor of that!"

"Does that mean I am trapped here? After all, I now know of your existence."

Karuk paused at that, having no answer for the man.

"That is not for us to decide. For now, you are our distinguished guest, here to enjoy our sanctuary, here to have a reprieve from an apocalypse," she said, reminding David of his alternatives.

"We are just soldiers and will do as ordered, and right now, that order is to make our home your home," Ponco said.

They fell into a somewhat uneasy silence at that and David fretted about his immediate future, the forthcoming audience with the leaders of Kasper. Then the next issue was what they would do with them and their knowledge.

After a while, passing a steady stream of streets and avenues, with the center of town fading in prominence, they paused at a small, rectangular building that seemed, on the outside at least, some form of beige adobe or stucco. Ponco withdrew a small copper disc and waved it over a carving of a jaguar. Its eyes flashed red and there was an audible click. She pushed against the door, which noiselessly slid open, and she let David walk in first.

He expected something Spartan, stone and wood, maybe with thatched bedding. Instead, there was a large bed, with a tapestry or quilt atop it. There was a low, wide chest of drawers, with inlaid tile work that represented flowers in bloom. A comfortable-looking chair and a writing table were to the left. Behind the wall and headboard, there was another room, which turned out to be a bathroom with a sink, toilet, shower stall, and a woven basket filled with soaps and creams. He noted it was spotless and a cooling breeze came from recessed vents. The lighting had activated as they entered and seemed to soften as they examined the surroundings.

"You'll love the bed. One thousand thread count sheets and a memory mattress unlike anything you've experienced," Karuk said with a grin.

David was stunned, feeling as if he were standing in a hotel, not an underground house, accompanied by Maya warriors. He stared at the large, dark screen opposite the bed along with what seemed to be a terminal of sorts on the writing desk.

"Is there something wrong?" Ponco asked.

"It's fine, better than fine, in fact; it's just not what I expected," he finally said.

"We're not savages or some backwoods people," she said defensively.

Karuk hastened to step between his wife and David, understanding the nuance of cultures a bit more than his counterpart. "Ponco, let him adjust. He's not trying to insult us," Karuk said soothingly.

"I think I expected something more...traditional," he finally said.

"Ah. I see. When it comes to formal matters, especially with our leaders and priests, the old ways are retained as much as possible. But, the further away from the center, the more of your modern world's influence can be found. We've had a century to make upgrades after a long period of embracing the status quo," she told him.

"The Vanishing." Jumping past the formalities, he had dove right for it.

"As you call it. We call it something else."

David indulged the setup with a slight brow raise.

"The Great Migration, that's what we call it."

"Okay, why did the Great Migration happen?"

She looked him up and down, quickly glancing at Karuk before concluding her response. "A question for another time," Ponco said. "More clothing for you and Betty will be along shortly. If there's something you would prefer or need, tell the central computer."

David's head was swimming with the notion of Artificial Intelligence, but it did square with the hints of advanced technology he'd glimpsed. He would have to make a thorough study of the tech in his room and see how it matched with what he left up on the surface.

"Do you need anything else before dinner?"

"What am I to do? Or, what am I allowed to do?"

Ponco looked at her husband, who shrugged.

"We have been tasked to accompany you when you leave this building, but we were not given any restrictions. We may go to the gardens. I would be pleased in knowing our botany outperforms anything you could have imagined. Or we can show you any aspect of Kasper you wish to explore. We will dine with you and introduce you to people as needed. Or, you may remain here and rest. If you need us, tell the computer." She then tapped her index finger to just behind her ear, suggesting there was an interface with the central computer. There was far more to Ponco than he imagined.

"I'll just rest for now and wait for Betty," he told them. "I think I'll be just fine."

"As you wish," she said and left, Karuk on her heels. The door slid closed and he knew he could run, but not without Betty. He needed rest, she needed to recover, and he would be damned if he left without knowing what the hell he had to do with Maya prophecies.

He kicked off the moccasins and lay on the bed, almost immediately drifting off to sleep. His dreams were a jumble and he twisted on the bed, reacting to the images that included Holtzer, the Ghost Squad, the dead on the streets, the constant look of hunger.

Then, the fever dream faded, a cool sense of serenity washed over him, and he rolled over and felt another figure. His eyes snapped open and lying beside him, dressed in a long lightweight tunic, was Betty. She seemed tired and pale, but she was smiling and there was life in her eyes.

"Hi," she said. She sounded perfect.

"Hi," he replied with eyes that spoke more than words ever could. "How are you feeling?"

"The medicine here is amazing. I was in and out of surgery pretty quickly and I was pumped with an IV of something akin to a miracle drug. I feel pretty normal."

"What about your wound?"

"Right now, it feels more like a sore muscle than nearly losing my liver."

He squinted in confusion, which resulted in a laugh. Clearly, their medicine was a match for their tech and that should not have been a surprise.

"I was pumped with miracle meds, blood, and antibiotics, so I'm not running any marathons, but I will be fine," Betty reassured him. "Pretty nice place they gave us. Gilded cage?"

"I really don't think so," he replied.

He leaned over and kissed her, delighted to feel the familiar pressure in return. They remained that way for several minutes until she broke contact and leaned on one elbow, looking expectant.

"So, I've been trapped in a hospital or clinic or whatever. You've seen the city. Tell me all about it."

He recounted his actions along with his observations. She listened intently, asking the occasional question, but her jaw dropped, mirroring his reaction when first told of their connection to the prophecies. In turn, he asked her all sorts of detailed questions about her medical care and the procedure she underwent. She told him what she could, the blurred memories bestowed on someone's brain who experienced a near-death occurrence followed by alien anesthetics and surgery.

"Do you mean Karuk carried me all that way on his own?"

"That he did. They grow them big down here."

"And down here being something out of Jules Verne. That's pretty amazing, don't you think?"

"Oh, I do. And there's plant life here. Things are growing and I can't wait to study them," he said, his eagerness making him speak faster.

On they talked, sharing anecdotes, observations, and speculations. He lost track of time, not believing that his recently shot wife could heal with nothing more than what seemed like magic. But here they were, healthy with a bed and each other. Finally, their conversation was interrupted by a tapping at the door. He arose and walked over, looking for a portal or peephole. Seeing none, he just said, "Enter."

The door slid open and a teen boy stood there with a large woven box in his arms. "This is from the High Council," he said. "Welcome to Kasper" as he stared at David. David wondered if the teen had ever seen a white man before. The fixated stare said all David needed to know about the scarcity of his kind in this place.

David gestured to the dresser, and the teen entered and placed the basket down. He studied Betty, which didn't make David jealous, not at all, and he wondered about tipping the kid but had nothing. He didn't even know if the Maya tipped. He suspected not, so he said his thanks and the curious teen reluctantly left them alone. Betty had already rolled off the bed and headed for the basket, which had alternating bands of gold, blue, and red on the top third. She used both hands to lift the lid and David arrived in time for them to study the stacks of clothing. Some seemed to be woven cotton, others felt more like fine wool. The sizes indicated male from female attire and she chuckled when beneath the tops and bottoms were more traditional Western world underwear. What amazed David was how they knew their sizes and had access to such items.

"At least they're not crotchless," she said as she held up the pale pink underwear.

"Well, someone is feeling better." David grinned.

They both laughed at that and then each withdrew small boxes. Within, each held an assortment of bracelets, necklaces, and earrings. Betty admired them, holding several pairs up to her ears, using the large screen's reflection to see how they looked.

"Maybe there's a hairdresser," she said hopefully. "I need to do something with this mop. You too, mister."

He bowed low. "Your wish is my command." David was the happiest he'd been in some time, joking and laughing. He couldn't believe what was happening and spent every ounce of his will to freeze this moment forever.

A short time later, there was another tap at the door, and as it opened, Ponco and Karuk entered.

"You look well," Ponco said to Betty.

Before replying, she went over and threw her arms around Karuk, which was an effort given his massive size compared with her small form. "Thank you."

He looked a little stricken at the display of affection, but Ponco's eyes shined with delight, an emotion David hadn't seen on her before. David made formal introductions and then Betty started in with a stream of questions, starting with what did they wear to meet royalty? Then she asked about the jewelry and got a crash course in its meaning and symbolism.

Karuk and David merely hung back, periodically exchanging bewildered looks. Inwardly, though, David rejoiced because his wife was not only alive but apparently feeling better than she had in some time. Whatever they'd pumped her with seemed to do her a world of good, and he was incredibly relieved at that. Not that he would ever forgive Holtzer should they ever meet again.

Karuk finally cleared his throat and mumbled something about dinner waiting for them. Betty took the cue and thanked Ponco, who seemed either amused or stunned by the fusillade of fashion questions, things she'd grown up on and clearly hadn't thought about in ages. She turned to slide her arm through David's, ready for the next experience.

As they walked, Ponco informed them that they were scheduled to meet with the King and Queen the following morning. Normally, David would be anxious to get his questions answered and would have preferred to be seeing them that evening. But he'd just had his wife, his repaired and healthy wife, returned to him, and he wanted to just bask in her presence that night. His destiny would have to wait a little while longer.

CHAPTER 12

King & Queen

Betty took the staring with better equanimity than he did, flashing smiles at all who looked. Karuk occasionally pointed out a landmark or religious symbol on a door, things that fascinated the teacher. David kept looking at plants, bushes, and even small trees that somehow were growing down beneath the crust, a mystery he desperately wanted to understand.

"I notice a lot of the sculptures seem to venerate mothers," Betty said, noting the many stone columns featuring women nursing babies or their breasts suckling birds or other life forms.

"Our ancestors believed breast milk had magical powers. They went so far as to encourage teens to lactate without babies, to share their milk," Ponco said.

"No wonder they all look so large," she said. "You're loving it." She leaned into David, who felt a flush in his cheeks.

"I, my dear, am a scientist. I look with clinical detachment," he said with great solemnity.

"Uh-huh," she said, not at all convinced.

The meal was thankfully less spicy than his first one and the soldiers led them to a table where a few other soldiers, now off-duty, dined. Ponco politely introduced them after returning the salutes that her arrival sparked. The conversation was as banal as any group of strangers getting to know one another despite the otherworldly aspect. There were questions about duties performed, where they lived, about families. They probed Betty about life on the surface and asked David about his work.

All through the meal, though, Betty's knee kept nudging David, rubbing against him. He reached under the table and squeezed her hand. Her fingers traced lines up and down the hand, gently. He was no longer as hungry as he thought.

"What do you do for fun at night?" Betty asked a soldier to her left.

"What you would do above, I suppose," he replied. "Play games, read, talk with friends, clean our gear for the next day."

"Drink."

"Fool around," another said, which brought chuckles from everyone.

"If you are here long enough, we can teach you our sports," Karuk said. "Our death ball is something to be experienced, not watched."

"That sounds dangerous," David said.

"It can be, but it gets the blood flowing and keeps us competitive when we're not at war," he replied.

"And we have not been at war for centuries," Ponco said. "We keep the peace; we protect the borders and access portals."

"Our ancestors made war with neighboring city-states," Karuk added. "We'd raid one another, collecting prisoners, several of whom were used in ritual sacrifice. Spilling blood is a frequent way of appeasing the gods."

"We honor them with the death ball games," one soldier added.

"And today?" Betty asked. Her hand and his knee remained still; she was now focusing entirely on her rescuer.

"We continue to honor the old ways with tattoos, spilling blood then. There remain a few priests who hold to the old ways, and the terminally ill among us volunteer to be sacrificed to honor our people."

"Incredible," David murmured, uncertain how to reconcile such technological sophistication with such barbaric practices.

"Your world continues to wage senseless wars, often over ideologies," Ponco said. "You fight over ideas rather than things that make a difference, such as access to water or grazing or land. You hurl long-range weapons at one another rather than face one another. It seems too sterile, losing the meaning of the fight."

"I see your point," he conceded. "We've made it too easy to press a button from thousands of miles away and annihilate a town. Fewer fights would happen if we actually had to meet on a battlefield."

"Better just the leaders meet in a stadium and duke it out," Betty said. "The war would be over in minutes, let the youngest and strongest win."

"Then each country would be led by literal strongmen and might makes right. Isn't that what you say?" Karuk interjected.

David didn't have an answer for that and the conversation veered away from battle and back to sports. There was an apparent robust series of leagues throughout Kasper that mixed Maya and other Native American games with soccer. They were both invited to come and play for practice and exercise. These were welcoming people despite some of the Council's wariness.

A part of him thought he and Betty could find happiness alongside them, but not today. There remained an urgency in using the APLS to help the victims of Alliance aggression. That rarely strayed from his mind, even now as they relaxed, and he remained relieved that his wife was not just healed but clearly feeling better than she had in a while.

They were invited to join Ponco and Karuk for an evening walk but Betty asked to go back to their rooms so she could rest. Ponco agreed and said someone would be by to help her dress before meeting the King and Queen the following morning. At the door, there was an awkward moment as David didn't know whether to shake hands or salute or hug his hosts. He expressed their gratitude and Betty once again thanked Karuk for carrying her.

"It really was not a problem," he said.

"He'll want me to massage those sore arms," Ponco teased, running long fingers against his bulging bicep.

Taking his hand, Betty led her husband into the apartment. As the door slid closed, she wrapped her arms around him and leaned up to kiss him. There was a hunger to the kiss, her lips parting, her tongue probing his mouth. She squeezed tighter, one arm trailing down his spine.

"Are you really up for it?" he whispered in her ear.

"I am if you are," she said, pressing herself against him.

They kissed and kissed as they eased their way further into the room, heading for the bed. But she continued to stroke his back and arms, taking strength from him. His own hands left her face and hair, trailing down her sides. The fabric was soft to the touch and he sensed the heat of her body and he imagined the temperature rising. She tasted of the juice they drank at dinner, a tang of spice, and he returned her ardor.

Her hands tugged at his loose tunic, which easily came off and was tossed against the wall. Her fingers played with his chest hair and she broke the kiss to reach down and lick his nipples. He gasped at the sudden touch.

His own hands played with her huipil, the colorful blouse she had worn. Slowly, he was raising it so her warm flesh met his own. Then with a single pull, it climbed over her head and also met the wall. One hand grasped a breast, his tongue licking the other nipple.

They were both breathing fast but neither one was in a rush. This was not a race but instead was a celebration of living. She had survived, they were together, and for the moment, they were safe. He leaned down and took her breast into his mouth, teeth gently on the nipple.

"Do you wish I could suckle you?" she asked. "Do these disappoint you?"

"Never," he said and meant it. She was self-conscious about her modest breasts, but he was content as she was. He continued to suck and tease with teeth and tongue as her hands began to loosen the drawstring that held his pants in place. They sagged and she tugged until finally he paused and stepped out of them, his left heel kicking them away.

His hands worked on the faja, the sash that held her wraparound skirt in place. As it was also tossed away, he hiked the skirt up as it also began to fall below her hips. They continued to stand before one another, their breaths falling into a rhythm, touching their bodies as they interwound their lips gently holding each other in place. A sense of weightlessness came over them as their extremities locked in motion with one another.

The right hand held up the skirt as the left hand gently and slowly worked its way up her inner thigh, a direct path without interruption until he reached her mons, which he cupped, making her gasp in a short burst. He slipped a finger inside her and began to stroke her, and moments later, her hand found his shaft to match the movement.

Quickly, he withdrew and lifted her out of the skirt, which fluttered about her, fanning out on the floor. She leapt up, her legs wrapping around him and he hugged her tight as they eased back until his legs found the bed, sinking into the sheets that engulfed their figures.

She was atop him and eased him into her. With slow motions, she rode him, her slickness making the motion easy. His senses were heightened and he felt everything from the breeze on his arm hairs to the smell of her sex, the soft breaths she uttered, and that extra sensation as his body was tantalized, energized, and fully engaged with her body.

"I love you so much," he said, which seemed to cue her to increase her motion, so within moments, he exploded within her and she kept riding. He was spent, the post-coital exhaustion threatening to claim him, but he forced himself to keep his hands busy, running up and down her thighs, her hips, and buttocks. She rode further until her thighs tightened around him, squeezing, as she gasped several times, a soft shudder enveloping her.

When she was ready, panting slightly, she disengaged and rolled off him, lying on her back, next to him.

"I love you too," she whispered in his ear.

Naked and spent, they both fell asleep, the most relaxed slumber they'd had in weeks.

The following morning, a tray of fruits and juice was on a tray by their door. She used the wraparound skirt as a cape, covering her bare skin as she brought the food in. The day seemed bright, the temperature steady in a comfortable zone. They were happy, more often smiling at one another than not.

After they ate, still naked, they went to the shower stall, which might not have been designed for two, but they managed, carefully washing one another. When she turned her back to him, he saw the incision where the surgery and gunshot left the skin an angry red. His soapy hand traced around it. He marveled at how little damage there was to the flesh, the obvious lack of sutures, just some puckering around the edges, giving rise to new questions to add to his limitless supply.

"Does it hurt?"

"More like itches," she said.

As they dried, David looked at the clothing left for him, trying to figure out which looked best for meeting Mayan royalty. He settled on one that looked more elegant, relatively speaking, than the others and slipped it over his head. Karuk called it cumbi cloth, which was tightly woven with geometric designs of many colors. He added that it was considered expensive fabric, once used in days past, a sign of its value. A pair of dark, loose-fitting pants helped ground the rainbow top. He slipped back into the moccasins, brushed his hair, and considered himself ready. The last thing he did was retrieve the hard drive with all his data and add it to a pouch that he had seen others wear around Kasper.

Betty, still wrapped in a towel, was still sorting through the handful of women's clothing that had been delivered to them, when there was a knock at their door. David admitted two younger women who brought lidded baskets with them and introduced themselves as coming on behalf of the High Council. They were here to prepare Betty for the introduction.

Betty shot him a look and he shrugged, which didn't convey much of anything, but when in Rome...

He sat at the writing desk and spoke softly to the computer interface. It winked to life and a drawing of a Maya god he didn't know appeared. It seemed to be some sort of digital assistant, so he asked for information on the Kasper plant life, eager to start learning what he could about the world.

Images, videos, and text popped up on the screen, fascinating him as the two women buzzed about Betty. Apparently, they agreed her hair needed attention, there was a quiet conversation going back and forth, decisions, ideas and inspiration flooded the quaint chatter. Soon there was the distinctive sound of scissors at work, bits of her blonde hair, which the women found fascinating, one asking for a lock as a souvenir, fell. When they finished with the hairstyling, which involved gemstone festooned barrettes and feather combs, they set to work on the attire, which was brought with them.

Sheepish at first and then with a resigned shrug, Betty let the towel fall as the women set to work encasing her in yards of fabric. In response to her questions, the women explained this was a huipil, which they carefully wrapped about her lower body. They giggled when it was clear there was more cloth than needed for the petite woman. Then they slipped the cortes over her head, careful not to mar the hair design. Finally, a pair of moccasins, beaded with serpent designs, was slipped onto her feet.

"The huipil is unique; the color and style help identify the region or family plus the creativity of the weaver," one of the women explained.

"What does mine tell you?"

"The color pattern is not associated with any family or region but tells that you are from far away. The reptile pattern woven into the fabric also speaks of speed and deadliness, matching your footwear."

Betty laughed at that. "You think I am dangerous?"

"Anyone from the surface is dangerous," the other woman said.

They took her to the bathroom's full-length mirror and she admired herself, twirling a bit to see how the skirt moved. Despite the five yards of material encasing her, she was able to move freely and seemed delighted.

During all of this, David only managed to skim some of the entries, but from what he could tell, Kasper was dotted with hydroponic gardens, hothouses, and naturally growing trees and plants that were normally found in South America, Central America, or across North America. It was an unusual mélange, segregated by region with their own temperature-controlled environments. He had yet to figure out how they got the sunlight they needed, but that would have to wait.

One of the women whispered in Betty's ear and she looked over her shoulder and nodded. The other took the cue and walked over to David and grabbed his right hand, tugging. Uncertain, he rose from the chair and was taken to where Betty had been attended to. A hand on his shoulder directed him into the seat as she was joined by the other. Some sort of mister dampened his hair and then the scissors got to work. He remained still as Betty supervised, providing approving looks when the attendants paused. In fifteen minutes, they were done, and he rose to look in the mirror. The hair was shorter and neater, that was for certain. They parted it the opposite from what he normally did, but in seeing Betty's approving look, he kept his opinion to himself. One more thing to adjust to in Kasper.

The women declared the two were ready and Ponco was arriving shortly to escort them back to the palace. "Wait, I look so plain next to her," David complained. The women exchanged confused looks and then glanced in their supply baskets. One withdrew a few bracelets and some sort of choker. Each was filled with a mixture of stone and gems with leather thongs to close them. Carefully, she affixed one then the next to him and he winced once as she tightened it too tightly. He looked at the bracelets and nodded his appreciation as Betty thanked them profusely and the women bobbed their heads and left.

"You look amazing," he said.

"I feel amazing," she said.

David grinned; it had been a long while since there was a night like that. The fear from the surface world faded away for now. "I was that good?"

"We were that good, but I think it was also the medicine they gave me. It has, like, energized me."

More questions for his lengthening list.

Whatever he intended to say next was interrupted by a new knock and Betty headed over to admit Ponco and Karuk. Both stared in wonder at the transformed Betty. Ponco gave her an approving nod and Karuk beamed his approval with a broad smile, showing red and green jewels in his teeth, something David would never get used to.

"How are your arms?"

"I worked out the kinks last night," he said and shared a knowing look at Ponco. She actually winked at her husband, demonstrating a firm bond. "Do you need a lift?"

"I can walk on my own, thank you," Betty said with a broad smile.

David admired his wife and her rapid recovery, again thankful for the wonderous tech of Kasper. He even hoped he could speak with their scientists to help him complete and perfect the APLS, then return to the surface world—that was still taking time to get used to—and help his fellow citizens.

As they neared the temple, Betty gazed up at it, her teacher's mind examining it to understand the structure and the story it told. She carefully counted steps, levels, doorways, and windows, mentally cataloging them along with the large painted symbols she could make out as they approached.

"The thirteen doorways represent the levels of our heaven. The main entrance is the mouth of a fierce monster that protects the King and Queen," Ponco explained. "Those nine windows represent the opposite, the levels of Xibalba, our underworld."

"Like Dante's nine circles of Hell," Betty said to David, who nodded in recognition. Now that was an interesting coincidence.

"And the seven?"

"That is a mystic number, representing the world."

Palace guards saluted Ponco, who sharply returned the gesture and strode ahead of the others, her eyes keenly taking in the guards stationed around the structure. David and Betty once again absorbed the symbols and designs, and strained to make sense of it all, but even the most sophisticated translation program he knew of would likely fail. Anyone who could learn thousands of pictograms had his admiration.

They were led past courtyards to a building that stood on its own but was more heavily decorated and guarded than any other. This had to be where the royal family lived and ruled. David wished he had something more formal for the occasion but maybe he didn't need it.

Ponco proceeded up thirteen steps and led them into a chamber off to the right. He felt as if he had stepped backward in time. Where things were traditional for the High Council, here, the sovereigns looked as if nothing had been altered in one thousand years. No evidence of anything advanced was visible, but as he scanned his surroundings here, he noticed the barely dressed young men with large fronds fanning the King and Queen. Some sort of scribe, similar to the one on the mug he used the day before, sat ready to take notes on some form of parchment. There were stories told in the rough, white-painted stone walls, great battles against men and beasts. There was some jungle hunting party celebrated on the wall behind the thrones.

Each throne, glorious in its own right, was actually a wide, low stone bench that was well-worn, with a red cushion on the seat. David's gaze looked up and then into the eyes of the King, who sat cross-legged. Hakan Miwok was clearly a senior, maybe in his seventies or eighties, with sagging jowls and bushy gray eyebrows. Those eyes had seen much. His dark red skin was wrinkled here and there, the tattoos on his hands faded with time. He wore nothing out of the ordinary, which made David feel rather relieved. His badge of office was the ornate headdress he wore, with large white feathers encircling his head.

The Queen, Dakota Miwok, was decades younger and one of the more attractive Maya he had seen so far. She lacked the large nose most were born with, and she clearly paid attention to coordinating features, gems, and stones so she exuded Maya elegance. There was something suspicious in her eyes as she took in first Betty, then David. She leaned back on her own bench, hands on her bare knees, and watched with intensity.

Ponco made the introductions and then stepped back, standing beside her husband, a respectful ten feet away from the thrones.

"I am told you have many questions," the King said. "There may not be time enough to answer them all, so I will let the Queen begin with the answers we deem most pertinent." With a gesture, he turned the conversation over to his wife.

"You have heard of our prophecies," she began. David nodded, but he had to admit, he only had the smallest bit of knowledge about them. Even Betty admitted to him at one point how little she knew, as they were not part of her studies.

"Shortly before the event you surface-dwellers call the Vanishing, our calendar reached its end. To us, it was merely the end of an era and the beginning of a new one. To your world, it foretold doom. We were told how pockets of mankind panicked and prepared for the world to end."

Hakan let out a throaty chuckle at the notion.

"Each civilization counts time differently. For us, this was merely the conclusion of a Long Count *b'ak'tun*. Our thirteenth. Nothing more, although it has been misinterpreted as so much of our culture has been through the years," she said. Her tone signaled how much she disliked that.

"But we do have our prophecies, and as each one has come to pass, it reinforces our beliefs in the ones to come. The second prophecy reveals that the answers to everything reside within mankind. The prophecy shows two paths: one of understanding and tolerance, and one of fear and destruction." She paused and stared directly at David, who grew uncomfortable under her gaze, but he set his teeth and stood his ground. Betty slipped her hand in his and squeezed. He returned the gesture and held fast.

"Things do not simply start and stop with sharp edges, but they grow or wither with time," she resumed. "We end one count, we begin another. Such is the way. Our second prophecy suggests rapid change after a solar eclipse in your year of 1999. Considering the thousands of years man has walked the world, a century or more is a trifle. Still, your history shows a series of unfortunate occurrences that year, so things were beginning. Man has been increasingly dictated by his emotions over his reason, hence you reached the brink of climate disaster, and yet, your continued battles revolve around religious beliefs. It's pathetic.

"We believe the universe is connected and that energies travel between the stars and the galaxies. Since that eclipse, we have felt the rising energies coming from the center of the universe, and our galaxy is being realigned, which in turn will force man to change, to evolve."

"That interconnectedness is something many people believe is related to what we call string theory," David said, wishing Reid were here to back him up. This was not his element, but it struck him as interesting that the Maya had a prophecy about something science only figured out less than two centuries ago.

Dakota nodded, joined by Hakan.

"As with any prophecy, there are many interpretations, as priests come and go, each with their own view. Our study of mankind has also led to different interpretations of the prophecy. A prevailing view is that man will alter his behavior, reordering how he communicates with one another and his beliefs. He will face his fears and help Earth synchronize itself with the solar system and then the galaxy.

"There is said to be a great divide. There will be those who let their ideologies, religion, and models of morality or nationalism guide them. Then the other half will learn to control their emotions, becoming more tolerant and compassionate. Forever the two sides fight for balance and control. Since that eclipse, we have been in a waiting period, anticipating the next great change for man. Many of our priests have felt that our participation could influence the direction of all men and the future."

David thought about key world events since 1999, which he always felt was a big deal Christian thing since the dates were by their reckoning. There was the Y2K nonsense for starters, but soon after came 9/11, the 20-year conflict in the Middle East, the Vanishing, the dozens of nations that were reshaped as the polar ice caps melted and the seas rose and land vanished, the dissolution of the United Kingdom, the rise of a united Korea, the formation of the Alliance, and then the bombs. The Maya could have seen any of those distinct events as the prophecy coming to pass. But then again, they took the long view, each event a bead on a string until the necklace was complete. So, what made them think now was the time of the prophecy and how did he and Betty play a part?

"One rarely knows he is making history as it happens," the King interrupted. "To him, it is just another day."

"But to the keen observers," the Queen continued, "one recognizes when things build to a climax."

"You think the nuclear devices were at that moment?" Betty asked.

The Queen flashed at the interruption, but she nodded in agreement. Betty, he noted, remained silent and he thought better of saying anything further.

"This Alliance has changed global politics. We sought understanding of the countervailing forces, the balance the Prophecy talked of. Our intelligence suggested it was your intellect, David Anders, that would prove the difference. But that was not enough to convince us to act. We consulted the great priests throughout Kasper, held an emergency conclave, and reached a conclusion that finally meant bringing you to us. This cited the third prophecy."

"My favorite one," the king interjected.

The Queen ignored him, fixing her gaze on David. "Slowly, man has been poisoning the planet, since your factories first belched burned coal into the skies. Your logic leaped forward, with the five industrial revolutions—"

David broke eye contact to look helplessly at Betty. His wife looked at the exasperated Queen, who hesitated then nodded for her to explain.

"The first used water and steam power to mechanize production, which is what Her Majesty just referenced. The second was when steam was surpassed by the harnessing of electricity, gas, and oil. The next revolution was when information technology automated which led to the fourth, the digital age. The fifth followed more recently, coming fuller circle with the melding of solar, wind, and water energies to begin replacing the fossil fuels and coal," Betty concluded and gave the Queen a look, relinquishing her time back to her.

The Queen nodded with a small smile, conveying her appreciation that her time wasn't being wasted.

"Man's mind outran the planet; as a result, man warmed the world, which took centuries but finally brought about the geological disaster of the last 150 years. The harmony we need, and that so many of the people in Kasper knew going back to the first man, was that we live with the world. We damaged it and the world fought back, but that harmony is being restored. That is, until now. The nuclear war unleashed has set matters back immeasurably. Each man has to have a spiritual awakening and recognize this cannot be sustained. Enlightened self-interest has to be suspended in favor of loving one another and loving the world that birthed us. Where it took an Alliance to destroy, our research shows there was a single person who could change that."

The steadiness of her gaze at him and the enormity of what she just suggested sent David's mind into overload. Louder than the other cacophonous words flying through his mind were quotes from a very old television series. Without realizing it, he said out loud, "'One man cannot summon the future. But one man can change the present.'"

"Quite right, young man," Hakan said,

David let out a nervous laugh as he was processing being told he was deemed the living embodiment of an ancient Maya prophecy, told to him by none other than an ancient Maya queen in an underground city. This was far more than he could handle.

"You'll have to forgive him, your Highness," Betty said, grabbing David's hands and turning him to face her. She leaned back and looked into his wild eyes. He saw her steadying presence, her acceptance of the absurd, and behind it all, her abiding love and faith in him.

"This is all so much, I get it. But hold it together as we hear what they have to say. Then we can process it. I knew you were brilliant, David, and this merely confirms it. Just hold on."

All he could do was nod.

"Is he ill?" the Queen inquired.

"As you might imagine, this is somewhat overwhelming information to absorb. We will need time to digest this information. You have to admit it is quite a lot."

"Indeed it is," Hakan agreed. "But there is more he must hear."

"Please proceed," he said in a weak, soft voice.

"We have been made aware of your botanical experiments and your current project," Dakota continued. "Based on our priests' understanding of the ancient writings, the fourth prophecy, combined with the third, continues to apply to you. According to those writings, the great ecological shift may have been accelerated in 1992, by your reckoning. The consequences of global warming, starting with the depletion of the ozone layer, were changing the world. Since the earliest warnings of what man was doing to the atmosphere, a growing number of people wanted to change things. Change the world for the better and heal it. Things appeared to accelerate after the event you call the Vanishing. But it has been slow progress, a race to save a world that was rapidly dying.

"The fourth prophecy was all about changing man's mind, restoring the world, and repairing the green. Your APLS process is the catalyst for that change, for bringing health back to plants and trees, the ecosystem, which then extends to avian, sea, and wildlife."

"So I'm going to save the world," David said incredulously.

"You? Not on your own, and the APLS is just the start, but once it is deployed and others see its efficacy, then others will join you, following your lead instead of the leadership of those hellbent on self-destruction."

"Is that why Ponco and Karuk saved us?" Betty asked.

"We had been watching and observing, hoping to have this conversation under different circumstances. We could not reach your bunker in Iowa, but once you took to the road, we watched as you neared us. Those attackers forced us to act and I do not think you mind having your lives saved."

He heard the challenge in her cold voice. While she explained everything, he absorbed the information, but he was also processing the tone, which dripped contempt for mankind, and while she seemed happy to actually be watching the prophecies come to pass, she didn't think much of saving the world. She certainly didn't seem to think much of him. But she did believe deeply in their prophecies, and that made David believe every word the Queen had said. David took the room in, and while looking the Queen directly in the eyes, but speaking to Betty, he softly asked the question he knew was on everybody's mind.

"If I am the living being foretold by the prophecies, then what do we do now?"

CHAPTER 13
Realities A Bitch

"A very good question," King Hakan said. "The prophecies, you see, are not like an instruction manual. They guide our people and have done a fine job of that over the centuries. We determined we needed you, so here you are. It's not like we've been waiting for you to be born like some savior from stories. Ever since we established Kasper, our ancestors have prepared for a world yet to be born. As things looked bleak, we brought our brethren below to shelter them. Our world tripled in size, if not larger. It's been a constant series of adjustments and you are the most recent variable. But ruling, you see, is making decisions and living with the consequences. We are not a hasty people. We've learned to take our time, to plan and prepare, acting when we were clear in purpose. I wish more of your people acted in this way."

"We know you are here with a means to improve the world, but is it a world worth saving, hmm? Might it not be best if they just kill each other and then we can reclaim our place on the surface?" Queen Miwok added, juxtaposing the King's thoughts.

David blanched at the notion and his expression clearly conveyed his feelings.

"That is just one of the options," Hakan said. "We could send a force to protect you and let you use your miraculous technology to repair the world. Wouldn't that be nice, hmm?"

"Or," interrupted the Queen, "we could work in secret. There are many options and the High Council continues to debate the wisest course of action for you, for us, and for the world above."

"Shouldn't I have a say in these deliberations?" He did not want to be used as a pawn in some larger game. Holtzer tried that and he walked away. He'd walk from this too if he had no control over his discovery.

"After you learn more about us and our world, that certainly would be best, so we need to show you some more things. Ponco and Karuk will guide you."

David appreciated the Queen not giving him a voice until he understood the culture and people of Kasper more. Nodding with a disarming smile, he waited for what was to come next.

Ponco snapped to attention at the mention of her name. "Your Majesty, I am a poor guide given what is to be shown."

"Your companion, Karuk, has been briefed. He can explain what they need to know," Dakota said. Ponco shot her husband a glance then nodded in affirmation, although David could tell she still didn't like the task. He guessed it was because she was a soldier and not a tour guide. He sympathized with her.

"How long will we be here?" he asked. "I have people awaiting us and they are worried."

"Ah, it is good to have friends," Hakan said. "Allies are always welcome, hmm? Of course, they worried; you went off your path, I am told. You are far from home and not yet at your destination."

"Our presence must remain a secret," Dakota said sharply. "Even if we let you send such a message, it cannot contain information that compromises us or the people we are charged with keeping safe. Prophecies or not, violation of our laws will mean your deaths."

David didn't doubt it; she had a look that suggested how deadly serious she was. Betty's body language shifted and she even moved a step backward at that pronouncement.

"Today you will be shown more of our city including some of our own projects. In the meantime, the Council will continue their deliberations," Dakota announced. David noted the Council didn't provide a hint of this yesterday, so he saw they were going to be tightlipped about it all.

"Nacom, take our guests on their tour. By the time you return, we should know what comes next," she added.

Ponco nodded in affirmation and gestured for the couple to follow them. She did not bow or genuflect, so David and Betty chose to do nothing. Instead, they turned and left, hearing whispers between the sovereigns. They walked from the chamber but noted three figures watching from the shadows. While Ponco and Karuk ignored them, Betty was studying them, as David took in more of the architecture.

"Who are they?" Betty asked Ponco.

Without breaking stride, she said, "Those are the children, princes and princesses. The eldest is Mika, heir to the throne. She is followed by Titus, training for the army, and then there's Hiawatha, whose path has yet to be determined."

At that, David looked over and saw for himself that the children were younger than he imagined given Hakan's advanced age, but he kept that observation to himself. None of the children moved, staying as hidden as they could, in the dark, hidden from the sight of others. David appreciated the need for knowledge, and chuckling to himself, decided against outing them.

"May I contact our friend, the one expecting us?" he asked as they exited the palace and headed through the courtyard.

"No," Karuk said.

"Not now," Ponco added. "There will be time for that later."

As they left the tower, she took them east, into a section of Kasper neither had been before. David and Betty looked around, absorbing everything, waiting for Ponco to begin her narration. When it was clear she had nothing to say, Betty remarked, "I don't see vehicles. No transportation other than feet."

"There are bicycles and wheeled transport, but they are used rarely. Most sections or villages of Kasper stay in their respective places, so the need is minimal. When necessary, we use wagons to transport goods," Ponco said.

"Long ago, we developed the network of roadways to connect our cities," Karuk continued. "They were called sacbeobs, like your highways. We walked from city to city along these sacbeobs and prefer walking today. But, in the last century, as our population swelled, new forms of transportation were required. So as not to despoil our environment, we avoided engines, using our bodies to power ourselves."

"It takes time, but keeps us close to the ground, close to one another," Ponco said.

The pair fed off one another, with Karuk clearly the more technically minded of the two, hence the more detailed responses. Ponco was a soldier, a commander, and that was her focus and training. He liked their easy rapport, the way they worked together while remaining man and wife without any visible issues. As he considered this, he reached over to grasp Betty's hand and they walked onward. There were vibrant signs of life, the delicious aroma of spices and grains on the stove, sauces stewing and meats smoking, the sound of shuttles powering looms, the wheeze of bellows that fanned flames hotter, and the distinct electronic pitch of something being tuned. People smiled and nodded at them, the passing soldier saluting their nacom, the children running, playing catch, chasing after them with giggles. It was perfectly serene, Betty asked the occasional question, which mostly Karuk answered with a joyous, infectious smile.

"The various tribes that lived above us—the Crow, Shoshone, Black-feet, Flathead, Bannock, and Nez Perce among them—were hunter-gatherers. They lived in harmony with the birds, and the bison, and the fish, and the geysers," Karuk told Betty at one point on their long walk.

"What about the calderas? Weren't there eruptions over those years?"

"Now and then, but far apart. And when we began to build Kasper here, we prevented that from happening again."

"Wait, but I remember reading something about the ground rising, suggesting a massive eruption was coming."

"That was indeed a possibility," the soldier admitted. "But we brought our engineering know-how with us and tapped the thermal energies, redirecting it to power Kasper. Over time, that heated our homes and hearths, and allowed us to build here without anyone noticing. We've actually done the surface world a favor by tapping those energies for the last millennia."

"That actually makes me wonder," David said. "Your people were all over Mesoamerica; why relocate further north?"

Karuk and Ponco shared a glance before he replied, "There are some stories, some legends we do not discuss."

That surprised David given how open they had been about everything else.

"We found networks of caves and began building our new home," Ponco said, shifting the conversation's direction.

Karuk picked up the thread and added, "We sent exploring parties long before settling here. We knew of the calderas and our engineers determined they could link the Utah caves with this space and the work began. It was certainly a long time in coming, but we had plenty of workers."

David could only imagine slave labor and shuddered at the thought. Then again, if they could build those magnificent pyramids, then tunneling out a new city couldn't have been that hard. The scale of it, though, boggled his scientific mind.

"You were never fully united, as I recall," Betty said. "When did that change?"

"Time and wisdom," Karuk said.

"War can take its toll. Even a fierce people like ours can grow weary. The arrival of the Spanish helped unite our people in a plan for survival. We couldn't beat their rifles, so we learned a new way of life. A unified way that took generations to accomplish," Ponco said.

"Digging tunnels, fortifying roads, establishing all that infrastructure can wear you out, leaving the tribes too tired for battle. It was never going to be easy building a new world, but it became necessary," Karuk said.

"How could you do all that work without the local tribes not being curious or territorial?" Betty asked.

"There were fights," Ponco admitted. "But our ancestors bartered, traded, and even hired the tribesmen to come work on the tunnels and the beginnings of Kasper. All swore blood oaths to keep the secret, and the fact that you're asking today shows they honored their word."

"Unlike how your ancestors kept your word to them," Karuk said.

"I know, we suck," David said. "I get it. We didn't do right by so many people through the years. We still hadn't done right by so many even right before the bombs went off, even leading up to the event, it's amazing any-one still talked to us."

"You exaggerate," Karuk said. "But yes, your history is littered with broken promises. There are definitely descendants who were raised on those stories and your presence here has not gone unnoticed. As far as some of the people are concerned, you white folk should stay on the surface and reap what you sow."

"Not everyone here believes in the prophecies," Betty said.

"Not everyone here was raised Maya," Ponco reminded her.

"The Maya people perfected astronomical studies among other mathematical accomplishments, all of which informed our priests who wrote the prophecies. Their accuracy is pretty astonishing," Karuk said.

"But not everyone we brought below knows of them or accepts them. We honored a debt, one most were unaware of, so they see us as saviors and follow our rulers."

"And you, the army, ensure that's followed," David said.

Ponco gave him a look, assessing the words. "No, it's not like that. They came willingly and accepted our instructions. Few complained, and by now, generations later, everyone is living a fairly harmonious life."

A short while later, they paused for a brief, small meal. Ponco knew of a family that made a blend of fruits into a paste that was served atop maize flatbread, which was most welcome. They drank water, which was cold and refreshing, and answered a few innocent questions from the woman who was still stirring a boiling pot of fruits.

"Of course, some families were uprooted. It wasn't all perfect, but it was the best we had, and the climate back then was so hostile toward our people, we had to do something. While the migration itself was met with some pushback, the settlement was not. Once everyone arrived, it was clear that this way of life in this city was in fact more harmonious to our people." Ponco went on as she consumed the food she was given.

The walk resumed and David noted that the section of Kasper they were in seemed older, some of the earliest structures built. They were also descended, slowly and steadily, until an hour after their meal, they were brought to a fork of the sacbeob and a rougher path veered to the left, into a very wide cavern, still rough and natural. Twin strips of lighting panels, which David still wanted to ask about, lined the pathway, casting competing shadows as they walked. After a dozen feet or so, he began to hear the thrum of engines, a familiar whine of power, a flickering of light from something in action.

Finally, the quartet entered the main space, which was larger by half. A trio of scientists was working with a machine the likes of which David had never seen before. It struck him as an inelegant kludge of components, all advanced in their sophistication and connections from what he could tell, but exposed rather than neatly encased for aesthetics. One was tapping something onto a tablet not dissimilar to the ones he and Betty used. Another was using a long cylindrical tool to fine-tune something deep within the machinery, while the third was checking a readout, in Mayan pictogram, on a wide, shallow screen set into the far wall.

"Welcome to the RSN," Karuk said. His voice caught the technicians by surprise. They stopped their work and gaped at the visitors.

"What is the meaning of this?" the repairman asked. He was not of the Mayan race given his normally proportioned head and his long, black hair held in place by a beaded headband. He wore a simple tunic and pants although he had a utility belt around his hips.

"Supreme commander, you bring white people here?"

"By order of the King and Queen," she said in her commanding voice, the one that brooked no argument. "They are here to observe and learn."

"RSN?" David said, figuring talking about their work would quickly diffuse the situation.

The man reading the screen stepped forward and opened his arms wide, indicating the machine. "It is this. The initials in English are for the Reality Stabilizing Nucleus."

"What reality?" Betty asked. The man glanced at Ponco for permission and she nodded.

"Kasper was built as a refuge for the Maya," Karuk began.

"But in time, it became clear that the rest of those who shared our blood, if not our ways, would also need refuge," the man said.

"Without a war to fight or stars to study, our mathematicians and scientists set to work in other avenues," Karuk continued. "There were some interesting breakthroughs during the years. Each revelation meant a pause to build equipment to take measurements or record the data. We sent people out into the world to study where innovation was taking man. One day, our scouts returned with news of a machine to help us."

"You would perhaps know it as a Babbage," the man added.

David shot Betty a quizzical look and she considered a moment before her eyes widened. "You mean Charles Babbage's Analytical Engine, the first real computing device. He and Ada Lovelace developed something that few understood."

"Exactly," the man said, actually clapping his hands in approval. "While the surface people ignored it, we brought one down here and made it work—then improved upon it. While you were fussing with vacuum tubes to add two plus two, we were pioneering silicone technology and developed artificial intelligence long before you."

"What did you need to measure?" David asked.

"Our studies suggested there were energies to be harnessed, energies beyond our reality."

"Other dimensions, beyond the fourth?" David said.

"Yes, our ancestors pierced the veil between realities, revealing other planes of existence," Karuk took over. "Several seemed to be nothing but chaotic energy, so our scientists measured it and found ways to bottle it in small amounts and determine what it could do. With our computers, we learned that we could actually move matter. We could transmit it across spacetime."

David gaped, stunned at the revelation. "How?"

"We transmit a being's quantum state into another quantum object," the man said.

"Quantum teleportation," he said quietly. He knew that theories had existed for over a century about this possibility. He read briefly about it as he researched quantum physics while developing the APLS but really didn't recall much about it. This was definitely more Reid's area of expertise but being the third use of quantum fields to come up of late, he was increasingly convinced the quantum field where not only this RSN lived, but APLS as well, was the key to mankind's future survival.

"Our DNA scientists were able to provide us with the markers that set the Maya and Native Americans apart from non-Native Americans. We could then use it as a location device, scanning people on the surface and bringing them here."

"You're talking about moving hundreds of thousands of people and the event as we know it—the Vanishing—happened in an instant," Betty said in awe. "But how...." she continued.

"You proved very helpful with your data networks and cell towers, allowing us to actually piggyback our signal on yours, just at a unique frequency. As a result, after a few tests, we were ready,"

"Which is where the diplomats stepped in," a woman said.

Everyone turned around to see Itzel and Akna from the High Council enter the chamber. Both were in less formal garb, equally colorful, but better for walking long distances.

The younger councilor continued. "We sent envoys to the reservations and began discussing our debt to them, inviting them to come away from mankind's madness. It was an unpleasant time; as political gridlock choked the American government, the world was crying for help and was largely ignored. We finally had the means to help our people, the natives who didn't invite anyone to come and ruin the land."

"And everyone agreed?" Betty asked.

"No," Itzel admitted. "So, it took time for the tribal councils to meet and vote. When it was clear the majority desired this avenue, we obliged."

"What we couldn't do," Akna said, "was screen out the dissenters. It was all or nothing, something our envoys may not have clearly explained. As a result, there was a period of adjustment."

"And you wondered why we maintained a military force," Ponco asked Betty. "We moved seven million people in the blink of an eye." David's mind reeled at the kind of energy that had to be used to accomplish something on such a scale. First, it came from another reality, and second, it didn't destroy them or the city in the process. The technology was way beyond anything imagined. The revelations were once again overwhelming in their existence and implication.

"There was disorder on a scale never seen before. We were there to ensure an orderly adjustment. Those who didn't want to be there could not be allowed to leave and reveal our secrets. We had to convince them to stay without bloodshed. At that, we were less than successful." She bowed her head in her predecessors' shame.

"Nothing to apologize for," Itzel said. "What was done by our ancestors cannot be undone and now their children's children are here and happy."

While David suspected that was not universal, he had yet to see anyone in distress or less than content. He had to accept that for now, a minor matter in comparison with the scientific marvels he had just been introduced to.

"Let's back up a moment. You found a way to go between dimensions, so that means the multiverse exists in some form or another."

"Yes, David, but not as your entertainment depicts it. There are no 'mirror' images of ourselves in these realities. Life evolved in different ways or not at all. Some universes, it seems were just born, hence the chaos energy we could tap," Karuk went on. For a soldier, he seemed particularly good at explaining the science in layman's terms. It also showed he was aware of life beyond Kasper. There had been mention of scouts, meaning Mayan spies had been watching the world for centuries.

"Now that everyone is here and has been for a century, why is the machine still working?" Betty wondered.

"Progress," Itzel said.

One of the other scientists spoke up. "Councilor, am I allowed...?"

Itzel and Akna shared a look and then both nodded assent.

"The transportation was immensely successful," she began.

"The greatest migration since Noah," David said, which earned him a confused look from most in the room. Christian stories apparently were not well known in Kasper, which made sense as David reflected.

"Modifications and refinements allowed us to begin moving objects without a genetic signature. We used it in small ways to move materials and supplies from the reservations. That had our great minds considering other applications of the technology. Some considered trying to move materials beyond our world."

"You mean across dimensions?" David asked.

"No, we could tap the energy like sap in a tree, but could never manage to get anything across. Instead, we thought of the skies and considered how far our range was."

"The moon?" Betty suggested.

"Exactly. It didn't work. But we continued to experiment and explore with the RSN intelligence providing us with precise readings. This much energy was so powerful, it seemed to vibrate in ways we could not see but began to measure."

"The vibrations seemed to indicate we were entangling at a new level," the woman said.

"Quantum entanglement," David filled in. His mind raced ahead, trying to imagine the implications of this much energy on that level.

"The prevailing theory today is that we may be able to not just move people from place to place but from time to time."

"Time travel," Betty blurted a second before David.

"That's ridiculous," David said. "Our best minds, well, the best on the surface, are still theorizing about it. My friend, the one I'm trying to reach, this is his world, not mine. I am a botanist..." One of the scientists sniffed at the term, proving to him elitism existed everywhere. "I am here to help save people, not transport them, not send them into the past or future, but let them live today."

"Admirable," the woman said.

"Why show me all of this?" David asked Itzel and Akna. "Are you trying to show off your superiority? Impress me into working for you? Prove you are more than a handful of prophecies?"

Itzel sighed heavily at the angry questions while Akna stared with distaste.

"And why are you two here? I thought you were in debate over what we do next now that I am some sort of messiah."

"That is not what you are," Akna snapped.

"Well, we agree on that," David retorted.

"Yes, the debate continues and we will rejoin them. But we heard you were being shown the RSN. I wanted to see for myself how you would handle the revelations."

"Yeah, it's been a hell of a day," David said. His anger was getting the best of him, and Betty laid a hand on his arm to calm him. "And do what with the information?"

"Determine if we should return you, help you save mankind," Itzel said.

"Isn't it a moral imperative to preserve life?" he challenged.

"That is your moral paradigm, not ours," Akna said. "We live the best life we can, and when it is over, it is over. We ascend to the heavens or Xibalba." The notion of spirituality seemed most definitely out of place given the wonders filling the chamber.

"We were raised to cherish all life, preserve it whenever possible," David said.

Itzel cocked an eyebrow. "How does that explain the nuclear attack?"

David opened his mouth to say something, but there were no words. How could he argue morals when his fellow man annihilated millions if not billions with the nuclear rain that had polluted an already wounded world?

"We do what we can," Betty said.

"What you can do is not good enough." Itzel sneered. "You Caucasian lot have decimated our way of life for centuries, hiding the truth in fabricated histories of you being the saviors. Our people had massive, interconnected cities until your ancestors raped and pillaged the Americas."

"We can't deny that our ancestors were murderers, and we can't deny that our history books are skewed to the victor. But if you are going to blame Betty and me for every mistake every white person has ever made, then we are better off above the ground..."

"This has been a lot to absorb in a very short time," Karuk interrupted. "I would like to suggest we give David Anders and his wife Betty," Karuk gave her an endearing look of understanding, "time to internalize what he has learned today. Give him time to process information we learned over months and years."

"Thanks, Karuk." Betty gave him an appreciative look. "It's not just David who is trying to make sense of all this, you know."

It was Ponco who took note of this, cocking an eyebrow in Betty's direction.

"You bandy all this science around and pat yourselves on the back for figuring out all this 'stuff.' But I don't hear any of you discussing what is the right thing to do with that knowledge and power, only that you have had the ability to attain it."

"My dear," Akna began, "that is the purview of the High Council. We do not just carelessly use this energy."

"Okay, I know the genie is out of the bottle..." Betty paused when Akna and Itzel looked confused. "The energy has been discovered. You've harnessed it. But that means others can access it, and maybe you find ethical ways of using it, but not everyone thinks the way you do."

"The High Council speaks as one," Itzel argued.

"Gabor certainly doesn't seem to be in alignment with you," Betty argued.

"Gabor will abide by the rulings of the Council," Itzel said definitively. "He lives to cause trouble, but we know him and his ways, and do not let his empty words sway us."

"Fine, but he is just one example. How do you know what others are saying in the city, what dissent may breed in dark corners? Is anyone discussing if this raw power should be used? Or is the conversation only about how to use it best?" Betty finished, seemingly removing the rage from her soul.

The councilors looked at each other, and then back at Betty, unchanged by her words.

"Up top, on the surface, before things went to hell, there were great moral discussions about what to do with things, like your RSN. We didn't just split the atom and decide to use it as a bomb. There were great debates among the great minds of the time as to what should be done with such knowledge and power. Did that debate ever happen down here?" Betty continued. Her voice of reason had yet to be extinguished.

"Science has always been ahead of politics," David interjected from the other side of the room.

Betty whirled on him, exasperation on her face. Clearly, they'd had this argument before.

"No shit, David. But seriously, look at what is happening here, like splitting the atom," Betty turned her attention to everyone else at this. "You're dealing with primordial power here. Volcanic power, power I can't even comprehend. But I do comprehend history, knowledge, and patterns. We are one species, whether you want to admit that or not, and as a species, we are callous in our dealings with power once we discover it, so perhaps we need to pause for just a moment and reflect on its use before turning it on again." Betty finished, this time exhausting all of her energy into her argument. She leaned on David, still seemingly recovering from her battle wound.

"That does seem most practical," Ponco said, hoping to calm down

Betty, who seemed really stressed by the issue. "This would also give our councilors time to resume their debates."

"I agree," Itzel said. "You have learned much and we have observed much. We will speak again." With that, the two women turned and withdrew from the chamber. David just stared at the equipment, which seemed in some safety mode, not drawing on the extra-dimensional energies. The trio of scientists ignored them, returning to their work, their time travel work, he reminded himself. He shook his head and just looked imploringly at Betty, who seemed to be handling all this better than he was.

"Let us walk," Ponco said, and directed them to a different branch away from the chamber and opposite the councilors.

David desperately wanted to be alone with Betty to discuss the day's revelations. However, they were walking further away from their guest quarters and Ponco and Karuk were too close for a private conversation. His mind was aswirl with the information learned since climbing out of bed that morning. Out of billions on Earth, a collection of surviving Maya declared him the focus of not just one but multiple prophecies. That his APLS project, which had yet to work consistently, was a key to mankind's survival and its next age. That was enough to send the senses reeling. He didn't feel like a savior or chosen one, but more like an exhausted man trying to keep his head above water long enough to complete his project to see if he could help anyone. He was a part of the scientific community, he was a member of the human race, he was just...a guy. However, the thought of what he didn't do with Holtzer, what he did create in the lab and how he intended to integrate it into the world did have him wondering how true all of this actually might be. And that terrified him to no end.

But, not only did these Mayans anoint him in this unique and unasked-for way, they also revealed to him that other dimensions existed. They were real, no longer theoretical. He longed to speak with Reid, who would—what was the word his college roommate used—plotz. This was so much more for him than for David, who liked to feel the dirt with his fingers, enjoy the fragrance of new buds, and could wait an entire season to see a garden thrive with new life. Other dimensions, other energies were just the stuff of science fiction.

These energies, though, were said to have somehow magically transported seven million people from around the world to a hidden city in the depths of a caldera stretching from Wyoming southward into Utah. The existence of life underground was a given, so he supposed there was room if planned carefully, for seven million people plus the thousands who were already living here when the Vanishing was executed a century earlier. He knew full well how organized the Mayans were so had no doubt they had made room for each and every one.

And if that wasn't enough to ensnare the senses into overdrive, these same energies and equipment that performed the above miracle were now thought to be able to send things or people through time. He never even asked about forwards or backward because he was staggered. He was just stunned by the information, all of which sounded lovely, but truly was taking him away from being able to accomplish his own mission. Being allowed to do just that seemed to be in the hands of a council that had issues of its own to contend with, led by rulers with one who seemed unhappy with his presence and the other who seemed disengaged.

As he walked and thought, he grew increasingly tired and worn.

Betty must have sensed the swirling thoughts and emotions that threatened to shut him down as she wrapped herself around one arm and leaned into him. He didn't need the physical assistance, but he certainly needed the emotional support. He could only imagine what she thought of it all, of him. What did all this mean to her and for her?

They trudged along, no one saying anything until, finally, he noticed they were in a narrow tunnel, with minimal lighting and were ascending. He was so wrapped in his thoughts, his body on autopilot, that he hadn't noticed the change in their surroundings. Still, he walked and followed and asked no questions, knowing full well he already had too many to ask and certain he had learned enough for the day.

Ponco slowed to a stop then withdrew a copper disc from her belt and affixed it to a spot on the wall he couldn't see in the shadows. There was a small click then a grinding of rock against rock as a doorway appeared, letting in cool air and gray light. She then led the others out into the real, the surface world as they called it.

"We are in a different section of the park, one no one has claimed for themselves," she said. David surveyed the area, trees, dirt, rocks. So normal.

Ponco wrapped her arms around herself in reaction to the substantially cooler air. After a moment, she withdrew a variation of the tablet he'd seen in use in the lab. Her fingers swiped and scrolled and pressed things and then she turned it over to him.

"I have accessed an internet hub so you may inform your friend that there has been a delay," she said.

"Thank you," he said, taking the device into his own hands, avoiding shivering despite the thin fabric of his tunic. At least Betty had yards of fabric to insulate her.

Quickly, he logged into his university server and from there reached his contacts and sent a ping to Reid's computer. He had no idea of the hour and was even losing track of the day as time didn't mean the same below.

There was some static and then he first heard Reid's voice, followed by a somewhat fuzzy image of his newfound friend.

"Thank god you're alive," Reid said. "What's going on? Where are you?"

David hadn't had much time to order his thoughts, the day's revelations still commanding his attention. He didn't even know where to begin except with just some facts.

"We're fine. Honestly, we're better than we were when we were able to talk last. We encountered more of the Ghost Squad but thanks to some… umm, timely intervention, we were saved. And now we have a harbor in a place that Holtzer can't find us."

"Well, shit," Reid started, "that can't be good. For you or us. You're not in Seven Flags territory, so their attack was a violation of some law or another."

"Ya, I don't think Holtzer cares about the law, nor do I think anyone is enforcing them these days," David softly said back.

"Fair enough, David, but are you still coming? Please say yes. Linda would kill me if I sent you away, even with a posse after you."

"That is still the plan, but there's been a delay," David said, picking the words. "These friends have offered us shelter and protection for the time being, and the TAV is destroyed, so we are…assessing our options."

"Oh boy, the adventure continues, I suppose. Can you trust these people?" Reid asked.

"Some of them," David replied, thinking of Ponco and Karuk and maybe some on the council. He couldn't tell what the others thought and that worried him. He needed allies. "But we're fine. Healthy. We're still in Wyoming, so days from you whenever we head out."

"I understand," Reid said, sounding somewhat relieved at the delay.

"Listen, I've been shown some things, some amazing technology you wouldn't believe. A lot of it is quantum-based, so you'd understand it better than me, but from what I can tell, it will blow your mind. A real game-changer."

Reid blinked at that and leaned into the camera. "What sort of quantum work?"

"I'm really not sure how much I can and how much I might get right, but they seem to have sourced energy from somewhere beyond our space-time continuum."

"Holy shit! Do you mean extradimensional? That is a game-changer," Reid said. "What more can you tell me?"

"Trust me, you wouldn't believe it, and frankly, I don't want to do it over the net. This is most definitely a face-to-face discussion."

Whatever reticence Reid felt earlier was gone with the news and he eagerly said, "Well, get yourself in gear and come west."

From the corner of his eye, he spotted Ponco approaching and she didn't seem happy. He'd clearly said too much. Was it the location? The mere mention of extra-dimensional energy? What was it they were told earlier, death for divulging secrets? Had he made a fatal mistake?

"Once things sort themselves out, I'll be in touch. I gotta go." And with that, he cut the connection, leaving a no doubt disappointed and curious Reid in the dark.

"Are you a fool or an idiot?" Ponco asked.

"I hope neither," he said but was worried at what was about to come.

"We said not to share our secrets and you tell your friend, this man you tell me you've never met, about the RSN?" Ponco seethed.

"I did not tell him about the technology, I merely alluded to the idea of futurism and technology in this place. How am I supposed to communicate if I can't even say what I said?" David retorted defensively, hoping to mitigate the situation as much as possible.

It did nothing to relegate Ponco to calmer tones. "I have to tell the

Council and they may be even less happy with you. What is worse, is you have now put a target on your friends. Just because we stopped those Ghost soldiers doesn't mean more won't come. Or find a connection between you and this man. They may think he knows where you are and I get the impression they aren't going to be polite interrogators."

"That's enough!" Betty cried as she put herself between the angry soldier and her bewildered husband. "Put yourself in his shoes for a moment. Imagine you learned what he did in a day. How would you feel? He's had zero time to process this. Yes, he may have slipped, but really, he didn't give away anything about you or even where you are. Give my husband a little credit."

"We should return you to your quarters, then," Ponco said coldly. Karuk seemed to be as torn with the situation as Betty was. Yes, David was foolish, but did he really say anything that put them in actual danger?

Everyone was cold, everyone seemed stressed, and now David had a several-hour walk back from here deep under the earth to where his bed awaited him. The comfort of sleep beckoned him, but as he walked behind the soldiers, his mind sifted through the consequences of his actions. He had, moments earlier, counted Ponco and maybe even Karuk as friends. Now he pissed them off, and if they withdrew their support, what fate would befall him and Betty once the Council learned of his mistake? Had he really endangered Reid?

Without friends and support, David now feared for his life.

CHAPTER 14

The City of
Forgotten Souls

"It wasn't much of anything," Karuk argued as he accompanied Ponco back to the Palace after depositing the Anders at their quarters. It was a long, difficult walk, with little discussion among the quartet, a marked change from the easier conversation previously. That weighed heavily on the military's supreme commander. She liked David and Betty; understood they were in an impossible situation. But Ponco didn't rise to her role because she turned a blind eye to violations of commands from the High Council or their Majesty. No, she rose to her role through grit and determination, besting four others in a fierce competition that left her with a lacerated arm and broken foot, but victorious.

Since taking command four years earlier, she drilled her forces, thousands strong, making certain they were all combat-ready. Their intelligence from the surface suggested tensions were rising, bubbling under and ready to explode, much as the calderas they lived amongst threatened to do before their violent power was tamed by her ancestors. Sooner or later, their sanctuary city might be breached, and they needed to be ready to mobilize in minutes. She'd established a command structure so each access point had a garrison with commanders who could act without awaiting her permission to defend Kasper.

She supervised drills, made surprise inspections, called for war games to keep everyone sharp because the tedium could lull the army into inattention. Once the nuclear warheads flew around the world, she placed the forces on high alert, just in case.

As a result, she rotated squads to patrol, accompanied by engineers who inspected each passage, each doorway to the surface, examining locking mechanisms and ensuring each operated smoothly. After studying reports about the attack, she determined the American Midwest was largely unscathed, so she provided radiation detectors along with standard weapons and sent out scouting parties to see for themselves. The reports of the chaos and unrest were almost uniform in their sadness, something that pained her. Here, nearly seven months later, she was thinking they were finally able to relax a bit. Scrambling to rescue her companions, though, had her reconsidering that decision.

"He was told not to say anything and he did," she repeated. They'd been going back and forth on the issue as they walked back, her mind framing how to report to the High Council. With Akna and Itzel having witnessed some of this, she had to be certain her report matched what they observed. The Council tended not to occupy much of her attention; only recently had she been spending more time with them.

Ponco was a soldier, true, but that didn't rob her of the compassion she felt for the victims, the scores of people who never asked for a conflict they could not win, much as they did not ask for the drought that was already causing suffering. At one point, she was attending a Council session when Akna, the youngest, dared to suggest some form of humanitarian aid. No one else sided with her, although Gabor prolonged the debate, only to vote against her. She detested Gabor, wishing to rip his tongue from his mouth, the only person she actively wished ill-will.

"Would you act any differently after the day he had?"

"He is a guest and abused our hospitality. Should word get out..."

"It would sound like the ravings of a crazed person," Karuk said.

"David Anders is a respected scientist in his world," Ponco corrected. "Should someone have heard him, knew his name, then maybe our world is compromised."

"I heard a 'should' and a 'maybe,' so even you have your doubts," Karuk chided her and she fumed at his comment. He was right, of course, but the supreme commander didn't always have the luxury of lax attention. Her hypervigilance might mean the difference between Kasper's future success or failure.

By this point, they were entering the Council chamber and she could hear the murmurs of some debate going on. As they approached, the whispers faded and all eyes turned to her. Karuk fell back and she stood, centering herself before the seven.

"Itzel was sharing her observations of our guests," Hadwin said from the center.

"I fear he is a fragile thing and this has all been too much for him," she said. Akna was not nodding in agreement, keeping her thoughts to herself.

"Well, what would you expect of someone who survived a nuclear attack, marauders, and then was told he was our key to the future," Gabor said. "I say he's held on remarkably well." Of course, he'd have a countervailing opinion.

Xoc said, "He has promising technology but has yet to show how it works. We should just take it, perfect it, and forget him. He's not one of us."

"Oh, but he is my esteemed colleague," Gabor said. "Is he not, like us, part of the brotherhood of man?"

"You know what I mean," Xoc snarled. "He has no Maya blood. He's European—"

"By way of America," Zac-kuk interrupted. "Yes, his ancestors are from Europe, but that was generations earlier. Still, he does lack kinship with us."

"Just taking his life's work seems wrong," Aaapo said.

"He's young, he can do something new," Xoc said. "His APLS gives us a way to sustain our people. You've read the reports. Radiation is filtering into the water supplies. Already our water table is threatened. How do you propose we feed our citizens if the water is deadly?"

"The APLS is not a water filter," Aaapo corrected.

"No, but it gives us alternatives should our systems fail," Itzel said. "Still, taking it feels wrong."

"Of course, it does," Gabor said. "He should be given the tools to perfect it here, let our scientists aid him. Then we may share in its bounty."

Akna stared at her fellow councilor. "That may be the most sensible thing I've heard you say in session."

"You're too kind," Gabor said, nodding in her direction.

Hadwin looked at Ponco, who bore witness to the debate in silence.

"You didn't come here to watch. What brings you?"

Ponco took a deep breath, honoring her commitment to her people, and prayed she didn't doom a good man.

"Councilor, I need to report that David Anders made reference to the RNS when speaking with his would-be host," she said evenly. There, duty was done.

The surprised and angry reactions pretty much went as she anticipated with Xoc and Zac-kuk the least happy, Itzel and Akna surprised, and Gabor smiling slyly. They burbled amongst themselves for another moment before Hadwin asked for details. She then recreated as much of the conversation as could, having had hours to rehearse it in her mind.

"What do you know of this Reid Costa?" Akna asked.

Ponco looked over her shoulder, cueing Karuk. Her husband stepped forward, now side by side, and nodded in acknowledgment.

"Reid Costa is in Santa Barbara, California. He is an astrophysicist, a theorist trying to understand our universe. He is somewhat paranoid and suffers from Obsessive Compulsive Disorder. He is married to a woman, Linda, a sociologist." While she thought deeply about the consequences, which would be severe of course, the forthcoming research would round out their information. It was one of the many reasons she valued his companionship.

Thankfully, the moment David first mentioned Reid as his destination, Ponco had Karuk and his people do their diligence, researching him through the available records. Both paid attention to what David and Betty shared about them, during their conversations over the preceding two weeks.

"Is he a threat to us?" Xoc asked.

"As I just recounted, our location was not divulged. Nor was our existence," Ponco said.

"But the RSN's work was revealed. Its energies?"

"Referenced, yes."

"A smart man like that, he may intuit where we are," Gabor said.

"But he does not know we exist and cannot look for something he doesn't know exists," Ponco said.

"A theorist does exactly that," Xoc snapped.

"He cannot find us," Ponco said firmly.

"Are you willing to bet your office on that?" Zac-kuk challenged.

Without hesitation: "I am."

Hadwin seemed to be considering their options, which Ponco had already analyzed. They could leave things well enough alone, keeping them from speaking again. They could expel David and Betty for violating their safety. They could kill David and Betty if they were angry enough (the priests would love that). They could send a team to kill Reid and Linda Costa to ensure silence, but that struck her as the least likely.

"We should inform their Majesties and seek their counsel," he declared. This was too momentous a decision for him, too risky if he chose wrong and the sovereigns thought otherwise. He didn't want to risk his seat or the authority that came with it. A messenger was summoned, and everyone murmured to one another as they awaited a response.

"What do you think?" Karuk asked her.

"I think I did my duty and it is out of my hands," she said.

"Far from it," Karuk said. She cocked an eyebrow at him. "You're the supreme commander, you protect us. This is a security issue and your opinion has to carry weight. You never offered them your opinion of the situation."

"I was never asked," she said.

"They're not the King and Queen; you may speak without them speaking to you first. You had every right to have a say."

"Too late now," she muttered.

He squeezed her hand reassuringly. Despite their disagreement, he still loved her, and that meant a lot to her.

Minutes passed and finally the messenger returned and invited the Council, Ponco, and Karuk to the throne room. As before, the King and Queen sat on their stone benches, identically dressed as the last visit, the same courtiers along the periphery. It was a frozen tableau to the soldier. As they assembled, she noted the various alliances stood clustered together with Gabor standing apart, a man without conviction.

After Ponco recounted the facts, Queen Dakota looked as displeased as Xoc but without the smoldering anger.

"Quite the dilemma, hmmm," King Hakan said after a while. "What say you, Hadwin? What are our options?"

"Revealing our technology may lead to our existence becoming known," he began. "A serious crime, usually punishable by death."

"Death seems extreme in this case, hmmm," Hakan said. "David Anders is not of our blood, is he?"

"No, your Highness," Hadwin confirmed. To Ponco, his light attitude was another sign the ruler was growing beyond his ability to rule.

"Do our laws apply to him? Can we execute him?"

"Your Highness," Gabor spoke up. Hakan looked surprised at the interruption while Dakota tried and failed to hide a sneer of contempt.

"Go on," the King said.

"While he is an American and a Caucasian, therefore, not of our blood or our country, he is on our soil. That would make him beholden to our rules. He was, I believe, specifically told not to reveal anything compromising."

"And...?"

"Perhaps execution is too harsh."

"You recommend exile then, hmmm?"

"I do," Gabor said and received several assenting nods from Xoc and Zac-kuk. This seemed to fly in the face of David's importance to the prophecies. Something else seemed to be driving their thinking: fear.

"I do not," Dakota interrupted to Ponco's relief. To her, both options were too harsh for so minor an infraction. She regretted saying anything and now expected to endure Karuk's "I told you so" when they returned home.

All eyes were trained on the sovereign.

"What David Anders did was in violation of our instructions, but death or exile seems too harsh. After all, as his world burns around him, we need to be reminded that all life is sacred. Remember, what we decide will have immediate impact on not just him but his wife, Betty, and she is an innocent. We should not doom her descendants for his actions. Now, I recognize that this Reid Costa is aware of our technology, but truly, not enough to be considered a danger. Still, he is David's ally, and I may be proven wrong.

"I hereby suggest that we contain this by bringing Reid and his wife—"

"Linda," Ponco filled in the gap lingering in the air.

"Reid and Linda should be brought to Kasper. Nacom, organize Karuk and an expeditionary force and send them to California. Make all haste to retrieve them and bring them to Kasper."

The decision surprised Ponco, who had not considered that as an option. She also considered it an overreaction to the circumstances. In fact, the more she considered today's events and everyone's reactions, she concluded that the King, Queen, and the High Council had never had to make such consequential decisions before. There was little experience to draw upon and a lot of personal politics to color everything in. She was less than certain this was necessary or a well-considered move, but these were her orders and she needed to fulfill her role in the chain of command.

She looked at her husband, who nodded assent, a contented look on his face. Ponco noted this decree did not go down well with the others. After all, the number of Caucasians in Kasper was about to double, although it might help David and Betty adjust. There was definitely something in Dakota's pronouncement that caught her ears. Something hiding under words suggesting the Queen knew something the others didn't, or at the least, believed something the others didn't. Those thoughts would have to be shoved aside, for now there was work to do.

"What of the Anderses?" Hadwin asked.

"Have they not already had the day to consider the consequences and seriousness of their actions?" Dakota said. "Leave them be. Ponco will remain as escort."

That caught her up short, intending to be the leader of the force. Not only did she desire to do something meaningful, but this was a way to reassure David of their intentions as well as oversee the operation from the field. Now that responsibility would fall to Karuk while she remained on "babysitter" duty.

"Yes, my Queen," she said with a low bow.

With the sovereign's leave, Ponco and Karuk withdrew and headed out of the palace. On the way, she carefully considered the size and makeup of the expedition. With Karuk in the lead, she had every faith things would go well.

"My love, I would like you to bring Sasha with you."

Karuk seemed surprised by the request but didn't break stride. "As you wish, but why?"

"He's finished his training, and this gives him some practical experience. He needs it and I want someone I can entirely trust to watch your back. If I can't be there, he can."

"You don't trust your own troops?"

"It's not that. Of course, I do. But out there, up there, no, tensions are running hot and circumstances may prove challenging to all. It's for my own peace of mind."

"Fine with me. After all, we're on a there-and-back run. The toughest part will be convincing the Costas we have peaceful intentions."

"I certainly hope that proves to be the case."

CHAPTER 15
Strangers in A Strange Land

David and Betty were lying in bed, nervous for the decree from the royal family. Would they be exiled...or worse? Would they attack Reid and Linda? The thought of that horrified the darkest corners of David's mind. Betty, on the other hand, offered her opinion, understanding of the ways of these people and hoping reason would conquer all. As the night won the battle of their consciousness, the two dozed off, unsure of what the next day would bring.

Ponco and Karuk joined David and Betty for breakfast the following morning, informing them of the decision.

"You're bringing them here...?" David half-choked on his morning biscuit.

"Yes, the Queen thought it best. We will show up and explain the situation. It really shouldn't be a big issue, we believe. Honestly, this place is heaven compared to what they are dealing with up there," Ponco said in the most joyous tone they'd heard yet. Clearly, the idea of proving herself and her troops to the royal family had her excited. David couldn't blame her, and he was elated at the idea of his new friends joining them here, but he had his reservations.

"I am unsure Reid will come as easily as you think... he is, um, a bit eccentric, perhaps I should record a video, helping to explain the situation, and perhaps show the accommodations a bit. He doesn't do well with unknowns."

The two nodded in agreement before continuing to eat; happy, excited, and ready to assemble the troops for California. It was a persoal indulgence, but Karuk needled his wife into the plan because he felt she owed him something after adding to his already difficult day. Thankfully, he seemed rested, and having had time to absorb the revelations, in reasonably cheerful spirits. He appreciated that David and Betty came from very different circumstances and their morning conversation avoided the prophecies, the dimensions, and the RSN. Instead, he happily answered David's never-ending questions about life in Kasper. Every now and then, Betty elbowed her husband to let her ask some questions of her own. Ponco added little to the discussion, he knew she was feeling some lingering recriminations for her actions. She was constantly talking about her oath and obligations, but to him, she was a warrior with an army and had no way to fulfill their training.

Karuk, though, was a warrior more by happenstance than destiny, although it meant he got to meet Ponco while in training. They felt an immediate kinship, soon finishing one another's sentences, and battled to tie after tie, amazing the other trainees, who were easily bested by the rising woman. Soon after passing his final tests, they agreed to marry and rarely left one another's side until now. The trip to California was likely easy enough, and with a party of ten, should be sizable enough not to be bothered. The previous night, they discussed candidates beyond Sasha. Privately, he felt her younger sibling was too inexperienced, fresh from training, but he acquiesced to her request because it gave her comfort. Sasha was young and eager, fiercely proud of his sister, even though he called her by her name whereas others called her Nacom.

"Driving through Yellowstone reminded me of how incredible nature could be," he heard David say as he climbed from his reverie. "I'm almost thankful the Ghost Squad led us this way. I'd never been to the national park and would like to explore it more while it's still here."

"You think it's by chance the patrol led you here?" he asked David as he speared a slice of pineapple.

David paused and looked at Karuk, a searching look in his eyes. There were still dark smudges beneath each eye, but the eyes themselves were brighter and more alert, which pleased him.

"I believe our paths are set for us to follow," he told the scientist. "Mine led me to Ponco and service."

She smiled at that, but then her expression shifted to a more serious one, warning him about something. Betty was not religious, nor did she believe there could be forces at play that were unseen or unknown.

"Are you suggesting there was something divine in our being herded to the park, to be kidnapped by a, well, foreign power?"

"No, you were directed to the park so we could find you. There are other interpretations of those prophecies than the ones you heard yesterday. Some see a stronger hand guiding us."

"I think that's enough of that," Ponco said, cutting him off. Her eyes ablaze and he realized he had somehow overstepped. Thankfully, David and Betty seemed not to have noticed the silent exchange, but he and his wife needed to sort this out. He couldn't imagine leaving Kasper with her mad at him.

"Finish up," she said, her voice now lighter. "You have many miles to go today."

"I don't even want to think about prophecies right now," Betty said. "I want to do more exploring."

"Funny you should mention that. I would like to collect some samples and understand how these plants thrive down here," David said.

"Since there is just one of me, we will need to take turns," Ponco said, forcing herself to lighten the mood.

David and Betty insisted they see the traveling party off. Already the scientist had handed him a tablet with a recording for Reid, something to help convince him that Karuk and company meant no harm. They walked off, his arm draped over her shoulder, and the vision made him smile.

"Say nothing more of the prophecies," Ponco said in a quiet hiss. "That man has heard enough. Let him be a scientist today."

There was an inkling she knew something but wasn't sharing, which happened on occasion when dealing with the High Council or the sovereigns, and he had long ago reconciled himself to this. He didn't like it, but there was nothing he could do, so he shoved it from his mind.

They walked off to a different section of Kasper, one where the military maintained barracks and training facilities. He was proud of how quickly the newcomers a century ago volunteered to serve. During the merger, the percentage of Native Americans steadily grew in the once all-Maya army. That was reflected in the assemblage of the nine men before them. They stood erect, hands at their sides, suggesting they had been in formation for some time, just awaiting their arrival. The previous night, he and Ponco talked, settling on the eight who would join him and Sasha on the mission. He used the telecom system to notify the chosen that they were leaving in the morning and when to assemble. That gave them all less than twelve hours to speak with their own loved ones and check their gear.

Now, they stood awaiting orders. Most were in their twenties and thirties, wearing their warmest clothing, complete with heavy wool cloaks that looked wrong, lacking the color and detail of more traditional garb. These were special outfits, created for those who would enter the surface world, usually just the scouts. There were symbols and images of gods, but you had to look hard to find them as they were applied with charcoal gray thread woven into gray wool. Bits of red could be spotted by the keenest of eyes, and each pair corresponded with the eyes of the gods, added to the cloaks for protection and luck. They wore extra layers, which made them warm now but would be welcome topside. Satchels with essential supplies, including knives, first aid, rations, and communications gear were slung over right shoulders. On each forearm was a vambrace, copper in color and bristling with weaponry that had been designed and perfected over the decades. Settings allowed bursts of sonic waves that could damage hearing, rupture eardrums, and disorient their enemies. Different settings also allowed electromagnetic pulses to disrupt communications and scramble electronics. All wore a metallic collar that appeared to be jewelry but contained communications gear, allowing the soldiers to communicate over short distances and sending out a steady signal that could be tracked. Long before, the surface's weather satellites were located and hacked, letting the Kapserians track signals from the vambraces, allowing their espionage network to keep track of their global scouting parties. Today, four people were tasked with doing nothing but monitor the ten-member squadron as they headed westward.

He saluted the nine men and women and they smartly returned the salute. Karuk then approached and inspected each, looking for flaws before they set out. He was meticulous, careful, not willing to let poor preparation spoil the mission. They chose well, as Karuk found no flaw among them, from the most experienced woman, a top lieutenant, to the rawest rookie, his brother-in-law Sasha. The young man was nearing his twentieth birthday but was already covering his fingers with intricate tattoos, a snake coiled around one wrist, and a wicked red scar, seemingly fresh, on his neck. He had blazing blue eyes, very short black hair, and a lean face with high cheekbones, and just three earrings per ear, each in increasing size, all with jade embedded in them. Sasha smiled at him, revealing somewhat yellowish teeth with more jade on display in three teeth.

Karuk addressed them, quickly sketching out their destination, their goal, and whatever dangers they knew existed. None had questions at the end, although their expressions suggested each had something to ask, but dare not appear ignorant before the others. They would all come out in time, as it would take a day or two to reach the coast.

"How do you intend to get from here to there?" David asked.

"Not far from the park, there is a town, and we own a building there. Within are two vehicles we will use. I had them checked and serviced last night as I assembled this team."

That surprised both Betty and David, and clearly, they had more questions, but Ponco wanted to get things rolling, so Karuk left it to her to answer them. He gave a sharp command and the soldiers saluted her then turned to begin a march to the tunnel that would lead to the surface and the six-man electric vehicles. His last sight was of his wife; their eyes met, and he could sense her love, taking strength from it and silently promising her he would return.

• • •

Rodney Holtzer was meeting with a media specialist, planning an address to discuss the latest round of rationing that would be needed until their underground crops were ready. Despite all their planning, a percentage of their food stores had spoiled, far beyond the actuarial projections. It annoyed him because, without food, the people would rapidly turn on the new government. Full bellies meant no arguments with his laws.

There was a knock on the wooden door, and without waiting, a young woman, in the crispest uniform he'd ever seen, strode in. She was pretty, in her twenties, and wore her hair parted to the side, in a fashion that Elsa Ember had quietly turned into a fad, giving the new nation its first sense of identity among the populace. He eyed her and she approached without fear, nor did she stop when he glared at the interruption. She jerked a thumb over her shoulder, a signal the media consultant needed to leave, now.

"Well, aren't you bossy," Holtzer said as he leaned back in his chair.

"What I have here is something you want to see, and you don't want him to see it," she said. "One of our watchers tripped over a 375-megahertz conversation that gave us a lead. An astrophysicist in Santa Barbara has been burning up the ham radio—"

"That still exists?"

"It never stopped operating. They've got some nice EMP-shielded equipment and we've periodically learned things from monitoring their chatter. Several watchers were rapidly trained to infiltrate their ranks, engaging them in conversation to see how our people are handling the transition. We've also been listening along the border, making certain there are no surprises."

While he didn't know this specifically, it made perfect sense and he credited either Luna or Garrison with the operation. He nodded and waited.

"—burning up the ham radio network looking for David and Betty Anders. That was going on for a few days. This morning, though, we intercepted a signal where this man thanked all who answered and called off the manhunt. They'd been found safe and sound."

"So?"

"The watchers have been piecing things together and we now know who this man is and where he lives. And he seems to know where your targets are," she concluded.

"Where?"

"Santa Barbara."

"No, not that guy. Where's Anders?"

She seemed flustered for the briefest of moments but snapped back to form. "That remains unclear."

"Why on earth would Anders go there? Who is this man?"

"An astrophysicist named Reid Costa. Fairly unremarkable, more dreamer than doer."

"Why would Anders go there?" Holtzer repeated to himself.

"Does it matter? Either Anders is on his way or Costa knows where they are," she told him.

"You have coordinates?"

"Locked and loaded," she said, handing him her tablet.

"Thank you..."

"Aimee Lopez, sir," the woman said. "I work with the Watchers."

Holtzer eyed her, suspecting she was also in someone's pocket, someone who wanted to keep tabs on him, suspecting Garrison White. He knew Holtzer's type, and the attractive Lopez fit the bill to a T.

"Thank you, Ms. Lopez," he said abruptly and swiveled in his chair to activate his digital assistant. "Get me Varley."

The Ghost Squad was being given one more chance to snare David Anders and his technology.

• • •

The two personnel carrier TAVs were making good time, the armored vehicles smashing through barriers, riding over snares and traps set by desperate gangs. Karuk had never ventured beyond Yellowstone Park and was not immune to staring in wonderment and horror at the surface world. The lack of order and discipline among the people disgusted him, but the clear hunger in their eyes softened his heart. He could have paused their journey several times to break up fights or protect the weaker people, but they were not his responsibility. He wondered where law enforcement was, sad to see the once-great United States crumbling by the day.

What he and the others couldn't handle was the smell. The air was fetid, filled with obnoxious odors, from rotting vegetables, decaying flesh, burning chemicals and wood, and other, unidentifiable smells. He'd been to the surface before and didn't like the tang to the air then, but this was almost unbreathable compared to Kasper. The paradise below was a distant memory to the hell that was above. These soldiers had yet to experience true combat with actual enemies in unforgiving conditions, and almost every one of them complained about it. The only reason Karuk didn't make them stop was his knowledge that his squad needed this. They needed the catharsis to stay focused on the mission ahead.

They were making good time on Route 15, although all the interruptions did slow them, so the trip was definitely going to take two long days. They carried extra battery packs with them for the times they could find no functional charging stations. Still, it meant that they would cross through a portion of the Hualapai Reservation, where ancestors of the Tohono O'odham people, including his soldier Marie Chico, once lived. He studied the round-faced woman as she looked with longing at the land, which seemed scrubbed by time and wind.

Karuk rarely considered what life on the surface must have been like for the Native Americans. He was raised Mayan and knew of the history but really only knew a smattering of North American past. The tribes that roamed the Americas before the white man stole their land. The trade routes from the Dakotas to what's now Mexico and the intricate and subtle understanding of medicine that was not born from science but spirit. He knew of these moments but in the end, he was far more interested in the technological aspects of his world and the chronology of his people, but maybe he needed to broaden those horizons.

For now, he could daydream about what once was, as the vehicles closed the distance to California. Without resistance from Reid Costa, he figured they would be there and back home within three days. That would represent the longest he had been apart from his wife and her welcoming arms. Costa, he decided, had better not put up a fight.

CHAPTER 16
Come With Us

Reid's head was spinning. What he heard from David rocked his world and kept him in his lab later than usual. He'd been rereading books, articles, and watching videos of lectures, looking for some kernel that he had missed. How had David's rescuers found a way to pierce the dimensional veil? More specifically, how had it not been reported?

He had been working long past when Linda normally went to bed, so he was surprised when she came into his lab. It was a rare enough occurrence, partially because she was not invested in the work, partially because he needed things just so and her presence threatened to disrupt the arrangement of things. But there she stood, her dark hair loose around her shoulders, wrapped in the kimono she liked so much. Clearly, she hadn't slept and there was a bright look in her eyes.

"Aren't you coming to bed?"

Reid had been rewatching a lecture from his mentor, Dr. Katie Grenchik, rechecking a formula on his computer. Her voice startled him, hand flying to the screen to pause the video.

"More porn?"

"What—? No. Not porn," Reid said quickly.

"She's not your type anyway," Linda said, stepping further into his realm. She looked around, surveying his workspace. Everything was squared off, nothing out of place, not a speck of dust to be seen. As she looked, he furiously reviewed the previous twelve hours and realized that other than the bathroom, he hadn't left his office. He'd missed dinner. He was always absorbed by his work, forgetting to eat, or his chores, or he missed something she said, which angered her.

"I'm sorry I missed dinner," he said, hoping it was why she was there. But a look at the clock suggested it was later; she normally was in bed by now, so this was something more than missing the meal.

She worked her jaw before speaking. "I was hoping we would open a bottle of wine and talk. Celebrate."

"Celebrate? That David and Betty are alive? That we discovered other dimensions are real? Did I miss a birthday or something?"

She leaned over him, throwing her arms around his neck. "You didn't miss a thing. But we do have something to celebrate."

Reid continued to think hard, reviewing the last few days, which remained a jumble of thoughts, mostly centered around David's announcement. He looked deep into her brown eyes and saw her love.

"We are going to have a baby."

She hugged him tight as the words washed over him. They had hoped for one, even were going to try just before the bombs flew but hadn't discussed it since they entered the fortress. Neither one wanted to bring life into this hellish world, not now; yet, here it was, evidence man was destined to survive.

But with the news came a swirl of considerations. The fortress wasn't built for a baby; they had no furniture or equipment. What was worse, over the last few nights, roving bands of scavengers had been prowling the neighborhood, and if they ransacked the house, might find the access to the fortress, and that wasn't going to go well for anyone. It wasn't safe with them around and it certainly wasn't going to be safe if David and Betty were pursued by more Ghost Squads. No, he couldn't risk it, not with Linda pregnant. He'd had to rescind the invitation the next time David contacted them, which he hoped was before their arrival.

A baby. Scavengers. Ghost Squads. Dimensions. His mind couldn't focus, and he felt a rising tide of panic,

"You need an OB. We need a crib. My God, where are we going to find diapers?" he said aloud.

She held tight and reassured him. "We have nearly nine months to figure this out. Apocalypse or not, we'll be fine."

He returned the embrace and then she mashed her mouth to his to cut off further words. They kissed, tongues woven, happy cooing sounds emitting from Linda. He enjoyed the moment, tried to lose himself in it, but was continuing to think, shuttling from concern to concern.

Whatever he was going to say next was interrupted by the proximity alarm, a shrill beeping. They broke apart, their eyes going from glee to concern in a heartbeat. He swiveled about and activated the exterior security cameras, fearing the worst.

What he did not expect was the face of a young, dark-skinned man who smiled, showing off what looked to be jewels in his teeth. Had society devolved in savagery so quickly? he wondered. His hand reached to the far right and opened a cover revealing a toggle that would activate the defenses. From hidden chambers scattered around the house and grounds, automatic weapons were revealed, their targeting using infrared to find heat signatures, assuring deadly accuracy. A series of screens took over the main screen in the lab and Reid worried at the sight of so many figures, all almost identically clad, wearing something akin to serapes, shoulder bags of some sort, and something clublike dangling from their hips, glittering in the lights. Reid noted heavy tattooing, a plethora of piercings all over their heads—nothing suggesting they were locals. There was something South American about them, from skin tone to adornments, but he had no time to consider their origins.

They seemed to be milling about, awaiting a response to their presence, when the largest of the group, and also their leader from the body language, spotted several of the guns now in view. He seemed to be shouting something as hands dove int bags and withdrew something rolled and cylindrical. Each snapped theirs open, and as they did, the object formed into some sort of personal shield.

Reid opened fire. A hail of bullets from numerous directions filled the air, finding their targets and then bounded harmlessly to the ground, several ricocheting off the shields and peppering the house. He could actually hear small popping sounds from below ground. The first salvo was clearly ineffective, so he went to manual control, figuring he might get lucky by aiming lower, getting legs and feet, anything to make them less of a threat.

As he did this, he saw the young man from the camera waving his arms and shouting something. Reid flipped open the mic and the speaker filled with a high voice crying, "—harm, we mean no harm! David and Betty Anders sent us!"

Linda, who had been leaning over his chair to watch the action, gasped at the names. Her hand clutched his shoulder, giving him pause. "Those aren't scavengers."

"And they're certainly not Ghosts. David described them as military. Those aren't uniforms."

"Well, they are of a sort, hun. And those shields are impressive. Answer him."

Reid flipped open the mic. "Who are you?"

"Me? I'm Sasha. I'm from...Wyoming...we're friends with David and Betty. Well, I haven't really met them yet, but Karuk—he's my brother-in-law—is really friendly with them."

The young man gestured to their leader and Karuk addressed the camera. "Are you done shooting at us?"

"Why are you here?"

"Yes, you are a scientist. Always so many questions," Karuk said, shaking his head, which made Linda laugh.

"See, I'm not the only one," she said. Her words were picked up by the mic and Karuk noted them.

"Is that Linda?"

"Yeah, hi," she said from over Reid's shoulder. As the exchange went on, he had squeezed out some hand sanitizer and was rubbing his hands, thoroughly covering every finger and knuckle.

"I have proof of my intentions," Karuk said, withdrawing what appeared to be a data tablet from his pouch. His thumb slid down one side and then he turned it toward the camera. Reid zoomed in just as David's face appeared.

"Hi, Reid. I really want to thank you for the offer of safety, but it appears we're going to be staying in Wyoming for a while. One reason is that Holtzer's men can't find us, so it's secure. The other is that I may be able to complete my work here and field test it. Now, I must apologize to you.

I really shouldn't have said anything about the dimension discovery. That was not my news to share and the government where I am was displeased. They do not feel the world is ready for such knowledge and as you know, should word get out, the repercussions could be devastating."

"What's he mean, government where he is," Linda asked over the recording. "Isn't Wyoming still in America?"

"Shh," Reid hissed.

"In fact, they wish to contain the knowledge and feel it is in their interest—and yours—to have you come stay with us. There's plenty of room and plenty of food and water. Please don't fight this; they will be rather insistent, and for that, I apologize. This is on me, and I can explain everything when we're together. Grab whatever you need, including copies of your data."

"I will be honest, Reid. We don't know one another very well, but I could really use a friend here. Maybe even help me with the quantum aspects of the APLS. I need to make it work and we can field test it here."

"I hope you say yes and I'll see you soon."

The image froze before fading. Karuk then lowered the tablet, stowing it in his pouch as he asked, "What do you say?"

"Do I get to discuss this with my wife?" Reid asked.

"Of course. But please do not waste time. The sooner we get back home, the safer we all will be."

Karuk walked off camera and Reid could hear the murmur of voices in the background. He cut the mic and turned to look at Linda.

"Did we just enter the Twilight Zone or something?"

"I would say something," Reid replied, refusing to admit he didn't know her reference, but he understood its intent. His world was being turned upside down with regularity that day and that wasn't sitting well with him. He needed order, needed things to be orderly and to make sense. The idea of just grabbing his things and leaving his fortress and his home seemed impossible. But, he also recognized they couldn't live in the fortress forever. Sooner or later, they had to emerge, to find supplies, and to have Linda checked by a doctor. If the baby was conceived in the fortress with its shielding, that should increase the chances the baby would be born healthy, but he wanted a doctor's assurances.

He could do his research anywhere with a computer and a telescope or access to satellites. But Linda needed proper care and somewhere safe to carry the pregnancy. That won him over, not David's pleas, but the need to protect his wife and unborn child.

"We trusted David enough to bring him here. Do we trust him enough to go with this...what are they?"

"I guess we can ask them on the trip to Wyoming," he said, trying to sound positive.

"Just like that?" Linda was stunned.

"Just like that. Look, Linda, your safety and health are what matter now. It sounds like David is somewhere with a functioning government and military, a place where they have made amazing advancements in science. That's better than here. Do I trust David? Enough, I suppose."

"I'll grab the essentials," she said and turned to leave.

Reid flipped on the mic and said, "Karuk? We're coming with you. We need some time to pack."

Karuk and Sasha stepped before the camera, both with assuring smiles. "If you need help, just ask, but pack light. Come out when you're ready."

While Linda fussed in the living quarters, he copied all his research data to two portable hard drives, and then wiped the memories. He made sure the drives were biometrically secure then pocketed them. He disabled all the equipment, rendering it useless to foragers and thieves, and because he couldn't help himself, wiped down the monitors, keyboards, and the tables and cleaned his hands twice.

Ready, he walked out of his lab for the last time, refusing to look backward. This was all about stepping into the next chapter of his life.

Linda had two small bags prepared and looked around the fortress with a sad smile. "This never felt like home, but you built it for us and with love. Thank you for doing that. It's time, hun. We got this."

He leaned to kiss her and then they ascended the stairs one final time, the lights winking out behind them. They emerged into their basement and proceeded up the living room and then the backdoor. They both kept moving, not stopping to wallow in nostalgia, Reid certain they would never be back. The memories would have to do.

Emerging from the backdoor, they nearly walked into a woman, broad and strong, but shorter than Linda. The others quickly surrounded them, many welcoming them with smiles and hellos. To Reid, it was a little over-whelming, but Karuk cleared a path to them and extended his hand. Linda shook it first, introducing herself, even though he already knew her name. Reid followed and then surreptitiously used a pocket tube of sanitizer to clean his hand. Karuk frowned at that, and Linda touched Reid's bicep and cocked her head. He knew exactly what was coming next. Here was where she explained his OCD to Karuk, his compulsions, and then would come the request for kindness and consideration. He watched Karuk nod on cue, and he hated that she had to do this time and again for him. While it helped tremendously, it also made him feel the object of pity, something he never wanted.

Karuk led them all to the two vehicles, which were a style Reid did not recognize but did note they lacked manufacturer logos or other identi-fying marks. There weren't even license tags on the trucks, although these days, he doubted that mattered much. He and Linda were helped into the vehicle and Sasha plopped down beside them as the other vehicles were being prepared. With his large hand thumbing the touchpad, the engines engaged, and they were headed east.

Reid exhaled, and with it, he came to realize just how exhausted he was. It had to be three in the morning, easy, and the further east they drove, the sooner the sun would rise. He needed some sleep, but this was also a chance to learn something about these people.

Stifling a yawn, he asked Sasha, "Where in Wyoming are we headed? Laramie? Yellowstone?"

"Near Yellowstone," Sasha said with a laugh. "You'll see."

"What can you tell me about it?"

"You'll be given the tour on our arrival in a day or so. We really hope not to need to stop for more than the bathroom. It's safest if we make a direct path, minimizing stops."

"Fair enough," Reid said, then eyed the bag that sat between them. "What was that shield?"

"That, I can tell you about. I think. Whatever. Okay, so, that was a shield made from flexible Kararien steel."

"I've never heard of that steel," Linda said.

Sasha laughed at that. To him, everything was light and amusing. He was clearly having a good time with this mission while everyone else looked alert and tense. Being the youngest, maybe he hadn't learned the harsh lessons that came with combat. Or so Reid had heard.

"I'm not surprised. The steel was developed by Dr. Helena Kararien some time back. She found a way to use a precious metal called Zendarian Crystal, which is the fusion of molten lava and natural crystal to create this incredible malleable multi-use substance. Much of what we use these days is made of Kararien steel, like this truck."

A man opposite them added, "This stuff is one one-hundredth of the world's lightest metals and easily a thousand times the strength of tungsten. Is that still your strongest steel?"

Reid blinked at the question, wondering if he heard the man incorrectly. It almost sounded like they weren't of the same race. "I think so," he said.

He was left to his own thoughts, which were even more jumbled than before, and then things faded away as he fell into sleep.

When the truck veered sharply, throwing him across the interior, Reid was rudely awakened. Linda screamed as she tumbled to the ground and one of the soldiers fell atop her. There was daylight coming through the portals, so clearly he'd been asleep awhile, but he had no idea where they were or what time it was. The squealing of tires, though, suggested something was wrong. Looking over to Linda, he realized something was very wrong. He gave her a look of despair as he tried to rise to his knees and look out the nearest portal, but Sasha cried out, "Stay down!"

Instead, Reid focused on the sounds around him. There was the somewhat familiar hum of the truck's electric engine, but there were more sounds, more engines, tires crushing glass and concrete. They were under attack. He left the safety of his bunker because David assured him they would be better off with Karuk and company. That was proving to be a lie.

He dared to glance out a window and saw three black, hulking vehicles bearing down on them, spraying dirt and dust in their wake— sharks coming straight for them. High overhead was what appeared to be a large, dark gray helicopter, also headed in their direction at tremendous speed. They were certainly outgunned and he wondered just how powerful his guardians were. Sasha's assured expression had shifted to one of concern, which didn't help his mood. He looked to the front of the vehicle, where Karuk was directing their driver while clearly giving directions to the other driver.

With a jerk, their vehicle left the road and tumbled over a rocky terrain at a forty-five-degree angle, as the other vehicle went in a different direction. Whoever was pursuing them would have to divide their forces, which, Reid suspected, Karuk wanted in order to improve their odds. He wasn't a gambler—far from it—so he wasn't that optimistic, even though he could appreciate the maneuver from his protector. He clenched his teeth to keep them from chattering and gripped the bottom of his seat, sharing concerned glances with Linda, hoping none of this would be bad for the new life growing within her.

Karuk loudly called orders in a language he didn't recognize but saw them all withdraw their clubs and twist their wrists, which seemed to activate their weapons. The woman opposite him gave Reid a vicious look, one eager for conflict. She then went to the back of the truck and opened its door, gripping the top with two hands, and twisted herself in a graceful flip that put her on the roof in moments. Next, he heard something like a whoosh and then a different truck engine whine in protest. Then, he managed a glance to see them gaining distance from the disabled vehicle, the sight of which prompted Sasha to let out a whoop. He also saw the other two enemy trucks pursue the second Kasperian truck as someone else was flipping atop its roof.

He was distracted from watching a repeat of the disabling action because the helicopter roared overhead, passing their truck, and settling maybe three hundred yards before it, hovering no more than five feet off the ground. Two panels had opened, and the muzzles of rail guns were extended and clearly taking aim at them. They opened fire, laying down a trail of bullets that was effectively a shot across their bow, not-so-politely asking them to stop. Karuk's driver slammed on the brakes and fishtailed to the left, gunning the engine to force the helicopter to follow. This gave the woman still on the roof opportunity to take aim. Unfortunately, whatever energy she unleashed missed, as the helicopter swerved, lifting a little and coming forward.

"Out!" Karuk shouted to Sasha, who scrambled to dive out of the truck's rear, showing no hesitation or concern about their speed and hitting the ground. Gaping, Reid saw the young man tuck and roll to minimize the impact, then miraculously spring to his feet and also take aim at the helicopter. A twin barrage of what he now presumed were sonic discharges made contact with the vehicle, actually forcing it to move laterally.

Reid dared look back and saw that the men from the damaged pursuit truck had piled out and were assembling some sort of large gun on a tripod. Each was identically dressed in brown and green uniforms, each sporting the emblem of the Seven Flags. He remained amazed at how quickly the breakaway states were able to form a new nation, one that retained America's deadly warfare technology.

He looked back at the helicopter to see it hover as four soldiers jumped to the ground, each with a rifle at the ready.

Karuk also spotted this and had the driver stop the vehicle. It was time to fight back because running away wasn't going to work. He also knew the Maya were warriors, so avoiding a fight was anathema to them. He hoped the truck's shell was tough and would provide him and Linda with protection because he sure as hell wasn't going into a firefight whether Linda was carrying a baby or not. He'd never held a weapon and wasn't about to risk their lives by starting now.

The men on the ground had completed their assembly and seemed to be loading a dull green shell of some sort. He called a warning to Karuk, who shouted a command to the woman atop the now still truck. A voice replied and the next thing he knew, a loud whoosh passed overhead. It pulsed, one shot after another. If the weapon was sonic, as he suspected, then wave after wave of sonic force was being projected toward the enemy. Depending on the thrust of the missile being fired, the sonic waves would cause it to detonate early or veer off course; either way, it would not threaten them.

Reid's hypothesis was proven true about twenty seconds later as he saw the incoming missile wobble and finally veer away from the truck, out into the desolated land where it harmlessly exploded, causing a geyser of dirt to kick into the already misty air.

The next thing he saw surprised him as Sasha was charging the soldiers with a war cry, followed by the woman from the roof and then the driver.

Karuk left the truck as he headed for the helicopter, dodging gunfire from the quartet of soldiers. His moves were quick, efficient, and designed to avoid anticipation, a frenzied ballet of forward, left, right, backward, tumbling, and leaping. One of the soldiers broke formation and charged toward him, so Karuk landed lightly on his feet and raised his club. The soldier kept coming, so Karuk met the charge but swung upward with the club, its dark metal blades easily slicing through body armor and flesh, gutting the man who crumpled in a wet heap.

He stayed low, avoiding gunfire, as he raised his left arm and fired a sonic pulse that took out another man. The remaining two charged, firing wildly, easily allowing Karuk to avoid the bullets. He closed the gap and let the club dig deep into the thigh of the first soldier as his meaty left hand grabbed the other soldier by the neck, squeezing. As one soldier fell clutching the leg, uselessly trying to stop the arterial blood from spraying, the other gurgled under the man's tightening grip. Karuk's powerful fingers kept squeezing until the man was rendered limp, a victim of the Maya might.

All the while, the helicopter pilot was radioing someone and stabbing at controls. She began lifting off the deck but not quickly enough as Karuk's powerful legs let him leap high, grabbing a piece of the hulk. His other arm swung and released the club, which hurtled into the main blade atop the chassis, and it was battered a bit as the blade spun quickly, but the deadly edges ate away at the blade and the helicopter wobbled, mildly at first, then increased its rate until it tumbled to the ground, just as he leaped away from it. The heavy machine landed with a thump and crunching of metal, the scream of the engines drowning out any other sound for several seconds.

The pilot was slumped in the cockpit, which Karuk noted before climbing atop the heating wreckage to retrieve his weapon. He slung it to his belt and jumped the ground, going into a sprint back to the truck.

Reid swiveled his head to seek out the others and saw a pitched battle was underway between the six Kasperians and the horde from the two Seven Flags trucks. Sasha and the woman were running to join in the battle. The scientist kept leaning forward to observe when he felt a hand clutch his shirt and yank him backward. He looked over his shoulder to see Linda's unhappy expression.

"I am not losing you just so I can be alone with these people," she said. "Don't be stupid." That last line was a favorite phrase of hers, words she lived by.

"Their weaponry is beyond anything I've seen," he told her, hearing the excitement in his own voice. "That Kararien steel is incredible. Did you see what it did to the helicopter? Its metallurgical properties suggest something far more important than tungsten, far lighter and more flexible. And from what I could tell, not a blade was chipped after disabling the rotors."

"What it did to that man was sickening enough," she told him.

"Bullets seem to bounce off their body armor, which has to be from the same material, worn like a second skin that's lightweight, which would give it an atomic structure of..."

"Now is not the time for a lecture, professor," she said.

He turned back to watch the fight continue. Both sides had drawn close enough that it became a brutal hand-to-hand contest with all the combatants seeming fairly equal in strength and tactics. The Seven Flags soldiers wore heavy, stiffer body armor, which did give the Kasperians an edge, their moves more like a martial arts demonstration than a brawl. Still, Seven Flags soldiers got in their blows. One soldier dislocated the shoulder of a Kasperian, while another clearly broke his opponent's leg with a brutal snap. Several were using knives that managed to slash clothing, and in one case shorting out one of the sonic vambraces, so things remained fairly even.

As Sasha and the woman arrived, they both jumped high and threw themselves into the melee with what Reid could only consider as gusto. The Kasperians were clearly having a good time in this fight to the death and Reid was sickened at the notion that all of this was on his behalf. They had come to collect him, protect him and Linda, and someone might die in his name. He had never asked for that.

Two converged on Sasha, knives slicing the air between them, but the young man crouched and swept a leg that entangled one man, who then stumbled into his partner. Sasha sprang up, his fists connecting with their faces, stunning the pair. But, as he pummeled them, he was unaware of a third who came in on his blind slide. The knife caught the dim sun, causing a reflection that made Reid blink, and by the time his vision cleared, the knife was sticking out of Sasha's back. He stumbled and was then piled on by the trio. One of them withdrew something rope-like from a belt pouch and with practiced ease, had Sasha trussed up, no longer in the fight. Two grabbed his arms and dragged him toward the nearer of the trucks as the third went after another Kasperian. The woman who accompanied him, though, finally reached them and flung herself at the man who stabbed Sasha. She beat him mercilessly, his face a bloody, pulpy mess by the time she dropped him. By then, though, Sasha was secured in the truck, as another soldier climbed in and gunned the engine.

Some signal must have gone out to the helmet headsets as the still-ambulatory soldiers suddenly spun and retreated to the trucks. Two Kasperian soldiers struck down two more before they could all get aboard and leave.

Karuk let out a cry that summoned his forces back to him. This was followed quickly by an anguished howl, one a leader might unleash when losing one of his troops.

Reid regretted the loss, having quickly come to like the enthusiastic youth. As he recalled, Karuk was his brother-in-law and didn't envy his task of reporting the loss to his wife.

Reid couldn't help but think "why": why get them, why go through the trouble of protecting them, and Oh god, he thought, if he and Linda hadn't been under the protection of Karuk and his army, what would have happened if these people had come knocking on his front door. He thought about his unborn child and realized it was because of that baby that they were alive. "No chance I would have left in other conditions," he murmured to himself. "I would have said our fortress was fine enough, thank you." He kept repeating words and phrases under his breath, replaying the altercation and thinking through what would have happened if things were different. All of it felt uncomfortable, all of this felt unnatural.

As Reid fell back to sleep on the Kasperian's shoulder as if nothing had happened, Karuk, driving still, felt the weight of the altercation, full well knowing he would have to deliver the news to his wife that her brother was now a prisoner of war.

CHAPTER 17

Repercussions

"Is it me, or is everyone giving us the hairy eyeball?" Betty asked as they strolled through a market.

David had noticed it and squeezed his wife's hand in reassurance. "The Kasperians are humans like us, and there is nothing transmitted faster than gossip," he observed. Clearly, someone from the palace spread the word that they had somehow violated some taboo and the High Council, let alone the sovereigns, were displeased. Or, it had been that they heard about the prophecies. Or, maybe it wasn't so complex. The answer could be as simple as they were Caucasians in a land full of Maya and Native Americans. "Take your pick," David thought aloud to himself.

Still, business was business, and the various vendors were offering them woven wonders or ceramics of increasing complexity and beauty. Whatever passed for money or credit in this culture was nothing that had been offered to the visitors so whether they wanted to buy or not, they couldn't complete a transaction. He made a mental note to discuss this with Ponco, who was nearby but speaking with another soldier who held some boxy device, carved with symbols on the sides. Her face was grim, so whatever she was being told could not possibly be good.

"For a friend of Ponco, only seventy-five," a vendor, his smile plastered to his hawk-like face, said, his filthy fingers caressing the deep green tunic, which boasted twin embroidered dragons in yellow and red.

"We're really only looking," Betty said apologetically.

"What do you think's wrong?" David asked her as she continued to examine the design. The dragons seemed to dance in the air, their tongues of fire entwined in a column up the neckline.

"It has to be the mission and that means something went wrong," she said, a frown crossing her attractive features.

"For a special friend of Ponco's, this is now just forty-five," the obsequious vendor said.

"She'll take it," Ponco said as she approached. "Wrap it quickly."

"But of course," the man said hastily, grabbing something akin to tissue paper to wrap the tunic.

"What's wrong?" David demanded.

As the man handed Betty the package, Ponco jerked her chin ahead, away from the man. How the transaction was completed, David couldn't tell, supposing it was something digital. The blend of the traditional and the ultra-modern continued to confuse and fascinate him. They walked some distance from the stall to the outskirts of the commercial section, when Ponco slowed her gait.

"I just heard from Karuk. He has your friends, but there have been injuries. There was a fight..."

"The Seven Flags?"

She nodded, her features still grim, but something more emotional was seen in her eyes, which glistened a bit.

"There's more, isn't there?" Betty gently prompted.

"Sasha...my brother...was injured and is...a...prisoner," she finished. This was the most emotional they had seen her; the stoic, proud supreme commander of the forces was also a protective older sister whose brother was now a victim of David's blunder. His face burned in frustration. Ponco had never had to send troops out on a mission, never had them involved in a fight, and now there were injuries, thank God no deaths, but her brother was a prisoner. David concluded that regardless of any other victories, this had to be a blow to her ego and her faith in herself as the Nacom.

"He's alive, right?" Betty asked.

Ponco nodded. "There are things I must do. More intelligence to gather. Can you find your way back?"

"Of course," Betty said as David nodded. His wife reached out and reassuringly squeezed Ponco's forearm. The warrior didn't seem to notice and walked off away from them.

"We do know the way back, right?"

Betty shot him an unhappy look then nodded affirmatively. They walked a bit in silence, each lost in their own thoughts before she finally spoke. "He'd better be alright."

"Of course, he will," David said.

"How could you possibly know that?" she challenged.

"Why take him? Holtzer wants information and needs someone to ask," David said.

"He'll be tortured, won't he?" Her voice sounded small and sad.

"Maybe...probably," David admitted. "If the kid's smart, he'll babble in Mayan and I will bet you anything, Holtzer has no one to translate."

"Won't they kill him?"

"If he can't be a source of information, then he becomes a bargaining chip. It's in Holtzer's interest to keep Sasha alive."

"You'd better be right," Betty said. "We've caused that woman enough trouble."

"This is all unfortunate, but it's nothing we had any control over," David said, not entirely certain how things got to this point. Was it when he first developed the APLS and defied Holtzer? Was it when the Kasperians founded their underground civilization? Or was it something that dated back millennia to whoever divined the tea leaves or whatever they used in order to come up with David Anders as the focal point of their future? Why him? Why now? His head continued to process the information learned over the past few days. It was mostly too fantastic to treat as real, but there was more than enough evidence to suggest this was all too real.

Betty did know the way back and they nodded greetings, tight-lipped, to those who still showed them positive signs of welcome. He could tell that, like him, she was also deep in thought, and he couldn't fathom what it might be.

In silence, they returned to the rooms, which he realized Ponco called their home, but was it? It still felt like a rental, a hotel accommodation, perhaps even a prison. Not a place where they were putting down roots. "Unless, well, unless the High Council had made a decision about their ability to roam the world, if they had decided they could not go free," David thought to himself. After all, they were bringing Reid and Linda here to contain the dimensional knowledge. Was this truly their future? While the space was nice, he already missed his lab and work. He'd intended to ask Ponco about getting back to work, but he couldn't, not until she had clarity regarding Sasha and that was going to take time. The weight of time was a psychic one, pushing his shoulders down, occasionally buckling his knees. There were people getting sick from malnourishment, something he might be able to alleviate, but only if he could perfect the APLS and do so at scale. Kasper provided safety but didn't seem interested in passing that along to the surface.

They entered the room, Betty tossing the tunic on the bed and slumping into a chair, hands in her hair. David sensed she was overwhelmed by something, but he was uncertain what that was. Instead, he kneeled before her, took her hands in his, and waited.

"Everything we've done seems to affect others," she began in a soft voice. "You develop the apples and the government wants you to become a killer. You refuse and now that man wants you or the apples. We reach out to Reid for help, now he and Linda have had to give up their shelter. With his OCD, you can only imagine what that's doing to him. Ponco offers us support and maybe even friendship and we go and get her brother stabbed. What if he dies? Is there some cosmic balance at work?"

David caressed her knuckles with his thumbs, waiting her out, sharing the same sense of guilt. Still, those last words struck a chord.

"What is being balanced? If Sasha dies, does that mean one of us has to? I don't think it works—"

"Nothing like that, you idiot," she said, tears in her eyes. "If he dies, does a new life balance the scales?"

The words hung in the air.

"What new—wait...are you saying we're pregnant?"

She cocked an eyebrow. "What's this we, white man?"

"Are you?"

Tears streaming down her cheeks, she nodded and fell into his arms. They'd tried so often, only to be disappointed. So of course, here and now when the timing couldn't be less opportune, they were being blessed.

"Are you certain?"

Betty sniffed once, using the backs of her hands to dry her eyes. "I asked Ponco if they had tests down here and I took it yesterday. I've been trying to find the right time to tell you, but with everything happening, and her always being around, I couldn't find the right time."

He wrapped his arms tightly around her, trying to be gentle. He was elated regardless of the timing. In fact, being in Kasper was better than being in the Iowa bunker or anywhere on the surface. There was fresh air and clean water, food aplenty, and no doubt good equipment to help sustain the pregnancy. Actually, the more he considered it, the happier he was that this was happening in a positive environment, a safe, secure one. He, Betty, and the baby would be far from Holtzer, beyond his murderous grasp.

"What about a doctor?"

"I need to tell Ponco the results...I waited to tell you first, you idiot, and then I can see someone."

He enveloped her once more in his arms and whispered in her ear, "Given the wonders down here, this one is going to stick around. I can't wait to meet him."

"Him..." Betty raised an eyebrow again.

"Yes, him, I feel it in my bones. If it's a girl, I will love her equally, but I can feel it, this place is going to give us a son."

Betty couldn't hold back her emotions anymore. Full-blown tears engulfed her dynamic characteristics as she grasped her husband and whispered in his ear, "A boy it is, then."

• • •

Night had fallen and still no one had spoken. The injured were quickly gathered, and while several argued about going after Sasha, Karuk, stone-faced, insisted they head back to the garage and make their way to Kasper. Reid and Linda were the mission. If the High Council wanted to authorize a rescue mission, he would proudly lead it after this assignment was over. That earned the passengers some glares, but no one raised an objection.

At first, Linda and Reid had offered to help tend to the wounded, and after some reluctance, the soldiers nodded in agreement. Karuk remained in the driver's cabin, relaying word to Kasper, probably Ponco, Reid realized. How it must pain him to say her brother was in the enemy's hands.

Reid shook his head, focusing instead on staunching a woman's wound. He was revolted by the blood and bits of gore he saw, but his gloved hands kept him relatively clean and each splash of antiseptic was like a personal balm. Thankfully, the Kasperian first aid was pretty similar to his own experience, so Reid could actually be useful.

Across the aisle, Linda was wrapping a bandage around the woman who had accompanied Sasha on the mad dash to help their allies. Her right bicep had sustained damage, bleeding from a deep cut, but butterfly bandages and gauze-like wadding helped staunch the flow.

Everyone worked in silence, and once the grim repairs were completed, a soldier reached into a compartment and withdrew a series of leaf-wrapped meals. There were dried fruits, nuts, and some sort of hearty biscuit, no doubt filled with protein or vitamins, something to sustain soldiers. Water canteens were passed around next. Linda took two of each for them, setting them aside as she rummaged through a supply locker. She straightened up, holding a large white towel in one hand and a bottle of disinfectant in the other, like a magician pulling twin rabbits out of her hat. She gestured with them and Reid held out his hands, fingers splayed. Gently, she poured some of the liquid on each hand, massaging the hands up to the wrists. She then wiped them dry with the towel before repeating the process, her eyes silently communicating her reassurance, saying nothing to call attention to his condition. Once done, she placed the towel atop the pile of medical waste and returned the bottle.

Finally, Reid was free to unwrap his meal, secure that he was clean enough to touch the food. After he ate, he gave in to his sense of exhaustion and fell asleep, unaware he was leaning against the wounded woman, who stoically put up with it as Linda gave her an apologetic shrug.

The trucks continued eastward, unimpeded, traveling through deserted towns, wrecked highways, and scores of begging people. Karuk remained vigilant the entire way home, refusing to sleep, on the alert in case there were more ghosts lurking in the wastelands.

• • •

The Seven Flags trucks made it to an abandoned airfield where a second helicopter idled. Two disembarked, hauling the limp form of their prisoner to the aircraft. As soon as they secured him to a seat and made certain he was still breathing, they left, rapping the side to confirm they were out. Seconds later, the helicopter gracefully lifted into the sky, its blades scattering the dusty air, actually clearing the space, revealing a slightly less dusty, hazy blue sky for a few seconds.

The trip through American airspace went unchallenged, and within hours, the helicopter silently slipped across the border to the new nation. As soon as it landed, a medical team took custody of the still-unconscious man and strapped him to a propeller-propelled gurney that glided into a building. The international red cross was emblazoned on the walls and roof to ward off any potential attackers. The gurney was swarmed over by doctors, studying the tattooed and bejeweled figure, recording devices beginning to take digital measurements. Several blood samples were drawn and placed immediately into analyzers.

Once in an operating theater, the man was hooked to an IV and one woman began to treat the stab wound. Two others worked their way up, removing his footwear, pants, vambraces, belt, and other clothing, until he was laying naked on the table. His macuahuitl was placed in a steel container and wheeled off for additional study. Everything was scanned, weighed, and measured before being placed in small lockers, red readouts identifying the prisoner number. Despite the new nation being less than a year old, prisoner numbers were already in the five figures and this foreign opponent was designated 24601.

As the suturing was completed, a wheeled device was brought to the head of the table and activated. Slowly, with a blinking blue light, it took exact measurements of the man as it wheeled its way from head to foot. As it reached the end, the medics turned the body on its stomach and the process was repeated. Once completed, he was flipped over again as one medic parted the patient's lips so recordings could be made of the jade embedded in the teeth. The jaw was forced open to study the mouth cavity then closed. His jewelry was carefully removed, each piece scanned and weighed, scrapings taken to verify the metallic makeup. These were placed in a glassine bag that was placed on the gurney.

When the examination and treatment were completed, still naked, he was placed in magnetic hand and foot cuffs. The gurney deposited him in a conference room, a simple space, with a metal table and several chairs.

Sitting within the room already was Luna Knox, today resplendent in a bright yellow dress, with fire red accents. She wore a red lipstick that matched the accent shade and was dictating a memo on her tablet when the prisoner arrived. Once he was placed in the chair, she signaled he was to be awoken. A nurse flipped a switch on the IV, which went from an anesthetic drip to a stimulant. Finally, the figure began to stir.

"I suspect you're thirsty," she said, pouring him a glass of water and pushing it across the table.

Sasha stared at it, then his surroundings, his eyes blinking rapidly, absorbing his situation. There was no doubt he was being surveilled and the conversation recorded. He seemed to accept this and took the glass, sniffed, then drank a bit. When it tasted right, he drank more. Still un-clothed, Sasha was preparing for what came next, what he had trained his entire life for, and yet, this would be his first real-world interrogation. He would be lying to himself if he didn't admit he was excited to play this game.

"My name is Luna Knox, a governor of the Seven Flags," she said. "And you are...?"

Sasha silently stared at her, his eyes shifting back and forth, evaluating his situation, the woman, the water, calculating his options. He spoke in Mayan, knowing full well they would not understand him. Sure enough, Knox blinked in confusion. He then switched to rapid Spanish and here, she reacted in recognition.

"I'm sorry, I am not fluent in Spanish. Would you like me to get a translator?"

"No, thank you," he said in English. She blinked in surprise.

"Are you showing off?"

Sasha flashed her a wolfish grin.

"Any other languages?"

Sasha stared at her.

"I will take that as a no," she continued, unfazed. "Now, do you have a name for me to use?"

"Sasha," he replied.

"That's a Russian name, but you don't speak Russian?"

"Nyet," he said with a smile, which she returned. Clearly, they were going to spar a bit if she intended on learning anything.

"You aren't from around here, are you?"

"It depends. Where am I?"

"Fair enough. You are in Kansas, one of the states comprising the Seven Flags," she explained. "And you're from?"

"That's a pretty dumb name for a country," he said, smirking.

"That's entirely your opinion. Now, if we're in Kansas, you're from...?"

"Not around here, as you said," he replied. He was having some fun with this, but it was bravado, hiding his concern for his well-being, his future. Still, he would not betray Ponco or his people.

"So, I can't find a record of anyone who looks quite like you," she continued, ignoring his jibe.

"Faulty records after the bombings?"

"Maybe, but I doubt it. Our experts don't recognize your tattoos or the interesting dental work," she continued.

"You have tattoo experts?"

"We're a full-service nation, Sasha, and your people attacked my people," Knox went on.

"As I recall, we were riding through the United States when we were attacked by your people. Isn't that some sort of territorial violation? Maybe I should ask to see the American ambassador to the Seven Flags."

"There is no such person," Knox said. "And yes, I will concede that we were not in our sovereign territory when we encountered you. But the interesting thing, Sasha, is that you were carrying a weapon the likes of which we've never seen. We know for a fact the US has no such weapon. That makes you a foreign agent of some sort. Maybe a threat to the US and the Seven Flags."

"Or, I was a visitor, a stranger in a strange land perhaps?"

"You know Heinlein?"

"Who?"

"Never mind," Knox said. "For our safety, we need to understand where you come from and what you were doing with the Costas."

"Who?"

"Don't play dumb and don't play games. You're sitting here weapon-less, naked, and on my turf. If you explain yourself, we might see ourselves clearing you for release."

Sasha said, "So you can just follow me to wherever it is I come from?"

"What if I give you my word? Safe passage."

"I was taught that trust comes from actions, not words. What actions will you undertake to earn my trust?"

A door slid open and a red-faced Rodney Holtzer strode into the room, walked up to Sasha, and wickedly slapped him across the right cheek.

Sasha coughed in surprise and then looked up at the general. "That's not going to earn my trust."

Holtzer slapped the other cheek. He then unbuttoned and removed his uniform jacket, making a show of rolling up his sleeves.

"Now comes the beating for information," Sasha said. "I've seen enough movies and read the books. She was the good cop, you're the bad one. Maybe my worst nightmare?"

"Listen, you little shit, you're a threat. I don't take kindly to threats, so I will learn where you're from and who designed that mace of yours."

"Maces don't have blades," Sasha said helpfully.

"I don't give a fuck," Holtzer said. "When you and I are done 'talking,' I will have your country, your location, and your cooperation."

"Or you'll kill me," Sasha said matter-of-factly, although underneath, he was growing concerned, actually beginning to fear for his life. He had been raised since birth to endure pain, to give as good as he got, and to know he was never alone. Yet, here he was, alone and about to be beaten, maybe lose his life. Still, he would never reveal his knowledge. He couldn't.

"I'll take it from here, Luna," Holtzer said, swinging the empty chair around and straddling it, arms on the top. He was eyeing Sasha as a butcher does a pig about to be slaughtered.

Knox silently left the room, stepping into the observation lounge where Elsa Ember watched. The women exchanged glances, each conveying worry.

"What do you make of our guest?" Knox asked.

"He's tough, well-trained, and clearly conditioned. But he's young, so I take it he's inexperienced. He might be able to handle a beating or two, he might be able to hold on to wherever he's from, but maybe not. This, I think, may be his first test."

Ember was compassionate but the deadliest among the governors. A superb tactician, she never entered a battle without assuring herself of a positive outcome. Sasha represented an X-factor, something unexpected and therefore worthy of study.

"Where do you think he's from?" Knox asked, settling into a chair.

"Skin tone suggests South America, but there's no country with those adornments. There's no country with anything like that battle club. Our analysis is coming up empty, more questions than answers."

"You hate that, don't you?"

"Hate? No. Am I concerned? Yes. And of more immediate concern is our esteemed leader. He's overly fixated on this David person, taking his eye off the ball, which is consolidating our power. Yes, this technique the scientist has could be a positive for us, but we're doing fine without it."

"What do you want? They've got history," Knox said.

"Yes, and that means he's got a grudge and isn't thinking clearly. If he continues to focus on David Anders, our momentum slows at a time when we can't slow. The world will not wait."

The two women fell silent, watching as Holtzer continued to ask a question and slap Sasha, who seemed to have stopped giving smart-ass replies. His cheeks were a raw red, and a trickle of blood fell down his chin from a split lip.

• • •

David wanted to be at the garage to welcome Karuk and the others, but Ponco refused. The surface was filled with background radiation and unexpected dangers. Her responsibility was for their safety, so she insisted they all remain at the tunnel. As a result, he was pacing with anxious energy as Betty stood near their protector. Several other soldiers were along one wall, standing by in case they were needed.

Betty leaned over to Ponco and asked, "How are you holding up?"

The supreme commander was stiff, at attention, a model soldier for the others and that would include her deportment, so David knew the truth was tucked away.

"Fine."

"Ha," Betty scoffed.

"Ha? What would you have from me, Betty? I cannot protect my brother; I have wounded soldiers. This mission did not go as planned. That reflects on my team...and me."

"You couldn't have anticipated three Ghost Squad trucks," David said, adjusting his pacing to come nearer so they could speak quietly.

"Shouldn't I have, from everything you told me about these Seven Flags people? Maybe twelve was not sufficient and that's on me," she said, not caring to keep the recriminations from her voice.

"We'll get him back," Betty said.

"How? I know that is meant to be reassuring, but there is no tactical way to do so without risking more people. The High Council would never authorize a rescue mission, so my brother is a casualty of war."

She turned away from them and David shot Betty a glance that said to leave her be. She wrapped herself with her arms and stood nearby as he resumed pacing, giving their friend space. With every passing moment of waiting, the tension seemed to thicken the air worse than any humidity he'd ever felt. He wanted to help while he continued to feel guilty for getting this sequence of events started.

The sound of a motor made him stop his pacing as he turned about on his heel, looking expectantly at the doors. Betty came up behind him, wrapping an arm around his own, leaning into him. Ponco stepped forward, taking the primary position in anticipation of her soldiers returning home. Finally, the motor slowed and stopped, the doors sliding open and Karuk stood, looking dirty and weary, dark rings under his eyes, which were filled with emotion. Still, he marched out and stood to the side as his fellow soldiers filed out.

David strained to spot Reid and Linda amidst the others, and finally, he spotted a mass of curly hair popping above the heads. Then the two emerged, studying their rocky surroundings. As he did initially, they noted the recessed lighting panels, the smooth walkway, and the reality of entering an underground civilization.

Reid stepped forward and paused, taking it all in, then his eyes found David's. His dark face brightened with a smile of recognition, and he took another step forward, Linda right behind him. David noted the man was thinner and taller than he was, older, perhaps he was unsure what to expect after countless hours on the radio, talking, planning, discussing, trusting to get to this moment. But Reid looked like most scientists, work fed him more than meals, and his posture showed his aptitude for lab tables. He was wearing thick, black-framed glasses and his black hair was shaggy, coming over his shirt collar. There was a keenness to his eyes, ever observant, which made him somewhat of a kindred spirit. Betty was right, he could use a real friend down here.

Linda was half a head shorter than her husband, with brown eyes, and that mane of auburn hair that nicely framed her face. She was thicker in build than Reid, far bustier than Betty, he noted, and seemed to be in good shape, far more the athlete than her husband. She looked fascinated and delighted, unlike her husband's warier gaze.

"Reid, Linda, welcome to Kasper," David said, stepping forward. He thrust a hand forward, which Reid took reluctantly, pumped once, and released it. Linda quietly slipped him her tube of sanitizer, which he used twice.

Linda rushed forward and enveloped Betty in her arms, saying, "Finally! Betty, I am so happy to see you."

"Me too," Betty said from underneath some of those curls. They both laughed and then straightened up.

David noted that Karuk had gone to his wife, but as a soldier, not a husband, and they spoke in hushed tones. Finally, he turned and gestured to his guests. The pair walked over and were formally introduced to Ponco, who nodded her greeting. She then turned to her returning troops and addressed them.

"Your service has been noted and appreciated. Those in need of the medical team, see them immediately. Get some real rest, real food, and clean up. I want your accounts of your actions by tomorrow morning. Dismissed."

The soldiers, accompanied by those who stood by patiently, walked out of the tunnel and into Kasper directly. Once they were gone, her duty discharged, Ponco exhaled and turned to the others.

"I apologize for the rough reception you've received," she began.

"You couldn't have known," Reid began but was cut off.

"Yes, I should have known, given David's warnings. What's done is done. We will escort you to quarters and let you acclimate yourselves. I will arrange an escort for a proper tour, but that will have to wait. Karuk and I need to discuss what has transpired and what comes next. No doubt, the High Council would also like a word with you all."

That didn't sound ominous at all, but David had no idea what was left to say. He was the focal point of their prophecies and had to make the APLS work to help humanity while staying far away from Holtzer and anyone from the

Seven Flags. Still, it felt good to have fellowship in the form of the Costas and he looked forward to spending time together.

As the six walked into Kasper, they paused to let Reid and Linda absorb the splendor of the city, the part they could see. They already knew the entire city-state of Kasper extended for hundreds of miles, so this was merely a piece of it. Still, what they saw filled them with the same sense of wonder David initially felt. And like David, Reid had a lot of questions, but Linda spoke for them both when she said, "I don't think we're in…"

"No, you're not," Betty said.

"If we're Dorothy, it's the Maya—they are the Wizards of Oz," David added as the four of them laughed at the cliché, fully understanding the feeling of the moment, while they all looked in wonderment at the scene before them.

CHAPTER 18

Salvation

The Costas acclimated to Kasper swifter than the Anders. A man of imagination, Reid found the whole city to be nothing short of magical, and Linda knew more existed than met the eye in the world and was just happy to have been gifted the pleasure of seeing beyond the veil. Neither had faced the horrors the Anderses had, allowing them to realize the magic of their situation faster. After being briefed by Karuk to a degree, they were just a little better able to adapt to the wondrous world beneath the surface. It helped that they could share the experience with one another as well as with David and Betty, who were now starting to feel more comfortable. The mere presence of these people acted as a balm, David realized. They had been given adjacent accommodations identical to their own which gave them their own private enclave in one corner of the sprawling city. Ponco had not been seen since she departed to debrief her team and report to the High Council. While gossip about the white people had spread, news from the palace was scant. The silence was of some concern given how much of a steadying presence the supreme commander had been, but Betty pointed out she did have responsibilities way beyond that of babysitting surface folk.

Throughout it all, Reid was practically vibrating, wanting to see the RSN and discuss with their scientists how it worked, how they pierced the dimensional veil, and what else was possible. Linda laughed at his childish eagerness, lightening the mood. The women insisted on coming along, not wishing to miss out on anything that might prove significant, although David worried even he'd have trouble keeping up with all the physics about to be discussed. They remained resolute. As a result, their guide, Yum Cimil, a middle-aged man who held some rank akin to that of a captain, with an especially elongated forehead and drooping earlobes from the stone earrings he fancied, walked them for over an hour to reach the lab where the RSN research was being performed. Along the way, Linda and Betty couldn't help but keep up a running commentary on the fashions, the colorful outfits, and amazing tattoos they saw. It got so that David was feeling embarrassed on behalf of the women and apologized to Yum Cimil, who merely shrugged it off.

The RSN lab took over an entire building, decorated with stars, moons, and planets, its signage in Mayan. It was three stories tall with a tower twice that height, filling most of a city block. There seemed to be little activity that made sense since the RSN's major work was a century earlier. However, just the notion that within those walls was a device that moved seven million people at once and might send others through time was mind-boggling. He'd already extracted from Reid a promise to help him look at the quantum structure of the APLS to see if they could perfect it and then run some trials.

Yum Cimil flashed some sort of badge of office to the young man who seemed to act as receptionist. In turn, he led them through narrow corridors deep into the building, nearing, from what David could ascertain, the tower. Then a door swung open and the oldest man he'd seen since arriving stood in the frame. He was short, stout, and surprisingly bearded, a crisp white beard that matched his bushy eyebrows and the forearm hair that peeked above faded tattoos. He was wrinkled and jowly, but seemed pleased to have the visitors, which relaxed David. He knew many scientists were extremely protective of their work, refusing to share or divulge what they considered trade secrets.

"I am Ixbalanque, the last surviving member of the original RSN team. We designed this apparatus as a way to bring our people home, and with the hope of expanding into new scientific realms," he said by way of introduction. David introduced the small party of four as Yum Cimil introduced himself, saying he would remain out front, seemingly disinterested in the

177

subject matter. David was sadly accustomed to such military attitudes. The crew looked on as a familiarity glistened across Betty's face.

"Your name is familiar," Betty said, which caught everyone by surprise. "Let me think a moment. There's a story about an Ixbalanque."

"There is," the man said in delight. "What do you recall?"

"You're a twin, I mean, the original is a twin. The hero twins, grandchildren to Xibalba. I don't remember the rest," she admitted.

"I'm impressed you know that much," Ixbalanque said with a throaty chuckle.

"I've been doing some reading."

"Well, being named after the devil's grandchild is fitting because, initially, some people here thought I was doing his work," Ixbalanque said.

"I have so many questions," Reid, impatient, interrupted, but Ixbalanque held up a hand.

"Let me share some thoughts before you dive into your questions about quantum tunneling. I have anticipated your arrivals," the shorter man replied. He waved the group to follow him, and they entered what seemed to be a circular chamber. Computers and screens ringed the walls. A giant chart took up a huge space at the opposite end. David discerned it was filled with astronomical markings, celestial annotations, and graphs with markings he couldn't make out.

"So, Reid Costa, what do you know of the RSN?"

"It somehow transported millions of people meeting a DNA standard from the surface to Kasper," he began.

"Yes, but how?"

Reid looked helplessly to David, who shrugged. That seemed to delight the man.

"Good, no preconceptions to dispel. Let me begin. We know there are four dimensions—height, width, depth, and time—but in times dating back centuries, our astronomers couldn't understand how the universe worked with just four dimensions."

"The same with us. We theorized a fifth dimension, but then we needed at least a sixth for some of the math to make sense. We got as high as eleven without fully proving it all," Reid added.

"Eleven?" Betty asked in wonder.

"Is that all you've found?" Ixbalanque asked with a smile. "Oh, there are more. Far more. We determined there were more, each with its own properties, its own laws of physics. Some seemed to contain life, some the chaos energy that existed after what you call the Big Bang."

"That's what you harness to power the RSN," David said, recalling what Karuk had told them.

"Yes, but first, we had to find it. And then harness it, and then put it to use," Ixbalanque said, clearly warming up to his subjects. The voice was old, scratchy, but filled with energy.

"We've been using LIGO," Reid said, pausing from practice. He glanced at Linda, who shot him a look that said, "Yes, we're idiots, please elaborate." He added, "It's a massive gravitational wave detector, which receives signals from objects such as black holes merging..."

"Black holes can merge?" Betty blurted out. "I'm a teacher, but liberal arts, not the sciences."

"They can," Reid confirmed. "We were hoping to understand the readings to see how energy transited space and find a way to control it."

"We did that," Ixbalanque said. "We found that sort of power and used it to create what you call a wormhole." He paused and looked at the women. "That is, boring a tunnel through space, connecting two distant points, allowing us to send an object from one point to another."

"Like folding space," Reid said, trying to help. Linda nodded, then Betty's face brightened.

"Like the tesseracts in A Wrinkle in Time," she said. In response to the blank looks everyone gave her, she laughed self-consciously and explained, "It was a science fiction, well, maybe a science fantasy novel that involved tesseracts—she called them tessers—which did exactly that."

Reid objected. "Tesseracts are a fourth-dimensional construct. Not at all the right term."

"Whatever," Betty said. "I get it."

"But, how do you do that?" David asked, refusing to be confused with the terminology.

"We decipher the extra dimensions by understanding their influence on the cosmic energy unleashed by the birth of the universe," Reid said. "By understanding those forces, we come to better understand the dark matter that fills the universe. That's a lot of what string theory is all about."

"He says that, I keep thinking he means orchestral music theory," Linda said to Betty, who giggled.

Reid was not amused but was also used to his wife's wry commentary. "Honey, while I know you know, you married a nerd. This is my life's work after all. Let's show some respect to the man's invention."

"Thank you," Ixbalanque added. Reid shot him an approving look.

"Sorry," Linda said.

"The best way to understand the six infinitesimal dimensions is, of course, to actually be there at the dawn of the Big Bang, but that would require time travel," Ixbalanque said.

"Of course," Linda said.

"We're working on that," he told them.

"You are?" Betty asked incredulously.

"We have been for some time, and I fear we will conquer it after I'm gone," he added softly.

"What exactly are you trying to measure?" David asked, hoping to get things back on track.

"Gravity is weak and we've been trying to measure scales of far less than a centimeter," Reid explained. "Scientists have managed to measure the attraction between objects just 0.2 mm apart, so those dimensions are below that."

"Yes, they are," their host said. "We discovered them about 150 years ago."

Reid and David both gaped at that, confirming the Kasperian technology was generations beyond the rest of mankind. The sonic weapons, the touches here and there, and the massive movement of people just added to the advancements. This impressed David, but Reid was genuinely excited by everything Ixbalanque was explaining.

"Did you use the torsion pendulum?" At the blank look from the Maya man, Reid corrected himself. "A copper disc and a pendulum were used, separated by just 0.2 mm, and a laser took the measurements."

The old scientist nodded in understanding. "We discovered the, I guess you would call them loops, that vibrate."

"String theory," Reid explained to the others. "The loops can be particles like electrons, quarks, and neutrinos, or carriers of nature such as photons, gluons, and gravitons. Each string vibrates in different modes, or splits or merges, all of which creates the universe's matter."

"They wiggle?" Linda asked. Clearly, she and Reid had developed a pattern, so David stayed quiet and watched. Their host seemed very interested in the byplay.

"Yes, but hyper-dimensionally. That's where M-theory comes in," he continued.

"Whoa, what?" Betty said.

"We know of ten dimensions that make the math work, but M-theory suggests there's one more, a Muon, that helps fill in the final gaps," Reid said.

"And more," Ixbalanque confirmed. "That has allowed us to harness the energies from those dimensions and power the RSN."

"I thought all these dimensions were like mirror universes," Betty said. "Our fiction is rife with such stories."

Ixbalanque looked at her, confused.

"I thought so too, hun," Linda said reassuringly.

Reid sighed. "You're talking about the theory of eternal inflation. As the Big Bang ignited, the singularity at the center was inflating in all directions faster than the speed of light. The cosmic inflation exploded outward to 1026 times its original size. Note that's all before the actual expansion of matter you understand to be the Big Bang. The matter is seen as a consequence of the inflation. Once the inflation slowed, there was a flood of matter and radiation as a fireball, and it is from there that the atoms and molecules formed and, well, here we are."

"What does that have to do with parallel universes?" Betty asked.

"The inflation never ended since the universe kept expanding," Reid went on. "Instead, it cooled in some portions of the universe. That's the theory of eternal inflation."

"Like this explanation," Linda quipped.

"Shh," Ixbalanque hissed.

"As each portion of the inflation cooled, a bubble universe formed, so as it cools elsewhere, more bubbles are formed and those are your parallel universes. They will never touch because the universe continues to expand."

"So, we will never meet an evil Reid," Betty added helpfully.

"I hope not," Linda said with a hearty laugh.

"Maybe," Ixbalanque said.

Reid glanced his way in surprise. "But, the eternal inflation and string theory combined suggests that each bubble universe may have its own laws of physics. Or, if we use quantum theory, whenever we tried to look at one of those bubbles, we actually will form a new one by the mere act of observation."

Betty shook her head at that one.

"What about the fact that there are so many ways to combine the elements, so the finiteness suggests parallel development may occur? Some even think that the Big Bang created a mirror universe going backward in time,"

Ixbalanque said, "We're looking into that too."

"Of course, you are," David said with a laugh. This was the most surreal conversation he had had since arriving in Kasper.

"Astounding," Reid said, absorbing the other scientist's words and ideas. This was going to keep him up at night, David realized.

"Well, I'd love to be a part of this," Reid said. "I'd even volunteer to test your time travel theory."

"I am sure you would," Ixbalanque said. "But there is nothing as of yet to test." There was a sad look in the scientist's eyes, realizing a new generation was on hand to continue his work, and he was regretting not being a part of it. David could sympathize, as his work built on the efforts of other botanists stretching back through the ages and there would be those who took APLS and improved on it. Such was the way with science. Such was the way of life. David pondered the thought: how would his creation be iterated and compounded by future generations... as the thought flew across his mind a darker one engulfed it. What if there were no future generations, what if they were at the end of the scientific road? The thought left as fast as it came, bringing David back to the present, ready to re-engage with Ixbalanque.

The chitchat and tour continued for another hour until Ixbalanque seemed to tire, something Betty noticed, and signaled to Yum Cimil it was time to return to their apartments. David and Reid enthusiastically thanked their host, promising to return soon, something the scientist seemed to appreciate. He promised the next time he'd include the entire research team. Then, the long walk back was undertaken with the men rapidly speaking to one another about the ideas they'd just heard, and David admitted that it might not be his field, but he knew enough to be excited at the prospects of using the Kasperian technology to perfect APLS. He did notice that Betty grew weary as they neared the quarters, so he suggested that the women go to one building to rest while the two scientists continued to talk.

"You just want to feed off one another's envy of their tech," Linda said.

"Wouldn't you?" David shot back.

"Why David, would you really leave this time, for another? Is our time not enough for you? Does the power of humanity's possibilities need David Anders at its front lines? But of course," she said as David shrugged. She exasperatedly closed the door on him, leaving the two women in his rooms.

As the door closed, Betty exhaled loudly and fell backward atop the bed as Linda perched on a large chair.

"Those two are in heaven," Linda said.

"They're likely to be like this for a while," Betty agreed. "I had my fill, fascinating as it was. I get the general idea of how it might help, but I still cannot fathom them moving seven million people at once. Even I know the energy required for this is astronomical."

"I'm thinking more about how long it must have taken to prepare for that. The number of buildings and supplies, the changes to their entire society," Linda added.

"Yep. All these big ideas make me want to curl up and read a good book," Betty admitted as she stifled a yawn.

"What're you reading?"

"Thankfully, I downloaded a bunch before relocating down here. I just started Let Me Help by Alvarez."

Linda laughed out loud. "That's pretty funny, because I'm about a third of the way through that very book."

"Have Gennifer and Hiro met yet?"

"No, they keep missing one another," Linda answered. "We're going to have our own little book club. It'll be nice to talk about something other than the radiation or the Seven Flags..."

"Dumb name," Betty inserted.

"Valid. But really, why are Reid and I here? What threat could we possibly be to the Kasperians?"

"David and I think it's all an overreaction. No one outside this city knows about the power they control. Imagine Fitzgerald or Holtzer getting their hands on that much power."

"Which one is Holtzer? Defense?"

"No, he's the guy running the Flags. He and David have some bad history, so I am glad we're down here, far from his reach. Frankly, Linda, I think this might be the best place for us all. The radiation is not reaching us, there's food, water, and an army that seems to know what they're doing. They're armed to the teeth with weapons any country would envy and best of all, there's genuine peace and harmony from what I could tell."

"Well, I could use some peace and harmony," Linda said. She let out a yawn and stared off into space for a moment. Betty couldn't read her expression, but clearly, something else was on her mind.

"You okay?"

"Yeah, yeah, fine, hun. It's, well, just as all of this went south, I learned Reid and I were having a baby."

Betty sprang forward, jaw agape, eyes wide.

"Me too."

"Seriously? That's wonderful. Congratulations." They hugged in mutual joy.

"Thanks. You too. The thing is, I've miscarried repeatedly, so I really want this one to survive. I won't risk its life, which is why being down here is such good timing. I can stay here for nine months and give birth and not worry."

"This wasn't even planned. Well, we wanted kids, but we had held off seriously trying given the shitty state of the world," Betty added.

"Valid. Totally valid. So, how far along are you?"

"Just a few weeks," Betty admitted. "There hasn't been a lot of time for lovemaking."

"Nothing like an apocalypse to kill the libido," Linda said.

Betty laughed and then added, "You're not going to have any trouble feeding them down here; the food is incredible."

"It doesn't seem like anyone goes hungry down here. You'll fill out nicely, I bet. Me, on the other hand—ooof. I don't know how I'm going to look with a ball on my belly," Linda said. "So, how did you know?"

"I woke up one morning just knowing something was different."

"How long ago? I did the test two, three days back, right before Karuk came for us."

"That was about when I took my own test," Betty admitted. "So, maybe it was the same day. Freaky."

"Yeah, freaky."

Both could sense there was something more than mere coincidence at play here, but Betty didn't even want to bring up the prophecies and the supposed divine hand at work.

Both fell into silence, each keenly aware that the synchronicity of their conception could have been a coincidence, but the way events had flowed of late, Betty suspected neither believed that. Given that Linda already knew about the portal and Kasper, she figured her newfound friend should know it all. She slowly detailed the various prophecies and how the interpretations pointed to David. How their unborn child may be at the center of this, and that David's discovery and his being could be the key to restoring the hope of a brighter future.

"That's just crazy talk," Linda said as she finished. "So, it's a reversal on Christ. He's the Madonna and you're just Joseph."

"Joseph didn't have to carry a bowling ball for nine months," Betty quipped, and they both laughed but quickly fell silent.

"Is there a prophecy about the babies?" Linda asked quietly.

"None I know of, but there were seven major Maya prophecies. I've been reading up on their culture. If this is to be our home, I figured we better fit in."

"I'm glad you're a teacher because you'll have to explain this all to me and do it slowly."

• • •

A pair of doctors were completing a very detailed, very thorough, and very invasive examination of Sasha's battered, bleeding body. They took biopsies from various organs, withdrew more blood and other fluids, took hair and nail cuttings, and only when they were done did they begin to treat the numerous wounds. Their orders were not to do more than stop the bleeding; the broken bones were to remain as they were, the lacerations remain unsutured. Throughout it all, Sasha drifted in and out of consciousness, deprived of any topical or general anesthetic.

From a different room, Holtzer watched the procedure, sitting in the dark by himself. He was interrupted when a doctor entered the room, holding a tablet that glowed brightly in the dim light.

"He's perfectly healthy and totally human," the doctor, a middle-aged, gray-haired man, said without preamble. "Our rapid DNA sequencing says he is a pure-blood Mayan..."

Holtzer blinked, taking his attention from the prisoner and focused for the first time on the doctor. "Mayan? Aren't they extinct?"

"The culture may have been wiped out centuries ago, but it didn't mean descendants didn't survive and pass along their genes."

"What's with the head? And the teeth?" Holtzer gestured to the prone body.

"I did some research on the race, and apparently, this was their preferred look, and shortly after birth, babies had their heads forcibly reshaped."

"Barbaric."

"The tattoos and the jeweled teeth also date back to the original Mayan culture, but the dental work here is exquisite. Something perfected over the years."

"Would you do that to yourself?"

"No, sir. But his dental exam was exemplary. No cavities and minor tartar and plaque. The stool sample suggests a primarily plant and vegetable diet, but so mixed, we cannot suggest a region."

He made an unhappy face at that. "Can you tell where he came from? We don't know of any people like this existing today."

"Nothing in his DNA or bloodwork. We ran a spectroscopic study, but he came up with a human baseline. No radiation, no example of genetic engineering."

"I hate mysteries," Holtzer grumbled.

"Has he shared anything with you?"

"He's a pain in the ass, quipping his way through the interrogation whenever he says anything. He certainly has a high pain threshold; I'll give him that."

"Are there any other tests you would like performed?"

"Anything you recommend?"

"Not at present."

"Dismissed." Holtzer snapped his attention completely back on the figure opposite him as the doctor silently let himself out. As a result, he missed that the doctor was replaced with Elsa Ember, who entered and stood several feet back, watching the proceedings.

"What's next, finger removal?"

Holtzer blinked once, acknowledging her presence without looking at her. He was growing unhappy with being second-guessed about his approach. He was a soldier, she was not, end of comparison.

"He's a threat," he bluntly said.

"To whom, exactly?"

"He's a Mayan, so we have a squad of Mayans, maybe coming through the mists of time, to collect the very people we wanted because they were a lead to David Anders. That's a bit outrageous of a thought, don't you think? There's a third party involved, and to me, that's an unacceptable unknown. We're not prepared for it."

"The mists of time? Do you hear yourself? Get real. Why do you think they wanted Reid Costa?"

"That's what I'm trying to find out," Holtzer said, his voice dripping with cold fury. "I need to get in there and start again."

"Let him recover a bit, feed him a bit, and then you can start. It might make him more susceptible," Ember suggested. "Right now, he's in a mass of pain, so more pain won't make him talkative. Renewed pain, though, that might help. Now, let me pose a question."

Finally, he looked at her.

"What if this Mayan—and I find it very odd we still have Mayans in the world today—actually wanted Reid Costa, or even Linda Costa, for reasons totally unrelated to David Anders? What if this was all some cosmic coincidence, a matter of bad timing?"

She left the room and he seethed at the question and its implications.

Still, he knew she was a fine tactician and followed her directions. The prisoner was to be taken to a room, fed, cleaned up, and given ten hours rest before the interrogation was to resume. He continued to sit in the dark, pondering why an ancient race of warriors, long thought extinct, would suddenly surface. When he prepared the Seven Flags plan, he studied geopolitics thoroughly, so he saw in advance the Alliance being formed. He knew the corrupt South American and Central American countries would scramble when things went to shit. Australia would barricade itself from Pacific Rim threats. Africa would continue to fracture, come together, split apart, as they had for the last 150 years, so this would throw them off kilter. Nowhere did he note any organized group of Mayans, and that was troubling. Anything unforeseen could upend their plans.

What made it more challenging to his worldview was the weapons he carried. They were being analyzed, carefully reverse-engineered for potential replication, but so far, his best engineers were stumped. Add to that, the metallurgic studies of the blades affixed to the club were unable to fully identify all the elements—they were no metal or alloy they'd ever seen before.

This spoke of secrets, something hidden in plain sight, and that suggested a deadly force somewhere in the Western Hemisphere. Where were they, what did they want, and why emerge now, months after the Alliance attack? Who the hell was Reid Costa, on the off-chance Ember was right? He'd asked his intelligence people for a full briefing scheduled for tomorrow morning.

With his prisoner resting, reports being compiled, and nothing resolved, the questions ate away at his fragile equanimity. Underneath it all was his rock-solid conviction that David Anders was at the center of all of this. But why this single botanist whose scientific invention, APLS, didn't even work that well, not yet at least? However, if David did figure it out, and these people that Sasha was with had David, it could and would be the game-changer he needed to become an instant super-power. He doubted the Mayans wanted it, or even needed it. If these were indeed Mayans, their technology would have to be so advanced that it wouldn't even make sense to use what Anders created. So they wanted him. Why?

What made David Anders so important? The question ate at Holtzer like a worm consuming an apple, slowly decaying as it spiraled into disarray.

• • •

"Do you want to know the sex?"

Quanah was an attractive man in his thirties, with a perpetual grin and terrific bedside manner, the perfect doctor for the two somewhat nervous women. After Reid and David finally returned to their homes, the women shared the coincidental good news, not that David saw it as a coincidence or necessarily good news. Of course, he was thrilled they were both expecting, but the timing struck him as bizarre. In turn, they asked Yum Cimil to arrange a medical exam for the following day, explaining it needed to be their equivalent of an OB-GYN. Neither woman could stop chattering through their breakfast, eager to be examined and able to reassure themselves, and then their husbands, that all was going to be fine.

Betty looked at David, repeating the question with her expression, and he nodded. The more information the better, he felt. Dr. Quanah glanced again at his monitor and confirmed, "It's a boy."

"So, the Anders name will live on," he said to no one in particular, but he'd always wondered about his legacy. The Anders family line was modest: some soldiers, some pilots, some economists, no one exceptional. If APLS worked and could feed a starving world, he would change that and privately wanted someone to inherit that legacy.

"And you," Quanah said to Linda.

She didn't hesitate to say yes.

"A girl."

"Hot damn! Reid, a girl."

"She better look like you," he said. He seemed pleased with this news, which made David smile.

The women reached across the adjacent examination tables and held hands, bonding over this moment.

"They're going to grow up together and get married," Linda proclaimed. Everyone laughed at that, even Quanah.

"You know, we do have some fine-looking men and women in Kasper," he keenly said.

"Look, doctor, there has to be something to all this. Something about the way we came together, how both got knocked up at the same time…"

"Apparently the same day, from what I can tell," Quanah interjected.

"See? This is destiny. You believe in the prophecies, so maybe there's something to this, the babies being conceived the same day. Maybe they're destined to marry."

"And change the world," Betty said so solemnly that everyone broke into a laugh. For David, it was a nervous laugh.

David was not so certain he shared their mutual joy at how all these things seemed to be occurring at the same time. Something beyond his reasoning was going on, another in a lengthening list of things, and that was beginning to concern him.

"Have you considered names yet?" the doctor asked, putting away the diagnostic equipment. The women were healthy, the babies—little more than zygotes at this point—were also on course. There were no concerns whatsoever, which overjoyed the women and should have pleased David, but a darkening cloud filled his mind. He wanted to enjoy this moment, but it was all too much.

"Not me," Betty said and received a confirming shake of the head from Linda.

"When the time comes, you will present the babies to the King and Queen for a naming ceremony," Quanah said. "Their high priest will consult the Maya calendar, which is 260 days compared with your 365. The priest will examine the energy of the year and the day of the birth. Now, Betty, for a boy, the number of the day should precede his name. Linda, your daughter should have 'ix' before the name, signifying power and energy."

"I like the sound of that," Linda said.

"Ah, I am a little more of a traditionalist. No offense, doctor, but my family tends to select names from the Bible," David said.

"So, you slew Goliath," Reid said.

"If I can conquer the APLS, then yes," he admitted.

"Reid and I will have to talk it over," Linda said.

"You can both get dressed and we'll wait for you outside," the doctor told them, still smiling.

A short time later, they made their farewells, and after they left the infirmary, the group was surprised to see Ponco and Karuk, not Yum Cimil, awaiting them. Both looked expectantly at the group, serious expressions that didn't fit their mood.

"It's all good," David told them.

"We're pregnant for real," Betty added.

The stoic demeanor evaporated and both soldiers broke into broad smiles. "This is welcome news, yes?"

"It sure is, Ponco," Betty said. "David and I have been trying, and now that we're here, the change of scenery did us some good."

The news that ignited the smile in Ponco faded far faster than it did for Karuk, who was asking Reid and Linda about their news. David studied her quietly, realizing their moods almost matched, but he suspected for vastly different reasons.

"A boy and a girl," Linda said with amazement. "They're gonna get married, you know."

"Has a deal been completed already?" Karuk laughed.

"We'll get to it; one thing at a time," she said.

As the conversation continued, Ponco began to withdraw from the group, step by step. David decided to confront the matter and nodded his head away from the others. Ponco confirmed the nod with one of her own and they just walked down the street from the building, seemingly strolling in the fine morning air, but really putting distance between them.

"You're troubled. The babies?" David prompted after they were well beyond earshot.

"No, nothing like that. Of course, I am happy for your wives. It's an exciting time."

"Have you and Karuk considered it?"

She shook her head. "We are soldiers; there is little time for raising a family, especially now that we have begun to engage more with the surface."

"Well, knowing them, you'll be Auntie Ponco," David said, attempting to lighten the mood. When she didn't rise to the bait, he asked, "What's on your mind?"

"Sasha."

"Of course," David said, feeling foolish for not figuring it out on his own.

"We have no idea where he was taken. I want to send out a team to scout for information, but it feels selfish. That's what Karuk and I have been discussing before we heard you were taken to the infirmary."

"I can help with whatever I know about the Seven Flags," David offered.

"Thank you," Ponco said, then fell silent. They kept walking for another block.

"There's something else, isn't there?"

"You read me well," she admitted.

"It's not hard, although normally, I'm not so astute with people."

"You know there are seven major prophecies," she began. He nodded. "We have other prophecies, some minor, some questionable, but there are others that are considered heretical or apocryphal."

"Our Bible has apocrypha too. Must be universal," David said by way of confirming her words.

She nodded without questioning. "I need to go back and do some research, but I seem to recall there's at least one about children conceived and born on the same day, an intertwined destiny of some kind. Being that one is yours, and you are a part of the major prophecies, I am beginning to wonder about things."

"What kind of things?"

"I believe in the gods, heaven, and hell. I do not question my faith. So, when all this begins to happen all at once, in rapid succession, it makes me think we're at an inflection point of history. The end of one era, the beginning of something new. And when it comes to forces like this, something new concerns me."

David let that sink in as it mirrored some of his own thinking, without too much emphasis on his faith. While he wanted to honor his family's use of biblical names, he wasn't a devout man, preferring to let the facts guide him. Here, though, was a moment when the facts and faith were intertwined, when people were being brought together like pieces being guided on a cosmic chessboard. Of all the people to respond to him, it was Reid, who happened to conceive a child on the same day as him and Betty. Of all the moments to be hunted, it had to be where the Kasperians could intervene. It all felt...destined...and that rattled him. Ponco's concerns only magnified his own thinking.

He needed something to count on, something rock solid. That meant science.

"Ponco, can you or Karuk take me to the surface so I can experiment with the APLS? Now that Reid is here, maybe he can help me perfect it."

She was deep in her own thoughts that it took a moment for her to process the request. "Why not down here? It's safer."

"True, but I need to be testing it in the conditions where it's expected to do the work and that means the surface," She nodded in affirmation, swiveled on her heel, and directed them back to the others. The moment of shared concern had ended as abruptly as it had begun.

It took about an hour or so to get things organized, but Ponco, David, and Reid were taken to the same spot where David made his fateful call. He wasn't sure if she chose the spot for convenience, familiarity, or to remind him of his faux pas. Either way, they emerged into a hazy, warm, humid day, overlooking an empty swath of forest. This portion of Yellowstone seemed to be always devoid of humans, the days in which Yellowstone was swarming with fruitful life eager to engage in the ancient game of dominance had been, for a while now, a distant memory of a different time which suited all concerned, especially David given the unstable nature of the APLS process. Given its purpose, it always had to be portable, hence it being designed on a board that acted as a backpack, albeit a heavy, drab, gray one. Miniaturization was always the plan after the process was perfected. He had a series of nozzles, injectors, and flexible mesh tubes attached to the output compartment, which drew its energy from the complex circuitry hardwired to the power source. There were only two sets for the current version of the device, one stored on a hard drive he carried with him, and one in a safety deposit box at an Omaha bank using his mother's maiden name.

As he was bringing the device to lift, beginning a cycling process that hummed and whirred with uninterrupted regularity, David scouted the area and saw a small cluster of withered plants, clearly dehydrated from the lack of rain and sunlight, thin with pale gray leaves. He recognized it as the Yellowstone Sulphur Flower, a wild buckwheat variety unique to the park. It adapted over the millennia to survive around the park's thermal areas, including Old Faithful and the four calderas. It disliked the shade so was clearly suffering, not likely to bloom as scheduled in the weeks ahead. A perfect candidate.

"I did some reading on the basics," Reid said, watching with interest. "You've based the APLS on abiogenesis..."

"What?" Ponco asked.

"Abiogenesis is the evolutionary biology that led to life on Earth," Reid explained.

"Right. Part of the theory is that non-living matter slowly evolved to organic compounds that, in time, began to self-replicate, giving rise to cell membranes. The interesting thing is that it happened with RNA molecules first, proliferating well before DNA molecules existed. The RNA's ribozymes can accelerate the chemical reactions that are critical for life."

"You know, David, not all of that was in English," Ponco said.

Reid laughed at that and said, "Linda says that all the time. She mocks me for using the scientific terminology without translation."

"Well, thingie is far less precise," David said.

"But it might help those of us who do not have doctorates in botany," the supreme commander of the Kasper military said sternly.

"Fair point," David conceded. "Let me try again. The building blocks of life need energy to sustain themselves. We need air, food, and water. Plants need sunlight and water. About a century back, we discovered that plants actually use a form of quantum physics to harvest light efficiently. When I read about that, it occurred to me that maybe the same process could be used with hydration, and when coupled with the light, would allow plants to thrive despite the initial conditions. In layman's terms, we need photosynthesis to happen unnaturally while still tricking plant life to believe it's happening naturally, similar to how medicine engages with our bodies."

She nodded. "That I understand. Mostly."

"Ok, you're still with me. The photonic light plants absorb is actually channeled in several directions. In quantum physics, we call that superposition; the photon can seem to be in several places at once. It actually chooses the most efficient path and location, photon by photon, going where it is most needed. Some of that is to sustain life, some of that is fluorescence, and so on. It samples pathways two or three at a time and chooses the one that works best."

"Plant life never lost its ability to self-replicate cells, to appropriately use molecular building blocks to spontaneously self-assemble into larger structures. My process actually provides some programming, nudging the replication toward hydration and sustained life. Once brought back from stasis, such as these plants, they can produce new buds or, in the case of grains or corn, new food stuff."

"Pretty impressive work," Reid said.

"And this will work given the current atmospheric conditions on the surface?" Ponco asked.

"That's how I spent the last six months, experimenting with just the right configuration to coax things back from the radiation."

A series of lights on one side of the device cycled from amber to green, signaling it was ready for use. "Have I solved it? The first forty-seven attempts were an exercise in frustration, but I had one iteration to try when things went to hell."

"What happens now?" she asked.

To demonstrate, David settled the backpack on the ground near the flowers and kneeled next to it. He took two of the nozzles that ended with needle tips and placed them into the pale green base of a particularly weak-looking flower. He entered a security code, designed to prevent anyone other than him from using it, which he added after his encounter with Holtzer. He then selected item "forty-eight" in the memory and set a countdown for ten seconds. Standing up, he pulled out his own tablet and began recording, to match the one Reid was making. If it worked, he didn't want to miss the moment.

The machine gurgled a bit, despite the lack of fuel, and energy was pumped through the hoses and into the stem of the flower. After a moment, the process ended.

"That's it?" Ponco asked.

"Not quite," David said with a smile, satisfied things got this far. "Now comes the tricky part."

"By tricky, you mean dangerous," Reid said.

"Yes. I have to complete the fusion process within fifteen minutes for this to be effective," David said.

"What fusion?" Ponco asked, concern on her face, her body growing rigid in anticipation.

"You know how powerful fusion can be, right?"

"In theory, not so much in practice."

"Hydrogen nuclei, that is, single protons, fuse together in a chain reaction to form helium nuclei, that is two protons and two neutrons, releasing a tremendous amount of energy in the process," Reid said as David focused on the tablet's readouts.

"That's the basis of your nuclear warheads," she said, sounding confident. David was disappointed she only understood the process because of its deadly byproduct.

"Well, I am using cell fusion. In this case, I am directing several uninucleate cells...cells with a single nucleus...to combine, forming a syncytium...a multinucleate cell. Cell fusion is vital as I manipulate the cells to maintain their specific functions, which is to revitalize and reproduce."

"So, the energy you're about to expend..." Reid began.

"Is considerable, concentrated into micro-bursts to stimulate the plant," David finished as he triggered the device. This time, there was a whine of energy buildup followed by the pock-pock-pock sound of energy traveling through the flexible tubes into the plant. On impact, the plant shivered violently but didn't explode, which had happened on the first dozen attempts. So far, so good, David thought.

"Now what?"

"We wait a little to see what happens," he replied, turning to power down the device as Reid maintained his focus on the pathetic plant.

"Impressive," Ponco said, causing David to twist about and stare at the plant. It stopped vibrating, but stood taller, prouder. The green stem appeared far sturdier, and the grayish leaves were whitening rapidly, yellow buds brightening, spreading out in clusters.

"You're getting this," David asked over his shoulder.

"Every shiver," Reid confirmed.

"I'll be damned, it seems to be working," David said to himself. "I've rehydrated a plant."

"Well, you know what they say, the forty-eighth time is the charm," Reid said with a laugh.

"Far faster than Edison," David said.

"Elaborate," Ponco said, refusing to take her eyes off the plant, which now appeared hale and hearty, brilliant in comparison with the ones adjacent to it.

"Thomas Edison, inventor of many things, including the lightbulb. He went through something like a thousand substances to find the right one to act as a filament to provide light from the electrical charge," Reid said. She nodded in understanding.

"Ponco, I will need to come back tomorrow to take measurements and repeat the process on several others to ensure this is not a fluke. But, this is further than I have gotten before, so it's most definitely progress."

"I'm sorry Betty wasn't here to see this," Ponco said. She saw the look on David's face as he realized the breadth of his breakthrough in real-time, knowing that years of his life had built up to this moment, this one absolute. But just as quickly as the look of disappointment flashed across his face, he pivoted to one of caution.

"With the energies I am using here, I wasn't going to take a chance on having either woman here," he said. He began powering down the backpack equipment but was controlling his inward excitement, the culmination of a lifetime, and the promise of actually being able to help others. That Betty and Linda were carrying new life just as he was perfecting resurrecting plant life suggesting a synchronicity that lent credence to the Maya prophecies, but also told him there were forces at play here that he would never understand. No matter how clever David thought he was in this moment, and especially when it came to botany in general, he had the dark realization that he was a pawn on some higher being's chessboard, who always believed until that moment he was a knight.

INTERSTITIAL
Council of Time

David Anders, thinner, graying, was writhing in agony as some sort of electrode jutted from his neck. Betty's charred corpse was cooling at his feet, not that he could see it, having lost his eyes the day before. Beyond a barrier, his tormentor kept asking after APLS technology.

"Next," Ponco said quickly.

"Ten degrees left," Karuk said. The pair shifted their direction and took a tentative half-step forward. Images swirled and eddied around them, a riot of colors and sounds hurt their ears and eyes, but as they settled their footing, things calmed, fragments of images slowly floated, assembling themselves into, at first, a kaleidoscope, then kept twisting until a singular vision appeared before the pair.

Now, they were looking at a far more bucolic image, but it was wrong. There was Linda Costa, noticeably pregnant, but running her hands over David Anders' shoulders, fingers playing with his chest hair. They were on a plush backyard patio, steaks grilling loudly so Karuk could hear the sizzle, the laughter of children further in the distance.

Ponco and Karuk exchanged confused glances because Reid and Betty seemed entirely absent from the family image. Karuk winced as Linda bit David's earlobe, her hands running inside his shorts.

"Next," Ponco said.

The swirl began anew. Karuk had lost count of the scenarios they had witnessed. How many lives had they lived? Scene witnessed, Karuk's mind was racing as the variable futures hanging in the balance. Ixbalanque's successor, Chichuaton, a severe middle-aged woman, had completed his work, and the RNS was no longer able to redirect its energies through the infinitesimal dimensions, but just the fourth: time. After successful testing, it was clear people could enter the chamber and be projected ahead in time. As the studies continued, a new team of scientists went to work determining if going backward was possible, opening up new avenues of study as others began hysterical debate over tampering with time. Even now, the High Council was embroiled in public debate over the appropriateness of looking ahead. Some argued the very act of seeing the future changed it, others worried that any alteration to the future would create splinter futures that would take the Kasperians off their proper path. Others argued going ahead would allow the people to avoid pitfalls, creating a more per-fect future for the people. Theorists considered if all versions of time existed simultaneously, then you could pick which one to visit but not affect.

The Vortex Chamber, as it was named, was constructed in a remote and lightly populated section of Kasper, deep in the Utah section of the city-state. Extra energy generators were devised to work independently so as not to threaten the existing society. These chambers held the equivalent of 24 nuclear bombs' worth of power, while the Vortex Chamber was effi-cient for what it was, Chichuaton had been delving into quantum folding technology to reduce the required energy stores so that the chamber could be moved closer to town without fear of a catastrophe. Further experiments were conducted in cycle until it was time to send a volunteer into the future to find the proper course for their people. A decision that would wait until the return of Ponco and Karuk, from the claws of the chamber.

No sooner did the next image resolve itself into the smoking remains of Kasper's palace then Ponco forced them onward to the next future. Karuk wanted to see what happened to ensure it didn't occur in their prime time-line, but she was horrified at the sight. She might be a warrior and a leader, but she was also a person who didn't like to see others suffer.

Ever since David Anders showed that the APLS worked, and could help the world at large, everyone from the King and Queen on down were confirmed in their beliefs that he was chosen by the gods and his destiny was a special one. That led to the fifth prophecy and the exploration of time.

The next image saw a dead David, no older than when they entered the chamber, being cradled in Betty's arms, Reid and Linda dead behind them. What made this particularly horrific was the sight of men and women in Seven Flags uniforms standing over the figures, clearly in the throne room.

As Chichuaton explained it, whoever entered the chamber would be cut off from reality. Time would pass in its normal fashion outside the Vortex Chamber, but the person or persons within would remain their age as their loved ones and friends aged. Time dilation was not something that could be altered, she told the High Council. But it was imperative for them all to understand what the right course of action was while they had the means. Was David truly the harbinger of a new age? Did the APLS save the world, and how might that impact Kasper? Did the radiation seeping into the air, ground, and water alter any of that? The next steps were going to be well-chosen ones, rather than happenstance.

David was being lauded for his next discovery, his sons cheering him on, each tattooed in the manner of Kasper. Betty was nowhere to be seen but the pain in David's eyes told Karuk all he needed to know.

The High Council debated with the public for a time before sealing themselves off with just the clergy to discuss what came next. After several weeks of discussion, the priests were dismissed and the Council spoke among themselves.

Kasper was overrun with tourists as the residents catered to them with gaudy souvenirs, the streets overflowing, debris everywhere. A Kasper that was unrecognizable to both Karuk and Ponco flashed before their eyes. The city looked more like a relic of the United States than the glorious haven that the two had stepped away from to enter the chamber.

Finally, Hadwin summoned Ponco to his private chambers for a discussion. It had been decided, he told her, that one person would enter the chamber and see the futures, determining which one was to be followed. That person would step into the chamber and no one was certain, not even Chichuaton, how much time would pass during the visit. For the person within the Vortex Chamber, it could be hours or days, and outside, it would be years or decades. He made it clear that the person to enter the chamber had to be someone trustworthy, someone well-versed in the prophecies, someone who could be clear-headed about what needed to be done. To her surprise, Hadwin explained they wanted her to turn command over to Karuk and be that person. He was making it sound voluntary, but both knew there was no choice being offered. She was childless, and her siblings and parents understood what sacrifice was all about. Would she accept this role as a volunteer?

Kasper was being bombed, a great tear in the ground above the city showered dirt and bombs in equal measure. Buildings were on fire, others obliterated. People ran over the corpses to try and find shelter. A society that survived millennia was on the cusp of annihilation.

To Hadwin's surprise, Ponco refused the assignment. That is, she refused to do it alone. She insisted Karuk be at her side as he had been all along. Together, they would evaluate the potential futures, together they would support one another and be there for one another should something unforeseen occur. She hadn't asked him prior to the conversation, but she knew in her heart she couldn't do this without him. The presider nodded once, sealing the deal. They were given a few days to sort their affairs since no one was certain how long they'd be gone. There were prayers and anointing from the priests, family meals, wills, and other matters to sort.

Kasper had grown, becoming something more than it was, a gleaming, chrome-covered city no longer hidden by a layer of crust, but exposed to the light. The streets were filled with people who seemed safe and happy. But, as they looked more closely, the people were Caucasian, Black, Asian, Indian. Not a single Mayan or Native American could be seen.

The day before the process was to begin, they met with the Anders and Costas, talking over matters, reassuring them that the acting supreme commander would look after them just as well, if not better, than they had. David had reported that the various flora the APLS had been tested on were all thriving and things were looking good. Karuk handed each of the pregnant women small gifts, earrings blessed by the priests. They each hugged him in return, certain they'd see them soon enough.

Kasper was abandoned. Buildings were decaying, streets pock-mocked with potholes, no power illuminated anything, so shadows filled their vision. Where had all the people gone?

The King and Queen were there, in a rare appearance away from the palace, to see them enter the Vortex Chamber. Hakan held his hand over each, giving them a personal blessing. They bowed in return, then looked at the scientists and engineers to ascertain all was ready for them. Given the energies about to be used, their outside guests stayed away, much as David and Reid wanted to witness the event for themselves. The chamber wasn't particularly large, about ten feet by ten feet, with three-inch-thick walls made of the special steel alloy, designed to contain the energy should there be a surge. The conduits from the device that channeled the energies from other realms were vibrating slightly, creating a rumble. The air itself was charged with anticipation as Chichuaton and the others gave the signal that all was ready. The pair walked in, Ponco taking charge, and the chamber door was closed with pneumatic seals. Standing in the bare space seemed anticlimactic to Ponco, but the feeling was fleeting. The lights dimmed then throbbed, colors beginning to swirl around them. Within a minute, the first of countless futures revealed itself and the journey was underway. Karuk's hand slid into Ponco's as Kasper faded into view.

People were dying on the streets of Kasper, boils and pus marring their oblong heads, blood oozing from elsewhere. Dark-suited figures gathered the dead like refuse, placing them in containers that wheeled through the dying city. Ponco's mouth dropped when she noted the next body collected was an older, gray-haired version of herself.

As she gasped, the image faded and was not replaced. The swirling ended; an audible drop of power output could be heard. Their journey, it seemed, had come to an end. For that, she was most thankful, but then her mind was filled with new matters, starting with: just how long had they been in the chamber? She knew the glimpse into the fourth dimension would keep them from needing food or sleep or bodily functions. She was suddenly very tired, and her body was demanding food and sleep simultaneously. As a result, she was not feeling at her best as the door seals began to hiss. Looking over, it seemed Karuk felt much the same way, a hand rubbing the back of his neck, trying to stay awake rather than sleep on his feet.

The doors spiraled open and the room's light was soft, welcoming. Stepping into view were two people she did not recognize. The young man was tall and broad, with curly, light brown hair, a set smile on his handsome Caucasian features. He was clad in native clothing, thick, broad bracelets on each wrist, no visible tattoos. Beside him was a curvaceous woman with medium brown skin, long black hair, bright eyes, full lips, and a ready smile. She wore a beaded green tunic and a deep gold skirt that reached her ankles. They smiled in recognition and behind them, a series of engineers and technicians were busy looking at the readouts regarding the chamber's cycling down. She felt a pang of disappointment as there was no one familiar there to greet them. What had gone wrong?

"Ponco, Karuk, welcome home," the man said.

"Hi, come on out," the woman added. "Here, you need this." In her hands now were two bright red ceramic mugs, each filled with cool water.

Karuk and Ponco exchanged concerned and confused glances, their minds still processing the futures they'd seen, trying to guess how much time actually passed, all while fighting to stay awake. They slowly moved out from the chamber, noting the equipment had altered. Some devices were familiar, others brand new. Some time had definitely passed, more than days. She guessed a year or two, eager for the truth. She accepted the mug and drank deeply, enjoying the coolness as it went down her throat, flooding her body, giving her fresh energy.

"You have questions, so do we," the man said.

"Who are you?" Ponco interrupted, since he seemed ready to plunge ahead.

The woman elbowed the man and shot him an "I told you so" look. She renewed her smile and jabbed a thumb in his direction. "That's Noah Anders and I'm Isabella Costa. We certainly know who you two are."

"You...you're...what, twenty?" Ponco asked, amazed and alarmed at just how much time had passed.

"We're eighteen," Isabella told them.

"Eighteen years."

Karuk gaped and looked back into the chamber. "We were in there for eighteen years?"

"Where are your parents?" Ponco asked, feeling once more the supreme commander.

"They're all alive and on their way," Noah confirmed. "We were getting indications your magical mystery tour was coming to an end and we happened to be on monitoring duty."

"Clearly, we have much to discuss," Ponco said.

"Who's in charge?" Karuk asked.

"That depends upon who and what you're asking about. Chichuaton is still running the lab, although she's nearing retirement. King Hakan and Queen Dakota remain on the throne, but who knows for how much longer. Shándíín Alba is the current supreme commander of the military."

At least some things hadn't changed.

"Your home has remained intact, untouched. We're going to escort you there, let you sleep, and eat, and then we can all catch up," Isabella said, reaching out a reassuring hand, which gripped Ponco's bicep. It was a surprisingly forward gesture, but the young woman didn't seem to think twice about it.

"Not yet!" bellowed a rough voice. Shuffling into view, right hand gripping a beautifully carved walking stick, was a withered version of Chichuaton. She was flanked by two garbed in white, red crosses on their shoulders, devices Ponco didn't recognize in their hands.

"Chichuaton," Ponco said.

"You just spent nearly two decades inside the fourth dimension, that has to be recorded. We'll be fast," she croaked. With a gesture, the others went to work. Each approached the time travelers, waving the handheld devices in front and behind, from top to bottom. Both stood still, understanding the need, but her knees were beginning to demand rest. Next, the two took blood samples from finger pricks and withdrew, almost hiding behind Chichuaton, who watched with a curious glint in her eyes.

"How do you feel?"

"Exhausted," Ponco said.

"Hungry," Karuk said.

"And extremely overstimulated, so we need to go rest," she added, walking toward the teens, who had been quietly watching the proceedings.

As they emerged from the science center, which seemed to have grown during the time they were away, the figures of four friendly faces emerged from the darkness. Without waiting for any ceremony, Betty flung herself into Karuk's arms, reuniting with the man who had saved her life all those years ago. Karuk, realizing it was decades for her, embraced the moment with an endearing tug as the two shared the moment. Ponco then saw

David, who stuck out his hand, which she tossed aside and then embraced him as well.

"Eighteen years, the time dilation and energy consumption we needed to sustain you, was nothing short of a miracle," Reid Costa began, always running to the science to break up awkward moments.

"The things we saw, the futures that might await us, they are not what any of us are prepared for," Ponco retorted in a tone that hinted at the future missions they would need to face. As they stood there in silence for several moments, Karuk finally spoke up.

"So, kids?"

"Yeah, can you believe it, it's been a hell of a time here. We will catch you up further once you've rested. You both look like we did when we arrived here. Me shot and David exhausted," Betty added as she moved to allow her friends the space to get the rest they needed.

As the four of them said goodbye to their reunited friends, the quartet entered a bullet-shaped silver vehicle that hummed to life as they settled. Without directions provided, the vehicle propelled itself forward and at a good speed. Much as Ponco wanted to see how Kasper had endured the intervening years, the moment she settled in the leather seat, she fell fast asleep as a fleeting thought passed by: where was Sasha?

CHAPTER 19
S.T.A.N.

Year: 2121

Sasha awoke to find himself once more strapped to an operating table. He ached from head to toe, certain he had not only broken fingers and toes but at least one rib. There were contusions and aches everywhere, except maybe his eyelids. They scraped away at him, taking samples, even one of his jade tooth pieces. He was devoid of his jewelry, which made him feel more naked than the lack of clothing as he lay awaiting the next indignity.

Their leader kept asking the same questions, sometimes whispering in his ear, sometimes shouting. Often, the questions were accompanied by slaps or punches, each new bruise an unwelcome tattoo, a reminder of the suffering he had had to endure. Time lost meaning as his containment unit was always highly lit, accompanied by loud noise, something akin to music, but more mechanical and less melodious. What water they gave him was the only pleasurable thing about the experience, as it was cool, clear, and refreshing. He was given some bread, some vegetables, and broth, which tasted like chicken.

When he was left alone to recover, the intervals when it was just him and the noise, he contemplated his options, certain he would die before divulging anything, but he didn't want to die. He felt he hadn't lived yet. Sure, he'd been a good soldier, trained hard to impress his parents and his sisters. But, he also had to be perfect. After all, she was the Nacom, and anything less than perfect would bring disgrace to her and their family name. Instead, he awoke earlier, volunteered more often, and made certain he would bring pride to the family heritage. And where Ponco was always serious and stiff, he allowed himself to go in the opposite way, seeming not to take life too seriously. She was a military strategist, reading about great Maya wars and fighters from the surface. He read more broadly, devouring histories of the great nations, so each brought different perspectives to most matters, which certainly enlivened the rare family meal.

He hungered for a proper meal.

Time was not on his side. Sooner or later, they would tire of the torture and the questions and would have to make a choice: death or permanent confinement. Neither were optimal or desirable, so he needed the third alternative, the one thing Ponco always sought when making decisions. Life was rarely binary, she said more than once. Her troops and commanders had that drilled into them as they prepared for combat. While life in Kasper was peaceful enough, the military doubled as emergency first responders, while engaging in quarterly war games should circumstances involve them engaging with the surface world. Small squads were taken into the forests of Yellowstone National Park and let loose to engage one another in a contest to protect a prize or steal the other team's prize, often a small carved stone idol, easily hidden or protected. The first time he stepped onto the surface, he hated the way the air tasted but loved watching the native animal life. He had plenty of chances to observe them as he hid nestled on a thick tree branch, keeping watch on his team's perimeter.

Now he had to observe himself and his surroundings and find a way out. He was often allowed to walk from the small room, down three corridors to the operating theater. There, he was strapped to an operating table, and from there, he was poked, prodded, and interrogated. Those three corridors were, then, his only chance at freedom. He'd begun counting steps, noting where security cameras were installed, how many doors on each side of each corridor, trying to make out the signs, hoping there'd be some clue as to an exit. However, no bright red exit sign was visible, which did not bode well. Yesterday, though, came a clue in the form of one door opening at the T-juncture of the corridors, revealing it led to stairs both up and down. He memorized its location and determined that was his best option. He had the patience to endure and wait for his moment.

He also noted that the operating room had a diagram posted by the doors, indicating where the occupants should go in case of emergency. As he was taken to the room once more, he craned his neck to see the image and noted the red dot indicating the very door he needed. A path was presenting itself.

However, there was the matter of being groggy and awaking from yet some other procedure that left his abdomen sore. Probably some other biopsy as the doctors were analyzing his body much as they would a lab rat. The mind was clearing and he took an assessment as to which digits and limbs could be counted on and which ones would fail him. It seemed they preferred messing with his left side, which was fortunate, as he was right-handed and only had two broken fingers. Then there was the matter of running around the facility naked and weaponless, neither of which would do.

His tormentor, the man they called Holtzer, was not present this time, so he was in the hands of the medical staff, with minimal security, unlike the four who normally flanked the red-faced, unhappy general. That meant that this was his time. He needed to act now, not wait.

"Ah, you're awake. How do you feel?" asked a plump nurse, not making eye contact but poised to add his response to her tablet.

"I need a bath," Sasha said.

She sniffed and agreed.

With a nod to the other nurse, he was unstrapped and asked to get to his feet. Today, there were just two guards ready to escort him back to the tiny room with the blaring noise that might be music to someone's ears, not his. He'd come to appreciate the operating room, if only for its relative silence and dimmer lighting. The pair seemed of average height, older than him, but not by much. One was a woman with buzzcut red hair and a malevolent stare while the other was a man with a pock-mocked face, dark eyebrows that formed a single line over heavy-lidded eyes. Each had a gun of some sort, both holstered and, he noted, strapped. Key cards dangled in a bunch on their hips, and their brown and green uniforms did not have name tags.

"Off you go, see you tomorrow," the nurse said cheerily.

"Oh joy," Sasha said and got to his feet, shaking off the last of the anesthetic. Their doses didn't last long, which he considered fortunate. As he stood up, he over-dramatized how dizzy he felt, gripping the table for support. The soldiers watched impassively, waiting patiently for him to right himself and start walking out of the room. He delayed it, head tilted down but eyes sweeping the space and assuring himself of tools that might be available. Nothing presented itself in the room nor in the empty corridors. Hand-to-hand it would be, then, not something his battered body was looking forward to.

He straightened himself up and took a half-step toward the door, seeming to test himself, then he took several steps and nodded he was ready. They fell in behind him, flanking each side, as the three left the operating room. The tile floor was cold, but he clenched his teeth so as not to shiver. Every fourth or fifth step, he staggered a bit, shaking his head theatrically, then strode forward, never making eye contact with his escorts. The door he needed was just up ahead.

About ten feet from the door, he took a step, staggered, and then fell to one knee, forcing them to react. The woman bent down, roughly grabbing his right arm, while the man watched. He yanked down, dragging her off-balance as he kicked upward with his left leg, catching the man in the chest. He bounced off the wall as the woman fought back, her right arm reaching for her gun. Sasha rammed her midsection with his head, pushing her against the wall, keeping her hand off the holster. She let go of his arm and clenched her hands into a single fist to pound into his back, but he rolled, a stab of pain from the fresh incision reminding him how hurt he was. Still, he focused on the lesser injured parts of himself to do the work.

The man had recovered and reached for him, figuring brute force over weapons was all he needed. Sasha had sprung up from the roll and head-butted the guard's nose, hearing a satisfying crack. He whirled and swept his leg at the woman, tangling her up and forcing her sideways to the floor. He jumped up, landing with both feet on her stomach, causing her quite a bit of pain, so when she reached for those legs, they were easily kicked aside. He turned his back briefly toward her and fell backward, his right elbow crushing her windpipe and causing her to gasp for air.

He then ducked a swing from the man and held out his right hand, fingers as straight as he could make them, knowing it would really hurt, and jabbed at the man's neck, but he unexpectedly danced backward, avoiding the thrust. Instead, the man finally began to reach for his holster, but as he flipped off the strap, Sasha rushed him, once more thrusting him into the wall, his fingers now poking at his eyes. With flat hands, he then pounded the ears, disorienting the man, and followed up with open-palmed slaps to keep him off-balance. He heard the woman gasping for air but also struggling at her belt. He reached for the freed pistol, kneeing the man in the midsection, and the gun slid free. It hurt like hell to bend his fingers around the butt, and there was a jab of pain that traveled up his arm as he pulled the trigger, but that was followed by the satisfying electrical discharge that flooded the choking woman, rendering her dazed or unconscious. Either way, she was done.

He backed away from the man, kicked him in the groin, and then fired again, sending the man sprawling to the ground. Sasha then grabbed his head with both hands and with a cry of rage, twisted so the neck snapped.

With little time to spare, he yanked off the man's boots, then tore the pants as they came off the still legs, and finally the jacket. Clutching them to his aching chest, Sasha opened the stairway door and chose to descend as recommended by the emergency evacuation map. He paused at the first landing to struggle into the ill-fitting clothes, then he shoved the pistol into a pocket and continued downward. At the bottom, there was a door marked "north" and he tested the handle. It was unlocked, and then he eased it open, to find himself facing a parking lot. It stretched on as far as he could see. His eyes searched for the best route, then he heard the alarm klaxon sound and his choices narrowed.

He darted out and hugged the building's wall to avoid the cameras, inching quickly toward the corner. He looked around to see the parking lot's edge, which led to a field with picnic tables and beyond them, trees. He'd have to make it to the trees and hope to hide until he determined which way to go. The alarms seemed to grow in volume, and he heard faint shouts from personnel on the other side of the building and in the vast parking lot. Crouching low, he darted from the building to the first row of TAVs, scooters, bicycles, and other vehicles. He didn't dare try to steal something, too sore to pedal far. He worked his way between cars, row after row, zigzagging his way across to the edge. Once he got there, he paused to listen. There were shouts and some engines starting up, but none near him.

He took several deep breaths, prayed his body would hold out, and then, still low to the ground, he dashed to the picnic tables. He then fell to his sore belly and slithered between the tables, or under them, pausing to check for anyone's approach. The green and brown uniform and setting sun combined to give him some protection, and the further away he moved from the building, the safer he felt. After the last table, he rushed for the trees, which were tall, thick, and sturdy-looking, even if their leaves were curled, brown, and crying for sustenance. He let himself get deep before slowing down and then sought the thickest foliage, which was to his right, about ten yards away. As he got there, he saw it would take some doing to scale it, but it offered somewhere for him to rest before figuring out where to go next.

His fingers refused to obey, protesting with electrical shocks of pain as he gripped the trunk and scrabbled to reach the first branch. Once he wrapped his arms around it and swung his legs up, he was more easily, but no less painfully, climbing up until he was some thirty feet off the ground. With the hazy sun now kissing the horizon, the shadows would help hide him and he leaned against the trunk, breathing hard and collecting his thoughts. His war games taught him things like how to look for directions, how to use the foliage for clues, and some general idea of where he was. Prior to leaving with Karuk, the team had studied a map, not just of the park, but of the territory all around it. As a result, he had some idea where the Seven Flags nation was, and he recognized that it would be a long walk back to his homeland.

There was a chill creeping into the air, but Sasha took comfort in knowing he was free, the pain would soon stop, and he could find his way home.

Year: 2139

The next few days were a blur of activity and conversation, more conversation than Ponco or Karuk were seemingly accustomed to. They slept for fifteen hours and were then so ravenous, as word spread of their return, they were enjoying the feast provided for them courtesy of the King and Queen. Everyone decided they deserved twenty-four uninterrupted hours to rest and recover from their journey. The price for that precious time, though, was going to be a thorough debriefing on both sides.

Each was left to their own thoughts, processing what they had endured before speaking of it to one another. Neither wanted to turn on their computer and see what the world of Kasper or the surface was like. They were merely thankful that the horrific or distorted futures they saw had not yet come to pass. She considered the riotous variety of future timelines witnessed, some far more vivid than others. Her exhaustion meant none invaded her dreams and she had awoken feeling rested and even better after a long bath and putting on fresh clothes. The ones she wore in the Vortex Chamber, she realized, had been caked in dried sweat.

To maintain focus on the mission, her first priority, she dared not find out what had become of her parents or whether Sasha had ever been found. That would have to wait until later.

Their respite over, the time had come to be reunited with Kasper, starting with those most invested in their report of what was witnessed. As she ate and then rode the bullet car to the palace, she tried to order and prioritize what she had witnessed, as well as a methodical list of questions that began with what role they were to play in the grand scheme of things. She and Karuk had spoken little, each left to their own thoughts, knowing there was time to talk when circumstances allowed.

They arrived and were taken to a different space than the throne room. It was a vast chamber that was as nontraditional as the throne room was a tribute to the glory days of the Maya people. Gleaming screens were embedded in the walls, a row of touch interfaces beneath them. There was a mammoth round table in a donut shape, the center with a low-lit circle on the polished, smooth floor. The current configuration of the High Council were seated along one section of the ring, followed by the sextet comprising the Anderses and Costas, two empty seats, and then the much-older King and Queen. She didn't recognize a single member of the council and was thankful when introductions were made. Over the intervening years, it appeared that Native Americans were now welcome to sit on the Council with the Maya, a form of progress she approved of. Their leader was Yolotli, an attractive Maya woman entering middle age and she served with younger males, Aaapo and Yiska. From the Native American tribes, they were joined by Minda Black Deer, a middle-aged woman; Nawkaw

Dreamer, a large, broad man; and Tohopka Arrowkeeper, lithe with piercing eyes; and Enola Echevarria, a woman with very long, jet black hair, held in place by a traditional beaded headband.

Ponco then noted how time had treated the monarchs. Hakan Miwok, already a senior eighteen years earlier, now looked like a living husk, the jowls sagging further, the exposed hair whiter, but the eyes took them in, still aware. Dakota Miwok had aged much better, a handsome woman entering her senior years; there were gray streaks, but more artifice than natural. Lines curved around her mouth and lower jaw, extra earrings where she had limited herself to four per ear in earlier times. Their children—the successors, Mika, Titus, and Hiawatha—sat to the King's left. They were older, resembling one or the other parent in different ways. She never had gotten to know them, but soon one or more would rule, and that posed new questions for her.

As they entered, David and Linda both rose from their chairs, attempting to greet them, but their spouses placed hands on arms to remind them decorum was in order, so they nodded and beamed. David and Betty seemed to have aged gracefully, some lines here and there, a touch of gray in their hair. She'd put on some weight, but it filled out her once-thin fame. Reid had gone white-haired, deep lines running vertically on both sides of his face, while Linda seemed fuller, her hair colored an interesting shade of purple. The monarchs nodded in welcome and waited for them to sit before things got underway.

"We are most gratified that you have returned to us unharmed," Queen Dakota said to start the meeting.

"Our doctors report that nothing seems to have harmed you. Your trip through time apparently has left your body unchanged. No anomalies, no diseases, nothing out of the ordinary," a man said from the council's side. Introductions would have to wait, it seemed. But the negative report was welcome news.

"What did you see? Hmmm?" Hakan said, cutting off his wife, an eager expression in his eyes.

Ponco had prepared for this and recounted as examples several scenarios that were most vivid in her memory. She sketched out each one, showing divergences from the here and now. As each negative story was recounted, the expressions around her darkened. David and Noah seemed the most distressed, and at that moment, she saw how much alike they appeared. If anything, Noah was a more intense version of his father.

"Something seems to have...soured...time," Karuk said as she wound down the descriptions. "We saw nothing happy, no positive outcome. Something will happen or is happening that makes all futures seem bleak."

"Or has happened," Reid said.

Ponco looked over at him, noting the wrinkles that had started to crowd his features. There was a haunted look of some kind on his face.

"It is, as it should be, as foretold," Dakota said, regaining everyone's attention. "As you know, David Anders seemed to fulfill the third and fourth prophecies. His APLS device was indeed an important catalyst to help the world recover and we have been instrumental in helping him safely apply it. But, as the world should be on the road to recovery, blight remains. We fear something altered that and that brings us to the fifth prophecy."

Ponco shifted her thinking to try and recall what was contained in the fifth prophecy but was spared when Linda, who was aging gracefully, asked for detail.

"There is a clear reference to a divergent path taken by leaders who ignored the will and needs of their people," Dakota said.

"Certainly not us," the King stated defiantly.

"No, certainly not," Ponco agreed. "Leaders on the surface world focused on their self-interest rather than universal issues."

"Things like the North American drought," David said. To Ponco, he just seemed older, tired, and maybe a little haunted. The years seemed to have been hard on the scientists.

"And the Alliance bombing," Betty said. She remained petite, maybe a little more fragile in appearance, but still attractive and attentive.

"Their greed and ambition changed the world for the worse," Dakota continued. "Those wielding power were universally distrusted, institutions began to crumble, partisanship and anarchy began to spread. The tighter your Alliance..."

"Not my Alliance, never," David snapped. Clearly, this was an exchange he and the Queen had had before.

"The tighter the Alliance clutched, the more people wriggled through their fingers. A global crisis was exacerbated as regime after regime fell and the people hungered. As written in the Books of Chilam Balam, the drought was predicted, but so was salvation."

"What exactly did it say?" Betty, ever the teacher, asked.

Dakota looked to a member of the council, a middle-aged woman who appeared more Native American than Maya, certainly without the elongated forehead. The woman, who seemed prepared, quoted: "Drought will arrive everywhere, but the face of hunger will not be ravenous. Because the water in the canals will offer bread beyond the mountains. Beyond the rocky hills, this time brings frightening hunger, but not everywhere."

Ponco at first looked confused then realized there was a reference perhaps to the APLS, which David must have perfected.

"It was limited to the descent of the serpent at Chichén Itzá," Black Deer added. "That is hard to trace not knowing the great serpent's path."

"The prophecy went on to describe the state of the people. There has been a descent into primitive and impulsive behaviors as people fought for food and clean water. The social orders, forged through centuries by myriad cultures, dried and withered, blighted by the drought it seemed."

"But the life we have created over the last eighteen years is sustainable." David posed.

"Yes, it may be," said the Queen, "But, wasn't it you who told me all those years ago, that if I had the technology to save the surface world, that I should."

David recoiled at this, realizing his own hypocrisy.

"This all sounds terrible," Betty opined.

Dakota nodded, miffed at another interruption, which to her dislike had become custom in her halls, but proceeded. "This ushered in a period of darkness, but we're told is also an opportunity. The prophecy says this is the time we are liberated from our deficiencies and can give free expression to our true desires. We emerge from the darkness into a new era on a new Earth. Even with the Seven Flags nation now more firmly entrenched, this era should provide more fruits for us all."

"How?" Linda asked. "Are you suggesting David is also some sort of messiah, leading us all into the light?"

"Not at all," Dakota said. "All systems based on fear which affect our civilization, will transform simultaneously with the planet and humanity, to take a new step toward the reality of harmony. David brought us to this point." She paused, looking at the six from the surface. "You are here now to ensure this happens."

"How?" Ponco asked.

Dakota looked over at Reid, who nodded and took over the conversation.

"Since you stepped into the chamber, I worked with Ixbalanque and then Chichuaton. With their teams, we managed to further harness and refine the RSN energy, no longer confining it to the Vortex Chamber and no longer being restricted to only looking ahead in time."

"You've perfected time travel, backward and forwards?" Karuk asked.

"Yes. We call it Stabilized Temporal Autonomous Navigation—an AI time machine, omnidirectional through time and space," Reid said with pride.

"I just call it S.T.A.N.," Linda said.

Ponco looked at her.

"Well, Betty renamed APLS, apples; I just shortened that mouthful to S.T.A.N.. It's a name, short for Stanley, a common name for white folk," she said. Reid made an unhappy face but said nothing, so that aspect of their relationship had not changed and by now was ingrained into their long marriage. It oddly comforted Ponco.

"Are you suggesting we go back in time and change something so this dire world does not exist?"

"From what we can tell, and from what you have confirmed with your own visions, something has interfered with a harmonious future. It is believed that the Alliance's nuclear attack was never supposed to happen," David said with obvious distaste.

"And this...S.T.A.N....works?"

"It has passed all the testing, Ponco," Reid said.

"Is there a plan?"

"It is still forming," Queen Dakota said.

Ponco looked upon her Queen, unsure of the tasks that awaited them, but knew of the perils she saw in the chamber. The evil that festered in the conquerors who lived above the ground, and how their actions would affect her people. With a rare empathic moment, Reid caught on to his friend's concerns.

"Mostly because we need to target an exact time and place. We need to provide coordinates for the machine to work with, a North Star of sorts," Reid explained and then looked over at his daughter, who was smiling broadly.

"As it happens, I have been working with my father's notes and theories and may have cracked that," Isabella said brightly.

She seemed too young to be doing such advanced work, Ponco thought, but she was born and raised in Kasper, exposed not only to its wonders but her father's advanced work. She was proving to be an impressive young woman, that was certain. The son, though, seemed poised to act despite not having a target. Throughout the discussion, he fidgeted, shifting in his seat, uncertain what to do with his hands.

"You have something for us," the Queen prompted.

"Soon," she replied.

"The sooner the better," Noah said. "We have to fix this, fix this world, this timeline."

"We all understand that. We will find a way to send a collection of you back to June 2121 so you may repair the damage, restore the way things need to be," the Queen said.

To Ponco, June 2121 was months ago, but to them, it was eighteen years. This was a military mission, and she began thinking about what it would take to prevent a triumvirate of rogue nations from unleashing a wave of nuclear missiles. It seemed an impossible task no matter how many people were brought back in time.

"Who do you intend to send back?" Karuk asked.

The Queen looked about the room, eyes seeming to skip over those from the surface and slowing to sweep up Ponco and Karuk. She was once nacom after all, and this Shándíín Alba had supplanted her. She was now expendable and so, too, was Karuk. But she knew the odds were exceedingly against just the two of them.

"There must be people who were there then, who understand the forces at work, who can help," David said.

Reid picked up the thread. "Ponco and Karuk are great soldiers, but know little about the surface world, don't know the geopolitics as well as those who lived through it do." Ponco considered this and agreed it made sense, but that would mean there would be present and future versions existing in the same time and place and wondered if that was even possible.

"Agreed, Reid Costa. At least one of you four should accompany my nacom," the Queen said, and hearing her title gave Ponco an honorable salutation.

"Uh uh," Linda said. "It can't be Reid. And, no offense, neither can it be you, David. You guys live in your labs, heads in the clouds, or whatever. Betty and I lived in the real world, and it should be one of us."

"Or both," Betty said firmly.

"There is no way I am letting you go back there and take that risk without me," David said.

"You're welcome to come, but follow my lead," Betty told him.

"You three will not be going without me," Reid said. "It'd be lonely with you gone."

The Queen looked around, patiently waiting out the banter between them, obviously used to it over time. Time. It used to be linear, one moment followed by the next. In the last few days or years, she supposed, time suddenly changed all meaning. It now meant past, present, and multiple futures. If this worked, they'd be going back in time to fix something that would create a new future timeline, one that was supposed to be the real one, one that would replace this one. It posited there was a future they hadn't witnessed over the last eighteen years relative time. Ponco tried to process it all, trying to keep her feelings of unknowing about her brother buried until the mission was over, her need to learn what had become of Sasha ate at her, but she knew that knowledge either good or bad would cloud what needed to come next. These thoughts circled her mind, silence was between them all until Karuk spoke up.

"Your Majesty, if it were to be Ponco, me, and our four friends, that would be a start, but we would need additional support, younger and stronger people to help protect them." In other words, he thought that David and Betty and Reid and Linda were too old to do the fighting that might be required. Or the climbing or carrying or whatever the mission might require. He didn't know the current troops, and the ones she might still recognize were probably past their prime by now.

The other factor was Holtzer, David thought to himself, unsure where the opening would be, and how he could sanitize the situation from another time if they went back. Could he right a wrong that has been festering for so long?

"Queen Dakota, I have helped design and construct the portable S.T.A.N. units. I need to be there as well should something go wrong, and the units need repairing. I will not lose my parents to the past," Isabella said. She then pointedly looked at Noah.

"Of course, I am going too. I need to fix the timeline and let my parents actually live a little," he grumbled.

"You both understand that the new timeline might be one in which you do not survive or exist?" the Queen asked.

"People assume that time is a strict progression from cause to effect, but actually from a non-linear, non-subjective viewpoint, it's more like a big ball of wibbly-wobbly, timey-wimey stuff," he said.

The Queen blinked. "Timey-wimey?"

"It's a quote I taught him from an old video program," Linda said as she laughed.

"I'm hanging on to the non-linear, non-subjective stuff and hoping for the best," Noah said.

"So be it, Noah Anders. If the six of you and my trusted soldiers are willing, we will correct a cosmic wrong," she solemnly said.

"Prepare yourselves for the ride of a lifetime," said Hakan, whom everyone thought had dozed off but clearly hadn't.

• • •

As it happened, the S.T.A.N. team of engineers needed a week to use Isabella's computations to determine the fourth-dimensional coordinates to send the party backward. In between tests, the young woman oversaw the fabrication of mobile S.T.A.N. devices that maintained a quantum tether to the mainframe machine that would remain under 24-hour supervision for the duration of the mission. Linda helped customize the outer casing of each wrist device to make them appear fashionable, with touches to help make them look less than identical, which would arouse suspicion.

Ponco exercised and trained, getting to know her successor, Shándíín

Alba, a Navajo descendant, and finding she approved of the no-nonsense man. She and Karuk worked together, honing their teamwork, sharing their thoughts and concerns about the mission. In doing so, the burden of truth fell to Karuk who first learned, both sets of their parents had died peacefully in the intervening years. Sasha's saga left them concerned, but it would have to wait until the mission was over. They allowed themselves one night for prayer and grieving, then she put family matters far from her mind. Once again, the mission became her sole focus. It was a talent Karuk envied more than any other of hers, as he needed more time to process the losses than she was willing to give him.

Whenever possible, she also took time to visit with Linda and Betty, seeing her friends grow older into the proud mothers they'd become. Betty had steeped herself in Kasper lore, learning passable Mayan, while Linda remained the sarcastic wit, volunteering with various groups to contribute to the society.

Their children had made them proud. Noah's determination, fearlessness and innate curiosity for life made him distinctly different from his mother or father. He was not a scientist or a teacher, very much unlike either parent despite his physical resemblance to David. Isabella, on the other hand, was brilliant like Reid and gorgeous and lively like Linda. She remembered the two mothers talking about an arranged marriage, but no such union had occurred as yet. Still, they grew up side-by-side and had an unshakeable bond she hoped would not be tested too much while back in time.

The eight met every other day, reviewing maps of America and the Seven Flags territory, which had started expanding outward at the fringes of the Dakotas. David and Reid pointed out key locations while Ponco marked where the Kasperians had located supply caches for their scouting parties. The data was stored on tablets, each biometrically secured to ensure no one else could access them. There was a tutorial on how to use the mobile S.T.A.N. devices with Isabella making it clear they were delicate and had limited lifespans, so each use had to be a calculated one. Then there was a discussion over weaponry. Noah wanted the sonic vambraces, but Ponco refused, not willing to possibly let their tech be discovered in the past, further altering time. The arguments about time and space went on for hours, what could be changed, what couldn't, what would create paradoxes, and were those even possible.

Instead of debating for the rest of time, they agreed to take multipurpose tools, made from the lightweight Kararien steel. Karuk carefully showed them the retractable blade along with a screwdriver, small electric charges, and other tools that might come in handy. He decided against the macuahuitl, preferring a one-meter Kararien staff. Ponco had decided on a shorter rod along with a belt that secreted darts made from the same metal, sharpened like the blades on the macuahuitl.

10 Days Later

Finally, over dinner one night, Reid and Isabella announced the work was done and they could leave the next morning. She even giddily said the royal family would be on hand to see them off, which felt very ceremonial. As a soldier, Ponco needed orders, not a fancy send-off. The last time they saw the two of them off, it proved an unpleasant experience that haunted her dreams.

But, the following morning, as they assembled before a new and improved version of the Vortex Chamber, located in a lab built just for the S.T.A.N. project, the King and Queen arrived, early no less, to see them off. Reid and Isabella consulted with the stooped figure of Chichuaton, finalizing the coordinates and energy discharge required.

"I know you understand the importance of this mission along with its dangers," Queen Dakota said.

Everyone nodded.

"When you come back, the world you see will have changed in ways you will note, both great and small. I hope it's a better world, one in keeping with our beliefs. A new age is due to this world and its people. You are my agents of change and I wish you all success."

The chamber opened and Ponco stepped in, feeling as if she only entered the first one a short time earlier. But seeing the older forms of her friends enter, it was clear how much time had passed. The teens entered last, standing near each pair of parents. She met the Queen's eyes and nodded that they were ready.

"King Hakan, will you do the honors?" Chichuaton asked, gesturing to the controls.

He shuffled over and was shown which series of buttons to press. One by one, the King's gnarled fingers followed the directions, and the machinery hummed to life, building in power. Familiar color swirls began even before the chamber door was closed.

As it sealed itself, things sped up, the sound grew sharper, and there was a twisting feeling as vertigo seized them for several heartbeats. Ponco felt her breathing go from shallow to heavy, her heart pounding, her breakfast threatening to make an appearance. Her steel will forced all things to remain as they were and she clenched her fists, nails biting into her palms to focus her thinking. This was most unlike the last journey, and she didn't like it, glad she would only have to endure it on the return trip.

CHAPTER 20

Let's Go Back to 2121, It'll Be Fun

I sabella was the first to throw up. But she wasn't alone. The trip backward in time was literally a gut-wrenching experience. Folding time onto itself through quantum variance manipulation was not like going to a theme park. Their insides were rearranging, trying to align with the dimension they were in, let alone the street where the S.T.A.N. chamber lay had yet to be built.

Thankfully, this was a sparsely populated section of Kasper, so their appearance out of thin air caused no alarms. Ponco oriented herself to the space and made certain everyone had time to recover from the journey.

"Whoa," Noah said as he placed his hands on his knees, looking about.

"Everyone okay?" David asked. Nods and assents reassured Ponco, until she squinted in the distance and saw a moving vehicle rushing toward them. She recognized its markings as those of the very military she was, in 2121, commanding.

"We are about to be greeted, which is unexpected. Everyone stand firm and let me do the speaking," she told them. No one argued, for which she was thankful.

Soldiers emerged from the troop transport, a gleaming red and orange steel vehicle that ran on magnetic tracks buried under the street. They gaped when they saw their nacom and immediately stood at attention.

"What brings you here?" Ponco asked.

"Our radiation detectors showed an anomaly, and we were dispatched to investigate," the woman said.

"Do you have any further details?"

"No, nacom," she said. "However, we were asked to bring interlopers directly to the High Council for questioning."

She cocked an eyebrow at that. "Are we interlopers?"

The woman hesitated at the question but replied, "Of course not. I know you and your husband, but who are your companions?"

"They are with me. But it appears our matters match. I need to see the High Council. Bring us." There was no quibbling about the command and the woman nodded, then gestured for the people to follow her. Everyone piled into the vehicle, and the driver, someone Karuk knew, gave everyone a friendly smile then conducted them to the palace. Along the way, the teens whispered back and forth regarding the changes that had occurred by noting things absent or different. It grew wearisome but understandable. Ponco surreptitiously glanced at the dashboard readouts projected on the windscreen and confirmed the S.T.A.N. device worked as programmed, which was incredibly reassuring.

The eight were escorted into the High Council chamber and were announced by the door guardian. They entered single file and Ponco was pleased to see the familiar councilors in the very seats where, a day earlier, she recognized no one. She nearly stumbled in her path when she also saw the Council was meeting with Ponco and Karuk, their 2121 selves. Astonished expressions were rippling across the room along with a murmur. If the High Council overreacted to David's slip of the tongue, this even more inexperienced collection of people would totally panic, so she needed to gain control of the situation.

"Let me speak and all will be made clear!" she shouted, her voice quelling the murmuring.

Hadwin raised his left hand, signaling the room was to be silenced.

"Explain," he commanded.

In short strokes, Ponco provided an edited version of events, sharing that the RSN experiments led to the creation of S.T.A.N. and how time travel allowed there to be two Poncos and Karuks in the chamber. She introduced her fellow time travelers, explaining that they were soon to become residents with Kasper, which set up a new wave of noise as the concept of Caucasians living among them was heretical.

Itzel asked the inevitable. "If time travel is indeed possible, and I applaud our engineers for devising the means, how can there be two Poncos and two Karuks existing in the same space at the same time?"

"Wibbly wobbly, timey-wimey," Noah muttered, only to be elbowed by Isabella.

"This actually works with quantum theory," Reid said from the back of the crowd. Hadwin gestured for him to step forward to explain. As he moved, Linda said sotto voce, "Small words."

"Let me start by establishing there is no such thing as objective reality. Instead, let us suggest that time is fluid, malleable to a degree. An object, or in this case, a person can exist in two places at once. We call this superposition. There is a photon, which exists on the vertical and horizontal axis simultaneously. Now, let us suppose your chief scientist Ixbalanque is studying a photon. He sees it spinning vertically on its axis, so it is now fixed as far as he is concerned. However, let us say his assistant is in a different room, also studying the same photon, unaware that Ixbalanque has seen it vertically, so it remains in a state of superposition."

Ponco appreciated the deft way Reid slipped in Ixbalanque's name, helping to confirm her wild story.

"The power we had to focus to even get the RSN to work nearly took Kasper down trying to achieve," Itzel jabbed. While believing it was possible, the mere presence of these duplicates did not define absolute certainty in his mind that they were who they said they were.

"But doesn't the existence of two Poncos and two Karuks in the same place at the same time alter time? Doesn't it create a paradox?" Xoc challenged.

"It does. Our being here is creating a new timeline forward, one we intend to assure is the right one. We are existing in a closed timeline curve; we cannot stop ourselves from being born. But, our choices going forward affect the sequence of events."

"Are you sightseers, then?" Gabor asked.

"Not at all, we've come back to ensure the right path is followed," Ponco explained, starting to feel a bit out of her depth. This was not her forte. Karuk could explain better, but she was nacom to them and they would heed her words.

"Why are you here, then?" Hadwin said.

"This man," she began, gesturing toward David, "this man is the answer to our prophecies."

Again, there was a hubbub of noise until Gabor spoke over them. "A Caucasian? Maya prophecies are for Maya. What is this nonsense?"

She heard Linda lean over to whisper to Betty, "I never did like this bastard."

"Not nonsense at all. This man has technology that will address the third and fourth and appears to be connected to the fifth as well," Ponco said, shouting down the crosstalk. "If you do not believe me, bring us the High Priest, bring us Chimalmat, mother of giants. She will help me make you see the sense of it all."

Hadwin gestured to the door guardian, who hurried out to fulfill the task.

"The people above are ready to destroy one another. Are you here to prevent that?" Gabor asked, a sly smile on his face. "Just you eight against eight billion. I admire your pluck."

While she wanted to rip his tongue out, Ponco stood her ground as her contemporary self came closer to examine her. She stared at the earrings, the clothing, and her hair. Finally, she said, "Where exactly are you coming from? You seem no different than I am today."

Ponco sighed. "I am from seven months from now, having traveled from 2121 to 2139 in an early version of the RNS time travel machine. Now, I have come back to this point."

"What did you see?"

"Enough to convince me that we are doing the right thing." They locked eyes, reading one another, so similar, and yet her earlier self, even by months, had yet to learn of all that was portended. Hadn't lost Sasha to the Seven Flags. She would be willing to risk more alterations to save him from what was to come, but didn't dare, given his role in the future.

"That is for us all to decide," Gabor said, turning to Hadwin and smiling superciliously. "Is that not right, councilor?" Gabor, who distrusted all progressive ways, seemed to be feeling the power of the moment.

Just then, there was the sweeping of robes against the rock floor, the familiar jangle of jewelry. In walked Chimalmat, mother of giants, High Priest of Kasper; tall, regal, with jet black hair, blazing blue eyes, neck, wrists, and ears entirely covered with rune-covered jewels. Her teeth bore jade and silver jewels, each in a different shape. Tall for a Maya woman, she looked down on all, eyes always seeming to judge.

"Why have I been summoned? I do not easily come at anyone's beckoning, even yours, Hadwin."

"I know, great priest, but we need a learned voice to help guide the conversation and help us with decisions," Hadwin said.

"You govern the politics, I govern the soul on behalf of the gods," she intoned. But her voice trailed off as she noticed the duplicates. "What devilry is this? What has Xibalba sent here?"

"Therein lies our issue," Hadwin said. He tried to call on Reid to help explain but seemed unable to recall the name. Ponco genuflected before the priest and then repeated her fantastic tale. When she finished, she concluded with, "Karuk and I saw dark futures. None good for the people of Kasper. As nacom, I am to protect them, and it is my judgment that we be allowed to go to the surface and prevent man from destroying man. It follows the prophecies and we need everyone to agree to this."

"Can it be true that a surface man, not a Mayan, is responsible for salvation?" Gabor sneered.

Hadwin shushed him and glared. It felt reassuring to Ponco that the honey-tongued councilor held little sway no matter how hard he tried to stir things up.

Chimalmat waited for silence and the attention to return to her. She was accustomed to being the focal point, demanding it even from the King and Queen, who acquiesced to her. "Many of our prophecies have been with our culture since its founding, others were developed in more recent times, thanks to increased access to the stars. Our astronomy was excellent long before the rest of the world and remains that way. As a result, my acolytes have refined the studies. As some of you may know, with the monarchs' blessing, we are writing new interpretations of the prophecies, based on our increased understanding."

"I can therefore take comfort in seeing people who have borne witness to the transgressions that have blighted our future, threatening our life as we know it."

"Are you suggesting that this man, David Anders, truly is a focal point?" Hadwin asked.

Chimalmat nodded once. "If what the future Ponco says is true, and there is no reason to doubt the nacom—" at this, both Poncos nodded their thanks, which brought a chuckle from both Karuks, which brought out more titters from the others until the High Priest stared them back into mannered silence.

"As I was saying, yes, David Anders from the surface will bring us prosperity once matters are attended to."

"What matters?" David asked.

"The blight Ponco and Karuk experienced is because of an event that predates today. The atomic attack you say you are here to prevent is a piece of a larger puzzle. This attack should never occur and happens because a world leader lives when he shouldn't."

As the words settled over the crowd, Ponco glanced at the people from the surface, who knew geopolitics better than she could. She cared little for the doings above, knowing enough in order to protect her people.

"Are you suggesting a president, prime minister, dictator, or premier alive today, 2121, should have died?" Betty asked in confirmation. "Who and when?"

"How far back?" Reid asked.

The High Priest said nothing, letting the guests work it out for themselves. Ponco suspected that, like her, the woman knew little of the surface nations but couldn't tell them that. It was something they were going to have to work out. Ponco had an appreciation that the High Priestess was less about providing the critical information, but more a spiritual fuse used to ignite situations like these where all hope loomed in the shadows.

"These refined astronomical studies, is that something I can get a copy of?" Isabella asked.

"For what purpose?" Chimalmat asked, eyes narrowing with suspicion.

"After we leave here, we're going elsewhere in time, and the more information, the more data we have, the better we can restore the proper flow of time," she said. This was a bright, impressive young lady, Ponco noted. If she was able to help her father with the S.T.A.N. project, it made sense she would be so gifted.

"How do we know which is the right time, the right person?" Betty asked. "I will not be responsible for someone's death."

"I don't mind getting my hands dirty, but getting blood on them is something else entirely," Linda added.

Chimalmat nodded at that and said, "That would be wise. No, the dark thread from your future to our today is something I believe can be traced. It involves a complex examination of star alignment. I have sent for my chief astronomer to come and explain."

Ponco blinked at that, having never noted the priest activating any device. This was one formidable woman that maybe she underestimated in the past. Her contemporary self seemed to pick up on this as well, for which she was thankful.

"David, what do you think..." Betty began but fell silent. Ponco realized this man, the center of cosmic events, had been very quiet during the discussion. The pained look in his eyes gave her a sinking feeling in the pit of her stomach.

"Oh," Betty said, a look of realization in her eyes. "Do you think so?"

"Maybe you can enlighten the rest of us?" Gabor prodded.

"If I am a focal point, then we have to examine my actions," David began in a strained voice. Ponco noticed her Karuk was paying attention as if he knew what was to be said and was sympathetic.

"My actions, well, all of our actions have consequences. You pick book A to read instead of book B will not disrupt time, but choosing not to act may do so, may upset the course of events." All eyes were on him, no sound evident in the chamber.

"In our native timeline, in our 2121, five years earlier, I was working with the United States military, using their cutting edge equipment to try and perfect the APLS, my method of restoring life to dead plants, a chance to grow food in barren areas. I saw hope in a broken system, I believed the APLS system could cure world hunger, and with the drought in America, the desertification of Africa and Asia, there was such a growing need for food..."

"I was asked by a member of the military to join him on a mission, using the APLS not to provide life, but to take it. The crazy scheme would have me take part in the assassination of the premier of the Korean nation in Asia."

"And you refused," Chimalmat said, not asked.

He nodded.

"Yes, that would be the kind of action that would have repercussions, changing time, poisoning the future."

David looked at his feet and Ponco's heart went out to him, recognizing what was about to be asked of him.

"For the future to fulfill the prophecies, to ensure our forthcoming new age, one single life must be taken. Is that not a fair bargain?"

"Spoken like a barbarian," Linda said, then checked herself. The council glared at her, Chimalmat turned to shoot daggers at her. The woman said "shit" and looked away, not entirely apologetic. Betty, whose neck snapped back at the shock of Linda's digression, gave her a look of mild approval, while both Reid and David seemed less sure of that perspective.

"The Maya are a proud people, but we are warriors. Death is as much a part of our life as is our textiles, as is our music, as is our prayer. To you, that may be barbaric; to us, it is the way of things," Chimalmat said coldly.

"Yes, that is your way, but not ours," Betty said, stepping forward, shielding Linda from the glares. "What is being asked here comes with a price. David wasn't willing to pay it then and maybe shouldn't be asked to do that now." For us, life is precious, regardless of whose it is. Would you go back and kill a baby Hitl…" She stopped herself as the words came out, realizing the answer to her own question would contradict her intentions. With a soft nod, she stepped back, retreating into the sea of arms beside her.

"It has to be done," Chimalmat countered.

"I agree," David said softly. "We have to go back to 2116, and I have to find a time and place to do this. It's the only option, isn't it?" His question was aimed at the High Priest, but Hadwin nodded first, speaking for his people.

Betty reached for her husband, drawing him into her thin arms, and hugged him tightly. Ponco looked away, unsure how to act in the moment of great understanding that had come over David.

After several silent moments, Hadwin spoke up. "You came from a time ahead, which confirms our people endure, and for that I thank you.

But your journey doesn't end here. You have a hard road to travel, and the sooner it begins, the sooner peace can arrive."

In other words, leave before your presence causes more trouble, Ponco thought. She didn't disagree, as she was discomfited at being in the same room with herself. At least in 2116, the mission would be on the surface and there was no chance of seeing her younger self.

At that moment, the doors opened again and a man hurried in, handing a tablet to Chimalmat, who nodded in acknowledgment. She held it out, aiming her hand toward Isabella. The young woman briskly walked toward her and accepted the device.

"Wow, an antique," she said, then caught herself. "Thank you, High Priest."

"Use it wisely," Chimalmat told her.

"We thank you for your belief in us and our mission," Ponco said to Hadwin and the priest. "If we can return to our starting point, we will take our leave of this time and place."

"I will arrange that," her other self said and hurriedly left the room.

Within an hour, they were reassembled and Isabella went from person to person, ensuring the wrist devices were properly programmed for the new location, a destination she worked out on the ride, further impressing Ponco. The ride was a silent one, everyone left to their own thoughts. Ponco had killed before, a result of a riot that threatened to get out of control, and Karuk had also taken a life. But these other companions, this act scared them, especially David. It was everything he stood against, and the weight of one more revelation seemed to force his shoulders down. He leaned into Betty but withdrew from the others. Noah sat on the other side, sitting ramrod straight, being there physically but not emotionally. Something was strained between father and son, she realized, something she missed earlier.

The group moved with haste from the vehicle, watching it vanish from sight on its return to the city center, Ponco finally spoke.

"Is everyone ready? We now know how this will affect us. That should help us. Once we get to our destination, we can survey the situation and form a plan."

Nods all around, although no one seemed particularly happy at the prospect of having their insides twisted into knots before going off to kill someone.

Reid cleared his throat and all heads swiveled toward him. From a pocket, he withdrew a fistful of papers and handed them to each member of the group. Noah and Isabella held the paper as if it were something foreign.

"Wow, old school," Linda said, looking over the folder document.

"We're going backwards, and we may not have access to technology, that is, electronics-based technology," Reid said. "I needed to make sure everyone had easily-referenced directions to properly use the devices should we get separated."

"On paper," Noah said, clearly unfamiliar with the printed page, nor was he happy about it.

"A user's guide," Betty said approvingly as she looked it over. "And written so we non-technical folk can use it."

"An idiot's guide," Linda quipped.

"Be serious for a change," Reid said sharply. "If we get separated, this may be your only means for using the S.T.A.N. device to get you home safely. Yes, it's on paper and written so you can follow it. We have to be ready for anything."

"Thank you," David said with a reassuring smile.

"Are you all done?" Ponco asked, clearly unamused. "This is nothing to joke about, nothing to make light of."

Somberly, everyone nodded in agreement, she waited a long moment to be certain before commanding S.T.A.N. A sharp look around, and with a look fit for a time traveler, Ponco eloquently said, "Engage."

CHAPTER 21

Let's Do the Time Warp Again

Year: 2116

Once everyone recovered from the transit, thankfully in a less messy manner, they looked at their surroundings. Isabella had wisely placed them in Yellowstone, above Kasper, and away from prying eyes. David was in no particular rush to fly off to Asia and somehow kill Bin Yun-Seo.

"Let me get this straight," Noah said. "We're here to kill some man in Korea, which will reset time on its proper path. What if something goes wrong? What if an even worse timeline is formed? Do I vanish?"

"Hard to say," Reid said. "You being here suggests your birth is a fixed event. But yes, we could fail and something even worse happens, such as the attack coming earlier in retaliation."

"How do we know we've chosen the right action? If we kill this man, how do we know time is corrected? Jump home and see?"

"I've been studying the files I received and I may be able to understand how they knew the timeline was wrong and how 2121 was not the right place for us," Isabella said. "I hope to have this figured out when we need it."

"That's an awful lot of hoping going on. Maybe we should just act and get on with it?"

"Noah, we're talking about taking a man's life. It's not like cross-checking your opponent. He won't get back up," David snapped. "We don't just kill so easily."

"None of us do," Karuk confirmed. "Yes, we're a warrior culture, but that has been more in name and in games than in reality. Sealing ourselves off from the world has also meant a singularity in purpose, no divisions, no wars. We haven't fought a genuine enemy in 1200 years. But it's instilled in us, it's why there's still an army."

"Let's get practical. How do we actually get to Korea and get close enough to this Bin Yun-Seo to kill him?" Linda asked.

"I'm already near him," David said. "My younger self."

"You're just going to convince him to do what you refused to do?" Noah challenged.

"No, I won't talk to myself. God, that's weird."

"There are younger versions of all of us," Betty said.

"Trust me, you don't want to confront yourselves," Ponco said.

"I dunno. The younger me around now was pretty hot," Linda said. She shot Reid a look and he quickly confirmed the claim.

To David, there were logistics to deal with. Exactly where was Bin? What was his security like? Where was Holtzer, who would cackle with glee if he knew his mission goal was being accomplished by the very man he grew to hate for being a "coward"? They'd need cash, contemporary IDs, maybe even different clothes. That would take time and planning, which suggested they'd need somewhere to stay, a vehicle or two for the eight of them.

Noah had stalked away from them, studying the sky. His mother walked over and leaned into him.

"The sky's blue," he said. "I've never seen it like that."

"The air is clean and fresher too," Betty said. "I was teaching in Virginia at this time. Your father was working for the Pentagon, commuting."

"I was taking extension courses," Linda recalled to Reid, who nodded. He was still a professor and researcher in Santa Barbara, his life the least different.

They listened to the birds chirping and the stealthy movements of some forest creature they couldn't see. But the sound fell into a familiar rhythm; not animals, but human footsteps. Betty looked over at David in alarm, and he felt his heart pick up the pace. He reminded himself it was the past, the bombs hadn't fallen, society was still intact at this point. It was probably just hikers.

What he didn't expect was to see himself and Reid emerge from behind a collection of trees. They looked to be roughly the 2139 versions of themselves, but something was off. Neither walked with pride or confidence. These were not happy men.

Then David saw his doppelganger's eyes. They were bloodshot, dark-rimmed, and so incredibly sad. Something had happened to these men, something terrible, and it was terrible enough for them to travel back in time. Being here and now was definitely not a coincidence.

Their approach was heard by the others and as Linda turned and saw them, she said, "What the actual fuck...?"

Reid stepped forward, joining David as they stared at themselves. Noah and Isabella stayed with their mothers, although the four of them caught the attention of the men, whose shoulders seemed to sag even further.

"When are you from?" David asked himself.

"2141," he said.

"Something happened," Reid said to the others. His double nodded.

"You come back here to alter the timeline and things changed," the future Reid said.

"Was Chimalmat wrong? Was the dark thread she saw not supposed to be pulled from the fabric of time?" David asked, sounding foolish with the metaphors.

"Time splinters," future Reid said.

"Alternate futures," Reid confirmed. "Our actions cause ripples. One such future is the one Chimalmat says is the right one, but others are created. It's like the study of the photon. I see it vertically, you see it horizontally, but it's the same photon."

"The quantum state vibrates, so it depends on who is looking at it and when," future Reid said. "So basically, we are confirming a multiverse exists..." both Betty and Linda said at the same time.

"Enough, please," David's future self interrupted. Both Reids fell silent and he briefly wondered how Linda endured the scientific talk all these years. No wonder she was a good social worker. Patience.

"In our future, you have killed Bin, so his successor does not join the Alliance. The Chinese try to destabilize the elections, which ignites a civil war that sees China invade on behalf of 'peace' in the region. They effectively annex the country, then partner with Russia and Iran and Sudan to strangle sea trade. The UN tries to ram the blockade and the missiles go flying."

"When?"

"2123," future Reid said.

"But those two years change everything, ravaging our world. I found Reid like you did, and we find Kasper, but in those two years, the Alliance has managed to overrun the USA. Their shock troopers eventually find Kasper. Ponco was a valiant leader, but inexperienced, and couldn't hold off the invasion."

Ponco looked startled to learn of a future self having failed at a task that was her whole life.

"But the RSN and S.T.A.N...." Reid asked.

"Both exist, obviously," he told himself. "And as Chimalmat studied the prophecies and the stars, she said this was not the right time. You were going to change events and make things worse, not better."

David blinked. The prophecies were the core to the Mayan society and had guided their actions and now his actions. How could they be right in his world and wrong in another? It hurt his head, but clearly, these future selves had it far worse off. He noticed how both men eyed the women, sad yet hungry looks.

"Betty and Linda," he began.

"They died in the assault," his future self said. "Early on."

"So, if we were to let Bin live, what would happen? What future emerges? The one we left is said to be the wrong one."

"Once she told us the way things were and somehow saw that you were coming here and now to change our past, creating this terrible reality, we had to come back and stop you," future David said.

"Just wait," David said, putting a hand to his head. He furiously thought about all that had transpired and what was said. Obviously, whatever they chose to do in 2116 was some sort of inflection point. It would erase the future he left and rewrite it and fulfill the prophecies as they were meant to be. But a different Chimalmat, in a different future, read them differently and said the 2116 assassination was not to happen because their dire future would be created. Could both be right?

"Doesn't the act of you being here suggest time is malleable?" Reid asked everyone around them. The others had stood in a semicircle, paying attention but not participating, letting the Reids and Davids sort things out. The only one not really paying attention was Isabella, who seemed to be focused only on the old tablet.

"Divergent timelines happen all the time," Reid said.

"And our choices now seem to suggest even more splinters will occur," his other self continued.

"Is David still a focal point?"

"Yes. His actions, his APLS, all seem to suggest he is spoken of in the prophecies."

"So, does it become their choice?"

Both Reids paused to look at their respective Davids, and he hated the feeling of being in the center, of being the one who had to make a choice. He looked at his future version and saw how lost he seemed, so terribly sad, and it looked as if he was along for the ride, having given up. He tried to imagine how the man felt, having lost Betty and still being in the center of the maelstrom. This future David, at least, didn't kill Bin or be asked to kill him. He still hated the idea that one resolution to this conversation would mean still taking a life.

"It can't just be our choice, because there are consequences," he said. "We have to consider the prophecies and the potential futures."

"May I?" Ponco interrupted, stepping toward them.

The four men looked at her expectantly, clearly hoping someone would help decide this for them.

"You..."

Ponco cocked an eyebrow.

"You died, quelling an insurrection," future David told her.

Karuk, startled by this statement, watched a tear run down his right cheek as David saw Ponco swallow hard, keeping any other emotion to herself.

"Karuk and I spent eighteen years in the Time Vortex and we saw so many futures, none good. Listening, it struck a chord. I think I saw this reality, one of the wrong ones, one of the blighted futures we are here to prevent."

"Think? That can't be good enough to make a decision," future David said quietly. "We need certainty."

At least he agreed with himself, but where could this certainty come from? What evidence could convince the group, starting with the four of them and then the others? He watched his other self, saw how he gazed with loss and longing at Betty, recognized himself in Noah.

"They live. Betty and Linda live. They live and give us children. Look, my son talks about time like it's made up with great regularity while our Reids stick to scientific theories, the quantum field, the theory of everything and so on. But forget both extremes. Look into your hearts, look at these people. They're alive. We have children. How can that be the wrong reality? Where we come from has to be a stronger, firmer reality, one that needs fixing, but your reality seems so lost. So, let me ask you both, look into your hearts. What do they tell you? Forget empirical evidence, but think about your souls."

The time-traveling David of a broken future stared upon his less damaged self in amazement and wonder, wonder leading to the quintessential question. It might be antithetical for any scientist to say that David was still a botanist by training, someone focused on life in all its forms. He wanted them to feel that, feel that life wins out and that they prove the point.

The future Reid and David looked at the women, who bravely met their gazes, sympathy in their expressions. Then, their eyes went to the teens, sizing them up, imagining that they were their children.

His other self said, "You have to fix this."

"We do."

All parties stood in silence for what seemed like hours, but for this group of explorers, time was just as relative as the leaves on the ground.

"Reid, we have to let them do this," he told his lifelong friend. Reid continued to study Lisa and Isabella, sharing looks and emotions. Finally, he nodded.

Both men withdrew their version of the portable S.T.A.N. devices, David noticing they were bulkier and far less elegant than the one Isabella helped design, so her influence seemed important. As they programmed them for a return trip, neither hurrying, it struck David that neither man wanted to leave. He could understand that. The air was fresh, a hint of fall in the air, sunlight and blue sky peeking through the tree canopy. All was peaceful and calm.

Betty and Linda seemed to sense that too, and walked over to the future incarnations of their husbands. They hesitated just a moment, then each placed kisses on their cheeks and walked away quickly. He could hear the men breathe them in deeply, savoring the moment.

Finally, without another word, they activated their S.T.A.N.s and the air started to shimmer around them, similar to heat waves, but they glowed with growing intensity. The waves enveloped them, making their forms increasingly indistinct until, finally, they faded from view, the colors fading slowly.

"Freaky," Betty said as she took in the moment, a dawning comprehension of her new normal striking her in a way that while having already experienced the sensation of time travel, witnessing it provided a whole different perspective that put her in a state of awe.

"Seeing them disappear like that, the technology, the movement, it's different when you watch it than when you do it."

"Amen," Linda said, already striding over to Reid and hugging him.

Betty walked to David and peered into his eyes. "I'm not going anywhere," she reassured him. He leaned low, kissed her with intensity, reveling in the physical contact, the reassurance her body promised him.

Isabella cleared her throat, interrupting the moment. The couples parted and turned toward her.

"What Chimalmat interpreted as the 'dark thread' from 2139 to today, 2116, was determined by her astronomers, following celestial alignments, as the Milky Way Galaxy rotated and moved further away from its origin point. What they did not take into account was the gravimetric alterations to the galaxy as a result of two black holes colliding further back in time. It caused changes to star positions and threw off their calculations."

Reid was fascinated as the others tried to keep up. David grasped the basics but was waiting to hear why this was important.

"I have made several adjustments, positing where the stars involved in this thread would have been otherwise. From what I can tell, the thread stretches further back. It's subtle and easily missed unless you know what you're looking for."

"And you do?" her mother asked.

"Yeah, I think so," she said, sounding confident, which reassured David. "As the stars are adjusted in my schematic, I see where they began to go off-kilter, creating this darkness that rippled through time. It's like a pebble hitting the water. The first concentric circle is tiny, but each ripple grows."

"Where does this pebble hit?" Reid asked her.

"I am still triangulating, but it appears to have occurred in the 19th Century."

"Wait, does that mean, if I killed Bin, things may not have been righted? Are we destined to live out the other timeline's horrors from this action, or does our timeline with our elements create new aberrations depending of a larger set of circumstances?"

"Perhaps," Reid said, following his daughter's way of thinking. "It's as if you put your hand in the pond and stopped the widest circles from radiating outward, but the inner rings remain."

"Got it," she said. Her eyes went wide as she studied the readout. "I'll have to double-check my work to be certain, but it seems the event that brings us to where we are today began on March 1, 1843."

CHAPTER 22
Above The Ground

"Run this by me again," Noah asked.

"Let me try, son," David said, cutting Reid off. He knew how to talk to his son, who was as adept with a lacrosse stick as Isabella was with quantum sciences. "The Maya studied the stars, using some of the most advanced techniques imaginable some two thousand years ago. Their entire faith system was based on the 260-day calendar, a critically designed pace that allowed the civilization to thrive, and with each iteration, the calendars of the time lasted for hundreds of years until a new era was to begin. There was quite the panic about that back in 2012 from what I was told. Anyway, as they developed their astronomical research after relocating underground, they refined their prophecies, and adjusted their faith.

"It seems their prophecies were based on a celestial alignment that was altered hundreds of years ago, that they missed or couldn't compensate for. As a result, when we were told to go to 2116 to correct the past and put the future on its proper heading, it was only partially complete. Now, it seems, we have to go further back."

"This thread is what, then? How do we just go back, fix it, and get on with our lives?" Noah reacted, frustrated with the task ahead.

"The alignment of the stars happens from time to time, and during those alignments we can observe and measure certain phenomena. It seems the Maya traced this alignment back through the years, matching it with existing prophecies and divine readings. Much as Greeks saw the stars and formed constellations by tracing lines between stars, the Maya traced lines to divine the order of things."

"So, it's like a matter of faith," Noah said.

"You'd be surprised at how much faith plays a part in most cultures. In this case, yeah, it looks like their faith and prophecies are closer to the mark than most societies."

"We go back to 1843 and do what? Did something happen back then?"

"It did," Betty said. She'd consulted her own tablet, and being the teacher, managed to sort through the histories to pinpoint the event that seemed to be the pebble in time. "Are you familiar with Morse Code?"

Noah shook his head. "Doesn't mean a thing."

"Me either," Isabella said, frowning at not knowing something, which amused David. All eyes turned to his wife as she shifted into teacher mode.

"Samuel Morse lived in a time when electricity was something new and everyone was figuring out how to harness it. He was far from alone nor was he the first to determine the simple truths of electricity. The pathways for signals to be transmitted from one another and the durability and strength provided through the use of copper wires. Where he succeeded ahead of others was determining with Leonard Gale that a series of repeaters would allow the signal to be sent further than it could on its own.

"He successfully lobbied Congress for funds in 1843, and on May 24, 1844, transmitted the words 'What hath God wrought' from the basement of the Capitol in Washington to the B&O Railroad in Baltimore. It changed communications forever."

"Huh."

"What are we supposed to do?" Linda asked.

"It seems that is the most significant event on that date, so that suggests that is the pebble in the time pond rippling forever outward. We need to stop the pebble from hitting the water."

"Stop Morse?" Linda said.

"No," Reid said. "Somehow stop Congress from authorizing the funds, delaying the project."

"And what would happen if Morse doesn't transmit on that date?" Noah asked.

"Once it is proven effective, it transforms America and then the world.

Now, suppose the telegraph is delayed," Betty prompted.

"Information is slowed, people continue to rely on what—horses, trains, boats?" Linda said.

"Right. It could possibly result in America not falling so quickly into civil war or something else," Betty said. "We won't know until we find out."

"You want us all to go back to 1843 America?" Ponco asked. "Karuk and I will stand out as anomalies."

"We can't let them go alone," Karuk insisted.

"I know the era best, so I have to go," Betty said. David saw where this was going and interrupted.

"Let's cut to the chase. I won't let Betty go alone; Noah won't let us old folk go unprotected. Isabella will be there to make sure Noah doesn't do anything she thinks is dumb and therefore her parents will want to come along. Ponco and Karuk insist they have to watch our backs."

"Do you have the first idea how to stop Morse? Or Congress?" Noah challenged.

"No one does, nor did we know how to go assassinate Bin. I'd rather kill a telegraph than a human being," David said.

"Okay, before we go back, let me update the tablet," Betty said. She then accessed the Wi-Fi, finding some information she needed. As she fussed with that, David approached his protectors and friends.

"What do you think?"

"Honestly, it all sounds kind of insane," Karuk admitted.

"If it is the will of the gods, it must be done. I saw those futures, David. They should not be allowed to come to fruition. You saw for yourself how devastating that can be. We have to try, and we'll figure out what to do when we get there. At minimum, we know Kasper is still there, and I can probably convince the High Priest or King we're not a threat. Maybe they have information or gear we can use," Karuk concluded.

"That's something to be thankful for," David said.

"You know I'm not an idiot, right," Noah said as the others moved away. The hurt and anger in his voice disappointed David.

"Of course."

"I was just never interested in science, or academics I guess. I'm good with my hands, fast, and really love lacrosse. So maybe I don't speak quantum or can't quote Angelou or Gorham like Mom does, but I'm not an idiot."

"No, you're not," David confirmed, placing his hands on the teen's shoulders. He could feel the tension amidst the muscles. He was definitely feeling like the odd man out when, in a few minutes, he might be the one to most easily fit into the earlier era with the Maya being the odd ones.

"I never thought you were an idiot. I never wanted you to be anything you didn't want to be. I wanted to push you hard in science, so that you could understand everything I loved, but I want you to be happy. I love that your interests are your own. That has never been a point of contention for me."

Noah looked at his father with love for the first time in many years, a mutual feeling of love washing over the men as an understanding of who they each were to one another came into focus for the first time.

"I've data scraped what I could find on the era," Betty said, snapping both the tablet and the men back into the group conversation, gently taking the device and stowing it in a pocket.

"And I've figured out coordinates to Washington, D.C., 1843," Isabella announced, joining them.

"We're really doing this, huh," Linda said. She had fully bought into being an agent of time.

"Safety in numbers, Mom," Isabella said. She then went from person to person, insisting she do the coordinate input for safety. No one objected and David was pleased to see bonds of trust forming all around, especially Ponco and Karuk, who hadn't seen the kids grow up around them.

"Stand by," Isabella said, taking a position between her parents.

"If you think the air is clear here, wait until you try pre-automobile air," Betty told her son.

He squeezed her hand.

"Engage," Isabella commanded.

The air shimmered around them all, as before, but just as reality faded from David's vision, he heard a loud pop.

• • •

The group appeared behind some low brick buildings, weeds and refuse littering the narrow space. A black cat scrambled away from the sudden arrival of people. Ponco took a deep breath to clear her head but gagged when she inhaled something fetid. Horse manure. Then she heard the whinnying of horses and the steady clip clop of many horses on the other side of the buildings.

She then heard the sound of someone vomiting. Each transit through time, at least one was severely sickened. This time, it sounded like Linda, who was being comforted by her daughter. She looked over to Karuk, who had his hands on his knees and was controlling his breathing from the transit. With Noah holding Karuk's shoulder for balance, Ponco's eyes locked with Betty as the moment revealed itself.

"David!" Betty shrieked.

Ponco's head whipped around to where he was standing when they left 2116. Betty was standing over the empty space where her husband had stood. Noah and Reid rushed over, the older man crouching to examine the area for any evidence of their friend.

Isabella instantly had her tablet out, syncing it with the portable S.T.A.N. on her wrist. Her fingers slid and jabbed across the screen as everyone continued to cautiously look for him, without giving themselves away. After all, they didn't have period attire and would stand out in public. As Noah and Betty started looking over at Isabella with increased intervals, her actions grew more frantic by the second. Finally, she slowed and looked up, eyes blurred with welling tears.

"I... I can't find any trace of him," she choked.

"Wha.. how... possible?" The words trickled out of Betty's mouth between her own uncontrollable sobs.

"I have no clue; this shouldn't be possible. Everything was linked..." she said as Reid came running over, wrapping an arm around her shoulder as she dissolved into him. Linda joined them and they held one another as Noah held his mother's hand tightly. Glistening eyes overwhelmed his stoic features.

David Anders, the key to righting time, was missing in time. The remaining seven were back in an era they didn't know, without a clue as to how they were to accomplish their task.

With the moment dissolving into history, the future patiently waited for their next move.

The End

ABOVE THE GROUND

Will Return.

Matthew Medney

An entrepreneur, prolific writer, and creative visionary, Medney has taken the reins of Heavy Metal with the singular goal of creating the next Disney; by amplifying Heavy Metal's unique ability to be the world's leading counterculture provider to mainstream audiences. In addition to being the driving strategic and creative force behind Heavy Metal, Medney has authored a best selling hard science fiction novel, Beyond Kuiper: The Galactic Star Alliance along with other works such as, Stable, Remnant, Dark Wing, The Adventures Of Adrienne, James, The Fifth Force with former Diplomat Catherine Loubier and more. He is the Head Writer for the #1 Metaverse AAA video game Star Atlas, he's the creative director for the Tupac & Ernest Hemingway estates in Web3, and he is the CEO, founder, and lead creative of Herø Projects, a boutique storytelling company that's worked with Floyd Mayweather, Rolling Loud Music Festival, the musician Shaggy, Disney and many more.

In addition to leveraging his creative expertise, Medney continues to transform Heavy Metal's business from a magazine to an Entertainment company by shepherding in new business ventures in Web3, gaming, live events, and collectibles having successfully executed deals with many high profile companies such as WhatNot.com, Crypto.Com, Live Nation, and many more.

Medney's creative success has also been translated to the screen, as three of his own graphic novel IP's have recently been optioned for studio development in TV and Film.

Find him at www.matthewmedney.com or @matthewmedney

Robert Greenberger

Bob is a writer, editor, and lifelong fan of comic books, comic strips, science fiction, and Star Trek. After graduating from SUNY Binghamton, he created the Comics Scene at Starlog Press, the first nationally distributed magazine to focus on comic books, comic strips, and animation. In 1984, he joined DC Comics as an Assistant Editor and went on to be an Editor. He later moved to Marvel Comics as its Director of Publishing Operations. Greenberger rejoined DC in May 2002 as a Senior Editor, where he grew their Collected Editions department. Bob has also freelanced for an extensive client base including Platinum Studios, scifi.com, DC and Marvel. He helped revitalize Famous Monsters of Filmland and served as News Editor at ComicMix.com.

He is a member of the Science Fiction Writers of America and the International Association of Media Tie-In Writers. His novelization of Hellboy II: The Golden Army won the IAMTW's Scribe Award in 2009. In 2016, Bob completed his Master of Arts degree in Creative Writing & Literature for Educators at Fairleigh Dickinson University. He helped cofound the digital press hub Crazy 8 Press, and he's written dozens of books, short stories, and essays that run the gamut from young adult nonfiction to original fiction. Most recently, Bob wrote the concluding chapter of This Alien Earth for the late Paul Antony Jones and the first chapter of Above the Ground, in collaboration with Matt Medney.

Bob teaches High School English at St. Vincent Pallotti High School in Laurel, MD. He and his wife Deborah reside in Howard County, Maryland.

Find him at www.bobgreenberger.com or @bobgreenberger

About Heavy Metal

First published in 1977, Heavy Metal magazine revolutionized comics with its fantastic worlds and visionary science fiction. Daring writers and illustrators from around the world took stunned readers to places they never dreamed existed. Since then, Heavy Metal has developed into the world's foremost illustrated magazine, a platform for countercultural artists worldwide, from European legends like Moebius, Enki Bilal, and Pepe Morena to subversive American stars like Richard Corben, Vaughn Bode, and Frank Frazetta. Its dangerous content — notorious for fusing science fiction with sexuality, psychedelia, and social criticism — has served as an inspirational epicenter for the world's most influential creators. Directors who credit Heavy Metal as inspiration include the likes of Ridley Scott, Guillermo Del Toro, Chris Columbus, Jon Faverau, and James Cameron; iconic films drawn from Heavy Metal's imagery include Alien, Blade Runner, Mad Max, The Fifth Element, and more.

After 45 years of mind-bending creation, the Heavy Metal brand, led by CEO & Best Selling Novelist Matthew Medney and an incredible team of misfits and exceptional creatives, Heavy Metal is expanding into modern entertainment by creating the next generation of groundbreaking science fiction, fantasy & horror. While Heavy Metal magazine continues to publish monthly stories from the best minds in comics, lead by Publisher, Associate Publisher & Executive Editor, David Erwin, Kris Longo & Joseph Illidge, Heavy Metal Studios is spearheaded by President and Head of Studio Tommy Coriale, as he and Medney develop TV and Films from Heavy Metal's rich library of IP. Heavy Metal is once again shaking pop culture to its core, by plunging headlong into revolutionary worlds and dizzying new futures. If you've been a fan of sci-fi, fantasy, and horror, for the last 40+ years, then You're welcome. Because this is our time to own the genre we have given so much to, Get ready....

This is Heavy Metal.... Buckle the f*#k up.